MW01008145

A TOWER FOR
THE SUMMER
HEAT

A TOWER FOR THE SUMMER HEAT

Li Yu

TRANSLATED, WITH A PREFACE AND NOTES,
BY PATRICK HANAN

COLUMBIA UNIVERSITY PRESS
New York

Columbia University Press
Publishers Since 1893
New York   Chichester, West Sussex
Translation and notes copyright
© 1992 by Patrick Hanan
and the Council for the Cultural Planning
and Development of the Executive Yuan of the Republic of China.
Preface copyright © 1998 Columbia University Press

Columbia University Press
All rights reserved

Library of Congress Cataloging-in-Publication Data
Li, Yü, 1611–1680?
[Shih erh lou. English. Selections]
A tower for the summer heat / Li Yu ; translated, with a preface
and notes, by Patrick Hanan.
p. cm. — (Translations from the Asian classics)
Originally published: New York : Ballantine Books, 1992.
ISBN 0–231–11384–6. — ISBN 0–231–11385–4 (pbk.)
1. Li, Yü, 1611–1680?—Translations into English. I. Hanan,
Patrick. II. Title. III. Series.
PL2698.L52S5213 1998
895.1'348—dc21   98–17764

CONTENTS

*P*REFACE

*#toocool
4thisschool*

I like the glasses

The stories of Li Yu (1611–1680) all claim to challenge traditional themes and conventional assumptions.[1] More than any other writer in premodern China, he stressed the absolute need in literature to "make it new." (And not only in literature—inventiveness had be applied to all spheres of life.) In the first story of this volume he employs a new device, the telescope, that revolutionizes courtship and enables its morally questionable hero to exploit popular superstition for his own ends; in another he offers us a maidservant who masterminds her mistress's and her own marriages to a handsome young intellectual; and then, to counteract these two novel and ingenious romantic comedies, he gives us an *anti*-romance that propounds a prudent, stoical attitude to love. Completing the volume are stories of a homosexual ménage

1. See Patrick Hanan, *The Invention of Li Yu* (Cambridge, Mass.: Harvard University Press, 1988), 76–110.

à trois that falls foul of a tyrant's lust, a confidence trickster of sublime inventiveness who becomes a Taoist immortal, and an extreme example of providential coincidence—so extreme it amounts to parody.

Near the end of the last story, the narrator disingenuously exclaims:

> Who would ever have expected the Creator's ingenuity to be a hundred times greater than man's? It is as if he had deliberately combined these events so that they could be turned into a play or a story—uniting the two couples and then separating them, separating and then uniting them, at a prodigious cost in mental effort. This plot rates as novel and ingenious to an extraordinary degree!

The playful address to the reader, the reflexive reference, the mockery, and the self-mockery are all pure Li Yu; he loved to load his fiction with comic interpretation (some of it contradictory) in prologues and interpolations, at chapter beginnings and endings. In so doing, he took the voice of the traditional narrator, which vaguely suggests an oral storyteller addressing his audience, and personalized it, so that it sounds not unlike Li Yu's voice as we hear it in his essays. (He was one of the great exponents of the humorous, but pointed, essay.) Even some of the views expressed in the stories, such as the bleak philosophy of the antiromance, are also to be found in his essays and letters.

The twelve-story collection from which these six works are drawn has two titles: *Jue shi ming yan* (Famous words to awaken the world), which is derived from one of Li Yu's pen names, Romancer Who Awakens the World, and *Shi'er lou* (Twelve lou). *Lou* is a term for a storied building or the upper story of such a building, and each of the twelve contains a *lou* that serves as its title. For want of a good English equivalent, I have resorted to ad hoc translations. Thus "Xiayi lou" (Lou suitable for summer) becomes "A Tower for the Summer Heat," and "Fuyun lou" (Cloud-brushing Lou) becomes "The Cloud-Scraper."

Unlike the stories in Li Yu's other collections, these are divided into chapters, like short novels—"The Cloud-Scraper" into as many as six. Li Yu was not the first to divide his stories into chapters, but he exploits the division more imaginatively than anyone else. In the title story, for example, the whole of the first chapter is devoted to the heroine's point of view and ends with a question asked of the reader. The second chapter supplies the answer to the question and then recapitulates the events from the hero's point of view. The third and final chapter oscillates between the two points of view, with the telescope and the matchmaker as mediators.

Like most fiction of the period with any literary pretensions, Li Yu's stories come equipped with emphasis marks, notes, and critiques, the last of which are included in the translation. The marks, the equivalent of underlining, indicate a judgment as to what is important or well expressed. The notes, humorous or appreciative rather than explanatory, appear in the upper margins above the columns of text they refer to; most are quite short, sometimes only a few words. The critiques, which follow the stories and amount to a paragraph or two in translation, praise the story and reflect, sometimes humorously, on its moral message. ("The Cloud-Scraper" lacks a critique.) Both notes and critiques were purportedly written by Du Jun, an eccentric poet who was one of Li Yu's circle of friends. Occasionally an author might write the notes and critiques to his own work, but these critiques are clearly not Li Yu's, with the possible exception of the critique to the title story, which makes the same point as one of his essays. In comparison with other commentators of the period, Du Jun is surprisingly candid, actually referring to Li Yu by a well-known pseudonym and mentioning another collection of his fiction.

I have translated the stories numbered 4–7, 9, and 11 of *Twelve Lou.* One may fairly ask what I have sacrificed by translating only half the collection. Does the whole work have a shape that has been lost? The fact that each story is named for a building is merely a superficial bond, stringing the stories together like ancient Chinese coins. A stronger objection could be raised to my omission of the twelfth story, which first describes Li Yu's experiences during the chaos of the late-Ming rebellions and the Manchu conquest, and then goes on to illustrate the dilemma of the artist in a society in which economic and cultural power is concentrated in the hands of officials. Li Yu made a good living—although he always teetered on the brink of bankruptcy—from his writings and designs, as well as from piecemeal patronage doled out by the officials who entertained him (and whom he entertained). But although the story has significance as a personal envoi to the collection, it is a lackluster piece of fiction by Li Yu's standards.

Twelve Lou must have been written in 1657 or 1658. Du Jun's preface is dated mid-autumn of the year corresponding to 1658. Li Yu's other story collections, *Silent Operas* and *Silent Operas, Second Collection*, were probably written in 1655 or 1656, while a copy of his erotic novel *The Carnal Prayer Mat* carries a preface dated early in the year that corresponds to 1657. He had written plays before turning to fiction, and he continued to write them after he had finished with fiction, sometimes drawing on his stories for subject matter. Of the stories translated here, "Nativity Room" was reworked into Li Yu's play *The Ingenious Finale* with some assistance from a story in *Silent Operas*. Li Yu spent most of the 1650s in Hangzhou before moving to Nanjing. It was in Hangzhou that he made his reputation with a sparkling kind of new comic drama, and it was there too that he wrote most of his fiction. *Twelve Lou*, his most famous work of fiction, was written in Hangzhou or Nanjing or both places.

Li Yu's first edition has not survived. I have based my translation primarily on the best available early edition, that of the Xiaoxianju publishing house, whose variants are generally superior to those of other editions. It is a well-printed edition that contains woodcut illustrations, one for each story. I am grateful to the Tenri Central Library and the Peking University Library for allowing me to use their copies.

I wish to thank the Council for Cultural Planning and Development of the Executive Yuan of the Republic of China for awarding me a grant to translate these stories. For their help I am also grateful to the following: Shang Wei, Wang Ch'iu-kuei, Ellen Widmer, Yenna Wu, Wu Xiao-ling, and Anneliese Hanan.

A TOWER FOR THE SUMMER HEAT

A TOWER FOR THE SUMMER HEAT

Ming /Qing period 1644 - 1911
↓
1368 -1644

CHAPTER 1

In which girls play pranks while bathing in the lotus pond,
And an immortal's eyes roam far in admiring their charms.

Poems:

There are pretty girls in both these hamlets,
With a bridge between and the river below.
They've sworn to be early for the lotus-picking;
Those who come late will have to row.

About to begin, they hesitate
And bend their heads in silent prayer.
The one with a double will soon be wed;
And who will receive a sign so rare?

I wonder whose daughter that girl is,
Who joins a boat along the way.
Too lazy by far, to pull on an oar,
But in flowers plucked she wins the day.

Sing but the lotus-picking songs
And tell no wild, indecent lies.
A man on the bank admires the lotus
And on the lotus-pickers spies.

Among the flowers you're unaware,
But at a distance their scent is clear;
She draws this lesson: to ensnare a man
Just let him look, not come too near.

The girls are summoned to the lotus early;
For grooming they have no time to spare.
Down fall their tresses and, home again,
They get their mothers to redo their hair.

These six poems, entitled "Lotus-picking Songs," were
composed by your humble servant in his youth.[1] Originally
there were ten of them, of which four have been omitted.
Now, anyone who writes a lotus-picking poem uses that
theme to sing of women, not of men, and of beautiful
women, not of ugly ones. Obviously the lotus differs from
all other flowers in that it has to be picked by women rather
than men, and by beautiful women at that.

I don't know how many thousand species of charming
flowers there are in the world, but the lotus is unique

---

1. The ten poems appear in Li Yu's collected works, *Independent Words (Yijia yan)* 5, in a somewhat different order.

among them. Not only does it abound in color and grace, it also possesses fragrance and charm in plenty. Not only does it delight the mind and eye, eventually it forms arrow-root to satisfy our hunger and thirst. The ancients dubbed it the prince of flowers, but I have another name for it: the beauty among flowers. And this beauty serves other purposes besides dalliance and lovemaking. It is also the frugal, diligent wife in the homespun dress, the sort of wife who is capable of bearing children as well as gracing her household. From youth to old age she knows not a single day of leisure, not one idle hour. Women ∠=7 Flower MERCIE

The flowering season is the lotus's heyday, and the blessings it confers then need not be recounted here. Instead I shall confine myself to the time before and after its flowering. From the moment it appears above the surface, it enhances the green waters with its *lotus coins,* to use the elegant term. And even before the buds have formed, you can drink in their pure scent; they deserve the accolade *azure cups*. Then no sooner have the petals fallen than the seed-pods appear, while the leaves, withered though they may be, are still not without their value. Although these marvelous features are mere addenda to the lotus's main contribution, they are admirable nonetheless. It differs markedly from ordinary flowers, which are not particularly attractive before they bloom and seem hardly worth saving once they fade. The ancients said, "Tend a flower for a year and enjoy it for ten days." From that point of view no flower is worth the bother. Only with the lotus do you get a real bargain, which is why I have likened it to a beautiful woman.

I once made a humorous remark that people at the time told me was worth preserving, and I propose to repeat it here, gentle readers, to see if you agree: "Frivolous and lewd behavior must have something serious and proper about it if it is to be perpetuated." And there *are* cases in which serious and proper results do emerge from frivolous and lewd behavior. For example, if sexual intercourse was not considered serious and proper in the very beginning, why has it been handed down from ancient times as a permanent part of life? Because out of the frivolity and lewdness of sex come sons to perpetuate the ancestral shrine and continue our lineage. How can anyone deny that the frivolity of sex supports a serious endeavor and that its lewdness is at least not inconsistent with propriety? This is the point to which my talk of lotus blossoms has brought me. I hope the reader will forgive me for rambling on so.

I shall now tell a remarkable story, and because I started off talking about lotus-picking, I shall take that subject as my lead-in, to avoid the danger of picking the wrong tree and finding that the graft doesn't take.

During the Zhizheng period[2] of the Yuan dynasty, there lived in Jinhua county of Wuzhou prefecture a retired official named Zhan Bifeng. He rose to be governor of Xuzhou, by which time his two sons, born while he was still quite young, were already launched on their own careers, so he retired at the top of his profession and transferred his remaining ambitions to them, spending his days on wine and poetry in imitation of Tao Qian and Xie Lingyun.[3]

In middle age he had fathered a daughter, Serena, who, after losing her mother in infancy, had been brought up entirely by nannies. Mr. Zhan refused to be rushed into an

2. 1341–1368.

3. The poets Tao Qian (365–427) and Xie Lingyun (383–443) celebrated the joys of private life in the country.

engagement for her. Instead he asked his sons at court to choose some young bachelor from among the officials, so that she would enjoy a lady's title from the moment of her wedding.

Serena was not only gorgeous, she was also completely natural and unaffected. Although she belonged to a wealthy and distinguished family, she had no interest in dressing up and flaunting her charms. Instead she was to be found with unpainted eyebrows in her boudoir busy at her needlework or her studies. Mr. Zhan's regime was exceedingly strict and required absolute segregation of the sexes. Servants' sons above the age of nine were banished beyond the second gate, and even when summoned, were not allowed into the reception room without permission but had to receive their orders from below the steps.

Since his daughter was nearly fifteen and still without a husband, Mr. Zhan feared that in her idleness she might feel lonely and start yearning for romance, so he devised a scheme to occupy her mind. Choosing a dozen bright, attractive young girls from among the servants' families, he appointed Serena their teacher. Every day she was to have them copy out a page of text and commit a few characters to memory. The scheme was designed to keep the teacher from feeling lonely and developing improper desires, but what its author failed to understand was that his daughter was a girl of exemplary rectitude, perfectly capable of restraining herself without parental control. Serena was only too well aware of how susceptible her heart was now that she had come of age, and she took constant care to banish any unseemly thoughts from her mind. Her father's decision suited her perfectly, and she threw herself into the task of instructing her young charges.

It was the height of summer, and the house sweltered

in a steamy haze. There were plenty of pavilions in the garden, but they all stood in the full sun and were useless for the purpose of escaping the heat. But there was also a spacious tower surrounded on three sides by a lotus pond and sheltered by sophoras and weeping willows that allowed not a ray of sunshine in all day long. The old adage warns us against climbing towers in summer, but this tower was well adapted to the season, a circumstance that had led Mr. Zhan to inscribe its name as *A Tower for the Summer Heat*.

Much attracted by it, Serena received her father's permission to move in and live there. She made one part into a classroom and the other into a bedroom, and spent all of her time in the tower, never going downstairs.

One day, feeling rather tired, she went into her room to take a nap. Her charges, incorrigibly mischievous, were excited to see her asleep and decided to go down and pick lotus from the pond. They had no boat, but one of them came up with a suggestion: "There aren't any men about anyway, so we don't need to worry about exposing ourselves. Why not just strip off and jump in? We'll pick some lotus and get a cold bath into the bargain, to cool ourselves off. Wouldn't that be *mar*velous!"

The girls, who couldn't endure the heat and were wearing dresses and trousers only because they had to, couldn't wait to strip off and enjoy the coolness. Moreover they saw themselves reflected against the green water and red lotus blossoms, and their number seemed to have doubled—how wonderful! They agreed to strip all at the same time, lest the ones who stripped first reveal something of note—and find themselves mocked by those who still had their clothes on. So they undressed together and proceeded

— Pleasurable —

to compare their treasures.[4] Peeking at one another, they dissolved into giggles.

By the time they got into the water, lotus-picking was the furthest thing from their minds. Instead they began larking about. Some competed at catching fish, others at swimming under water; some played with the pearls on the lotus leaves, while others drank the dew from the lotus blossoms; some stood close together and fondled each other's charms, while others hugged and had their way with each other; and there were some little groups that scuffled together in mock jealousy.

At the height of the hubbub Serena awoke and looked about; her pupils were nowhere to be seen. Then she heard a burst of giggling. She got up quietly, tiptoed outside, and found a bevy of mischievous girls skinny-dipping in the lotus pond. At sight of her, they went pale with fear. There was no escape for them, and they felt trapped.

Serena was afraid of causing an accident by scolding them too soon, so she shrank back into her bedroom as if she had seen nothing and gave them a chance to reach the bank. Only when they were fully dressed did she call them upstairs and make them kneel down in front of her. "The greatest virtue a woman has is her sense of propriety," she began. "If you're capable of this kind of behavior now, is there *anything* you'll stop at in the future?"

"The master's regime is so strict," they pleaded, "that no man would ever *dare* enter the inner quarters. It was only because we knew there would be no men about that

4. The text alludes to a mythical convention at which the rulers of the Chinese states compared their most precious gems.

we dared to do this. Please, miss, spare us this once! It's our first offense."

But Serena was in no mind to be lenient. After separating out the ringleader, she beat the others first, taking care not to break the skin. With the ringleader she continued until she drew blood.

Mr. Zhan heard all the shouting and sent someone over to inquire. On learning the circumstances, he declared that his daughter was perfectly right to beat the girls and praised her teaching.

Oddly enough, a few days after this incident a matchmaker arrived with a proposal for Serena. The suitor was one Qu Ji, styled Jiren, the scion of an old family and a well-known local scholar in his own right. A promising candidate for office, he had topped the list in the recent local examination. At the same time as he submitted his marriage proposal, he also prepared some handsome gifts for the girl's father in the hope that Mr. Zhan would accept him as a protégé.

Serena's confidantes told her that Qu was terribly handsome—a romantic genius, no less. But although Mr. Zhan accepted him as a protégé, he was studiously vague on the subject of marriage: "My sons are in the capital and may well have promised her to someone else, so I'm afraid I can't give you an immediate answer. Let's wait until the results of the provincial examination are out before we consider your prospects." By these remarks he was clearly implying that the Zhans, who came from a long line of officials, would be reluctant to accept a commoner as a son-in-law. Jiren would have to pass the provincial examination before a marriage could be arranged.

Full of confidence in his own abilities, Jiren had already set his heart on topping the list. The match will certainly be mine, he thought, I'll just have to wait a little longer. He told the matchmaker to give the young lady his respects and ask her to be patient and prepare to become his wife.

Serena was thrilled. If he weren't supremely capable, how could he be so sure of himself? she thought. I only hope he'll succeed and make good on his promise.

As soon as the results were posted, she bought a copy and studied it. Jiren's name topped the list. She exulted in the knowledge that she would become his wife and, as the saying goes, have someone to depend on for the rest of her life. Impatiently she waited for him to conclude an agreement and relieve her anxiety, but unfortunately new graduates are quartered in the provincial capital, and time must elapse before their return. Serena had looked forward to the engagement for so long without receiving any news that she now fell prey to doubt and suspicion, wondering whether he might have proposed again and been rejected by her father, or whether, following his success, he might have found a wife in some other well-known family. One should never allow a girl's heart to be stirred in this fashion, for once stirred, it cannot regain its equilibrium, and her anxiety will invariably lead to an illness. After several days of worrying, Serena did become ill. She was loath to tell other people for fear of arousing their jealousy, so she suffered alone, not daring even to sigh in the presence of her maids.

However, after a few more days the matchmaker returned with a message. "Master Qu is back. He knows you're unwell and has instructed me to ask after you and urge you to take good care of yourself so that you may become his wife. You mustn't fret over him."

Serena was astounded. I'm the only one who knows about my illness, she thought. Even my personal maids have been kept in the dark. He's just back from a long journey, so how could he possibly know about it and send her over to ask? She hesitated, then tried to dissemble.

"I'm perfectly well, thank you, and we haven't had a death in the family, either, to grieve over. Why would I be sick for no reason at all?"

"Don't deny it, miss," said the matchmaker. "I didn't believe him when he said you were sick, but as soon as I saw you, I noticed you'd lost a lot of weight and knew he was right."

"Supposing I *were* sick, how could he possibly know?"

"I don't understand how he does it, but he knows everything that goes on in your mind, as if you and he were Siamese twins. And not just your thoughts either, but everything you do—you can't hide *anything* from him. You've never seen him, but he knows exactly what you look like; in fact he gave me a description that fits you perfectly. I imagine you two must have been husband and wife in some previous existence and that that is the reason."

"Why don't you give me some examples, then, if he knows everything I do?"

"One example will be enough to astonish you. He claims he has the eyes of a god and can see *anything*, no matter how far away it is. On a certain day you were asleep in your room when a bunch of girls stripped naked and jumped into the pond to pick lotus. You came out and caught them in the act and gave each of them a few whacks, with the last one getting the worst treatment. Is that true?"

"That's just trivial gossip spread by malicious servants that he somehow got wind of. It has nothing whatever to do with previous existences and the eyes of a god!"

"The other points may have been gossip, but not your illness, which you haven't told anyone about. How could that be gossip? Besides he saw those girls bathing and said some of them were pale, some were dark, and others were in between. He also said there was one girl there with a mop of hair and a nice complexion, but who was disfigured by a scar the size of a bowl on her back. Is that true? Does it fit the facts? Think it over."

Serena was dumbfounded, aghast. Suppose we *were* careless enough to let someone sneak in, she thought. Why would he confine himself to peeping at maids and not try to seduce their mistress? What did he hear before he came, and what did he see while he was here? Anyway we're the strictest of families when it comes to access; a nine-year-old boy couldn't get beyond our inner gate. What sort of man is he, to get in here? If he wanted to smooth-talk us into marriage, why would he come out with all these details and get them so right? From that angle, there must be something predestined about our relationship after all. Even if he hasn't seen me himself, his soul must have visited me in his dreams in a kind of spiritual communion.

At this thought her heart grew fonder. "If that's so," she said, "why doesn't he just propose instead of sending you over to see me?"

"First of all, he's concerned about your health and fears that if he delays any longer, you'll only get worse, so he told me to reassure you, lest you become overwrought. Secondly, he suspects your father has set his heart on choosing a son-in-law from some rich and distinguished family, and although Mr. Qu is now a provincial graduate, he's afraid he might not qualify. He begs you to make your own choice, miss. He hopes you will take pity on him because of the bond you and he share from a previous existence, a bond by which his spirit never leaves you night or day. Should your father reject him and marry you to someone else, he will certainly die for your sake, and since his spirit never leaves you now and knows everything you do, he says that after his death he won't call it back but will let it continue to follow you all the time. He's afraid that you and the man you marry may not have a very pleasant time of it. You'd be far better off accepting him."

Serena had intended to marry him anyway, and now, on learning of these supernatural events and receiving this pointed advice, she was quite convinced and had no further qualms.

"Tell him to set his mind at rest and send in his proposal as soon as he can. If Father accepts it, well and good. If not, tell Master Qu to call on my brothers when he arrives in the capital. They appreciate talent and are sure to accept him."

The matchmaker took this message back to Jiren, who cheered up immeasurably and promptly sent in his proposal, uncertain though he was of its success.

Having come this far, gentle readers, please put aside all other concerns and focus on the question of how Jiren knew what was going on in the Zhan household. Was he man or ghost? Was it dream or reality? By all means try to guess the answer and then, when you find you cannot come up with it, turn to the next chapter for the explanation.

Cliffhanger!

CHAPTER 2

*A man of talent springs a surprise by impersonating
an immortal;*
*The Creator of Things does a favor by interrupting a
poem.*

Gentle readers, I expect you have been unable to guess
how Jiren came to know these things, so let me explain:
The incident was the work neither of man nor of ghost,
and the account given you was neither a complete fabrication nor the complete truth. It was the work of a certain
device that served Jiren as an eye, a device that allowed a
flesh-and-blood human being to impersonate a disembod-
ied immortal without any fear that people would doubt his
word. Although the device did not originate in China, it
was something that lovers of exotica were able to collect;
it was certainly no figment of the imagination. Unfortunately everybody looked upon it as a mere toy and ignored
its potential value. Only this man knew enough to conceal
its usefulness and not put it to work in other areas, but to
keep it for selecting a beautiful wife. For that purpose he
built an altar, appointed the device his commander-in-
chief, and asked of it a great service.[5] It proved capable of
picking up a great beauty ensconced in her boudoir and,
without actually removing her from that boudoir, placing
her right in front of him, and capable also of taking the rare
blooms from another man's garden and setting them in all
their glory before his eyes.

5. A reference to the appointment of Han Xin as commander of the
victorious forces in the civil war that resulted in the founding of the Han
dynasty. See *Shi ji* 92.

What do you suppose the object was? A lyric to the tune "Moon Over West River" describes it best:

It equals Lu Ban's dazzling sleight
And adds to Lilou's range.[6]
Its infinitesimal thread of light
Will let the eye take flight.

When new, it has no near or far
And needs to be set right.
Don't mock; the single-eyed
See with the keenest sight.

The device in question is known as a thousand-li glass and comes from the West. It demonstrates the same intelligence as the minute-revealing glass, the incense-burning glass, the makeup glass, and the lighting glass, all of which are capable of numerous strange and ingenious effects. Here is a description of these various glasses:

MINUTE-REVEALING GLASS
(MICROSCOPE)

Somewhat bigger than a coin, it is supported on a tripod. When the tiniest object is placed beneath the tripod and observed from above, it is transformed into something huge. Lice and nits appear almost as big as dogs and sheep, and mosquitoes and flies as large as cranes and herons. The hairs on the

6. Zhou dynasty figures. Lu Ban was the great artificer; Lilou had superhuman eyesight. The terms *microscope* and *telescope* in parentheses are the translator's additions.

louse's body, like the specks on the fly's wing, are so distinct you can count them. That is why it is called the minute-revealing glass—because it can reveal the most minute objects and set them before the eye with brilliant clarity.

INCENSE-BURNING GLASS

Also somewhat larger than a coin, it rests on an adjustable stand beneath which is a silver dish. A cake or strip of incense is placed in the dish below the glass, and when the glass meets the sun's rays, the incense burns without fire. As the sun moves in the sky, one tilts the glass to face it, which is why the stand is adjustable. The most delightful feature of the glass is the fact that it produces perfume without smoke, a single cake of ambergris lasting a whole day. This is the most useful of all of these devices.

MAKEUP GLASS

This is even smaller than the preceding two. It is used to check one's appearance and see that one's hair is in order. Ladies on an outing will find it most convenient. Attached to a fan or kerchief, it is readily available for titivating along the way, and they need have no worries about their hair being out of place.

LIGHTING GLASS

The one exceptional feature of this glass is that it can light a fire from the sun's rays, substituting for flint and steel. Smoking and drinking have recently become extremely popular, and people are constantly seeking to overindulge. It is a nuisance to summon a servant, but when you have this device with you, a light is always available. It is even more useful than the other glasses, owing to the circumstances of the time. Even when created in Western countries, it was not expected to be so popular.

THOUSAND-LI GLASS (TELESCOPE)[7]

This glass employs several tubes of different thickness, of which the smaller ones fit inside the larger. To adjust it, you extend or retract the tubes. The reason it is called a thousand-li glass is that the lenses are set at the ends of the tubes, and when you use it for looking into the distance, nothing is beyond its range. Although the term *thousand li* is an exaggeration—you can't really see from one kingdom into another—if you try it out inside that range, you will find the claim not at all fraudulent. If you use it for looking at people or things at a distance of several hundred yards to a few li, you'll find them more distinct than if they were sitting opposite you. It is a genuine treasure.

The glasses described above were all produced in Western countries. Two hundred years ago they were brought

7. A *li* is about a third of a mile.

to China only by tribute emissaries and thus were rarely seen and virtually unobtainable. From the Ming dynasty onward, some outstanding scholars from those countries, choosing not to restrict their activities to their own lands, chanced to come and establish their teaching in China. They knew how to manufacture these glasses and gave them to people as presents, and so collectors of exotica were able to obtain them. Wishing to extend this knowledge, the scholars also taught people how to manufacture the glasses. But China was unable to match the foreigners in this kind of intelligence, and few men were able to master the techniques. In the last few years only Zhu Sheng, cognomen Xi'an, of Hangzhou, a scholar well-known in literary circles, has succeeded.[8] His minute-revealing, incense-burning, makeup, lighting, and thousand-li glasses are all of superior quality, on a par with the finest products of the West, while his eyeglasses for

8. The Xiaoxianju edition leaves his personal name blank. (The other editions omit this whole section.) That the instrument-maker was the artist Zhu Sheng, known for painting bamboos in snow, is shown by a letter to him from Lu Jun. See Wang Qi, ed., *Fenlei chidu xinyu* (Taipei: Guangwen shuju, 1971) 22, p. 410. This work is the second anthology of letters compiled by Wang Qi and was published in 1667. (The *zhu* of the name is the *zhu* of *zhuwei*, Ladies and Gentlemen, and the *sheng* is *to ascend* with the sun radical.) The passage clears up a small problem in the history of Chinese science. Joseph Needham and Lu Gwei-djen, in their article "The Optick Artists of Chiangsu" (S. Bradbury and G. L'E. Turner, *Historical Aspects of Microscopy*, W. Heffer and Sons, Cambridge, 1967, pp. 113–138), note that two Suzhou instrument-makers of the seventeenth century made telescopes and microscopes, and speculate whether the telescope in particular might have been independently invented in China. Otherwise why would the first Chinese-made telescopes appear in a provincial city? This story supplies a neat answer. There is one additional point: In praising Zhu Sheng so highly, Li Yu may have been tacitly comparing him to his Suzhou rivals.

near- and farsightedness are even better. Those in possession of his products look on them as rare and remarkable treasures.

But what is the point of this digression of mine? I have extended my discussion of the thousand-li glass to cover these other objects as well, in order to show they are no figments of the imagination. Gentle reader, if you find all this too much to believe, I suggest you buy a specimen from a present-day shopkeeper and try it out. Jiren's intelligence was unusually rich in remarkable insights. He may not have been able to infer ten facts from every one, but he could certainly infer more than two. The selfsame object would be perceived by others in one light, but by him in another. People thought he was merely trying to be different, but in the end they came to realize that others' perceptions were shallow as compared with his.[9]

One day Jiren went out to buy books with several of his friends. Walking past an antique shop, they noticed a strange-looking object on a stand, and when they picked it up and examined it, found a strip of gold paper pasted on the front bearing a row of tiny characters:

WESTERN THOUSAND-LI GLASS

"What's this for?" they asked the shopkeeper.
"If you look through it from some high place, you'll

9. The text from the poem to this point is retained only in the Xiaoxianju edition.

find that it brings the scenery into view for miles around."

"Impossible!" they exclaimed in disbelief.

"If you don't believe me, gentlemen, you're welcome to try it," said the shopkeeper. He picked up a piece of scrap paper from an unsuccessful examination essay. "If I stuck this up in the doorway opposite, would you be able to read it from here?"

"Of course not! The writing's too small and the distance too great."

"Then try this."

He had an assistant stick the sheet of paper up on the gate opposite, then raised the telescope. His customers took one look—and were amazed. Not only was each character crystal-clear and plainly legible, they declared, but the brush strokes were much thicker than before, in fact several times thicker.

"If you'll step further away," added the shopkeeper, "they'll look even thicker. This amazing thing is at its best from a hundred yards to a third of a mile. I doubt that even the tablet on Eight Songs Tower or the scrolls outside the Star Goddess Temple have characters that size!"[10]

His customers clamored to buy it, but Jiren interrupted them. "I'm afraid you wouldn't use it properly. You'd better let me have it."

"But it's only for viewing the scenery from a high point," they protested. "What other uses does it have?"

"I don't think it's so limited. Let me buy it and take it home with me. Within a year at the outside I'm going to call on it for a great service: arranging a marriage. After that

10. The Eight Songs Tower (Bayonglou) and the Star Goddess Temple (Baowuguan) were two of the sights of Jinhua. The eight songs were composed by the poet Shen Yue in his Jinhua retreat in 494.

I shall have no further need of it and I'll pass it on to you for general use. How's that for an offer?"

His friends were mystified. "Very well, we'll let you buy it," they said at last. "When we need it, we'll come and borrow it."

Jiren agreed on a price, paid the money, and took the telescope home with him. It's not only for looking at distant scenery, he thought, it can also make people in the distance look clearer than if they were close at hand. It's not a telescope; it's a pair of long-distance eyes! Although I've come of age, I'm still not engaged. I hope to choose an outstanding beauty as my wife, but officials' daughters aren't allowed to meet their suitors and marriage to a commoner would hardly be appropriate for me. Recently the matchmakers have mentioned a number of girls, all from gentry families living within a mile or two of here, and now that I have these long-distance eyes, why don't I find some vantage point from which to view them? The houses of great families aren't likely to open on to brick walls and blind alleys; they'll be full of pavilions and terraces with doors and windows you can see into. From close up the view may be blocked, but not from a distance. I'll take this up to the pagoda of a temple and try it out a few times. I just may see something. If I *can* find the outstanding beauty and get a good look at her before I propose, I'll have saved myself from a terrible mistake.

With this scheme in mind, he rented a monk's cell in a nearby temple and, on the pretext of studying and enjoying the view, spent all of his time experimenting with the telescope. He peered into numerous courtyards and surveyed countless beauties, but found none that appealed to him. On that day, however, no doubt through a confluence of their marriage destinies, the young mistress of the

Zhan family was due to meet up with a fake immortal. A contributing factor to the meeting was the mischief of those young girls, who by stripping off and exposing their bodies first aroused the observer's passions.

Suddenly, in the midst of his excitement, out walked a girl whose beauty was of a different order altogether—a case of "when the tree peony stands alone, you know it at once for the queen of the flowers." Moreover this girl displayed calmness as well as rectitude. She did not take immediate action against the offenders, but waited before dispensing justice, an attitude that showed a nice balance between leniency and severity. As a wife she would surely be a capable administrator and a splendid helpmate. Jiren investigated and, on learning her identity, promptly sent off a matchmaker with a proposal. Lest Mr. Zhan refuse, he took the precaution of asking to become his protégé— emulating Nan Rong and Gongye in first impressing the girl's father with his looks and talents.[11]

Returning from his success in the examinations, Jiren was unable to put Serena out of his mind. Even before unpacking, he rushed to the temple, looked out, and found her leaning listlessly against the rail, her cheeks shrunken, to all appearances seriously ill. Realizing that he was the cause of her distress, he sent someone to ask after her health. (This was a trivial reason, of course; the critical need, as he well knew, was to find out how matters stood.) It would have been awkward to play this trick when he first proposed, but if ever there was a time for it, this was the time, which was why he sent the matchmaker to tell Serena

11. Nan Rong and Gongye were disciples of Confucius, who married them to his niece and daughter, respectively. See D. C. Lau, trans., *The Analects* (London: Penguin Books, 1979), p. 76.

about these supernatural happenings. They would capture her soul and fire her imagination, and she would never be tempted to change her mind.

When the matchmaker reported back, Jiren realized his triumph was due to the telescope, and so, after sending off his proposal, he took that trusty helper with him to the temple and looked out once more, only to find Serena leaning against the rail and nodding her head. On the table before her lay a brush, an inkstone, and also a sheet of special notepaper—a typical scene of poetic composition. He expected her to write her poem at any moment, and the thought occurred to him: I may as well play the immortal to the limit. I'll write a matching poem and send someone around with it as soon as she finishes hers. That'll take her breath away! Not even a real immortal will be able to beat me out then, let alone a mere human being.

At this point he began to worry that the matchmaker might be impossible to find at short notice. After an hour or two's delay his poem might surprise Serena but would hardly amaze her. So he sent for the matchmaker and asked her to wait in his study while he climbed up the pagoda to reply to Serena's poem. In the past he had stood on the fourth or fifth floors, and all he had had to do was to level the telescope. But this time he assumed she would be writing at her table with the poem lying flat in front of her—she certainly wouldn't hang it on the wall, lest it be seen—and unless he stationed himself on high, he would not be able to look down upon the world of men and read it. So he kept climbing until he could go no higher, adjusted the telescope, directed it at the Tower for Summer Heat—and examined Miss Serena.

He saw her slender fingers grip the brush and copy out a poem:

game involved *Pleasure*

Deep within the double gates, spring comes slow.
She longs for the buds to open and the butterflies to
   know.
                                          passion,
If the flower isn't touched by a butterfly's shade,   *attachment*
Why do butterfly dreams to the flowery branches go?

At which point, for no apparent reason, she suddenly took
fright. Crumpling up the poem, she stuffed it in her sleeve
as if she knew someone was spying on her from the skies
above.

The fake immortal was scared half to death. How could
she possibly know that I'm spying on her from up here, he
wondered. Then in the midst of his concern he noticed a
man climbing up the tower. From his hempen cap, simple
dress and stern, sanctimonious expression, Jiren knew that
he must be Serena's father and understood why she had
taken fright and hidden the poem in her sleeve—in case her
father saw it! She had heard his step on the stairs and tucked
the poem out of sight, lest her secret be revealed. Her aerial
observer, a long way off, had been able to see her expression but not hear her father's step and jumped to the wrong
conclusion. (His reaction was also the result of a guilty
conscience.)

Her poem appears to be unfinished, he thought; it
doesn't seem to end at the fourth line. I was going to write
a matching poem, but fortune has played into my hands
now that her train of thought has been interrupted. Why
don't I save her the trouble and finish the poem off for her,
as a symbol of our engagement? The traditional way is for
the wife to follow the husband's lead, but here the roles are
reversed. I'll just say that I saw her take fright and lose her
inspiration, so I finished the poem off for her. Finishing her
poem—how natural that is, yet how amazing! Quite unlike

writing a poem to the same rhyme which, although surprising enough, would seem a little too contrived. At this thought he jumped for joy and rushed down to his study, where he seized his brush and dashed off a conclusion to the poem:

All because the butterfly owes the flower a debt,
The flower has come to think the butterfly is slow.
Let me thank the east wind for our predestined bond—
For now no chance remains we won't together grow.

He copied it out on special notepaper, handed it to the matchmaker, and told her to take it to Serena immediately; the slightest delay would be disastrous. But quick though the messenger may be, the author insists on a delay at this point, so that he can start a new chapter. Like Serena's poem, which was broken off before it was completed, the story will be far more interesting than if it were told all in one piece.

[handwritten annotations: "Cliffhanger!" and "Playful attitude"]

CHAPTER 3

Half a poem fabricates a predestined bond;
A secret message gives rise to a brilliant lie.

When the matchmaker arrived, she found Mr. Zhan still talking to his daughter. She waited until he had left and Serena was alone before delivering her message: "Master Qu sends his love. He says you were writing a poem and were halfway through when you were startled by your father suddenly coming up the stairs. In your delicate state of health, this must have been a shock to your system, so he told me to come and see how you're feeling."

Serena shivered with fright on hearing this message. She was now convinced of Jiren's divinity, even though she still refused to admit it.

"I wasn't writing any poem! And my father comes up here all the time. Why on earth would I be startled?"

"Personally I have no idea whether or not you were writing a poem and whether or not you were startled. I'm simply telling you what Master Qu told me to say. He was also afraid that after the shock you'd have to rack your brains to finish off the poem, so he made a point of doing it for you and asked me to bring over the result. He's far from sure if his lines are good enough and begs you to correct them."

Serena was now even more astonished and felt almost certain he was an immortal. She asked to see the poem and then, on reading it, broke out into a cold sweat. As Jiren had anticipated, the poem took her breath away. For a long time she was struck dumb, but at length, regaining her senses, came out with an extraordinary remark: "In the light of this evidence, he really is an immortal, of that I'm convinced. And if I won't accept an immortal as a husband, whom *will* I accept? I have just one concern: I'm afraid his human shape may be only a temporary manifestation, not his true form. I don't want him flying off to Heaven after we're engaged, leaving me with no way to find him. That wouldn't do at all!"

"Nothing of the kind is going to happen! He never claimed to be an immortal as such, merely one who'd been reborn in human form. Of course it could well happen that after a long married life together he might revert to his original form and take you back with him to Heaven."

"Very well then, you can take my half-poem to him and leave his here, so that each of us has a token to keep. Tell him to propose as soon as he can; he mustn't delay. If ever I'm disloyal to him during my life, he can play King Yama[12] himself and snatch my soul away and do as he pleases with it!"

The matchmaker went back and delivered this message as well as the half-poem. Jiren was jubilant at the prospect.

But all good things in life are fraught with trouble. Jiren, good man as he was, received no help from Heaven.[13] The matchmaker reported back: "Mr. Zhan is still prevaricating. He wants to wait until he hears from the capital before making any decision. That clearly means he wants a national graduate for his daughter, not a provincial one."

Jiren wished to set off for the capital at once to sit the national examinations but was afraid some new development might occur in his absence, so he told the matchmaker to go and talk the matter over with Serena without letting on that the visit was his idea.

"As soon as Master Qu arrives in the capital," the matchmaker told Serena, "of course he'll pay his respects to your brothers and ask someone to act as go-between. But there *is* one problem. If your brothers are just as snobbish and insist on waiting for the examination results, what are we to do if Master Qu's name isn't on the list and they promise you to someone else? We need to come up with a plan and tell him about it ahead of time."

"Not to worry," said Serena. "In the first place, he's so

12. King of the netherworld.
13. A pun on the proverb *Tian xiang jiren* (Heaven helps the good man).

gifted he's bound to succeed. He qualified as a provincial graduate, and now he'll qualify as a national graduate. Secondly, he's an immortal in human form, and with all the magic he has at his disposal there's nothing he can't do. What's more, my brothers are devout believers in Taoism and Buddhism. Ask him to give them a demonstration of his powers and, in their eagerness for good fortune and fear of bad, they're bound to accept him. That's why I fell in love with him myself and want to spend all my days with him. You can't tell me that immortals can guarantee their future in everything except marriage, in which they allow themselves to be beaten out by mere humans!"

"You're right," said the matchmaker, who duly relayed this conversation to Jiren. She was unaware of the truth and believed he really was the immortal he claimed to be. After getting her report, she thought, he would display his powers and remove any further cause for worry.

Lest he reveal his secret, Jiren had to prevaricate, but privately he was intensely worried: this match is by no means a sure thing. I'm as much a human being as they are and have no supernatural powers to show them. All I can do is use my human powers to send off another proposal. If they accept me, so much the better. If not, I'll rely on my own abilities in the national examination. I expect that's what they really want after all. Once they see me in my silk cap, they'll consent! But if luck goes against me and I fail, I might just as well give up on this match altogether. I can hardly go on playing the fake immortal in hopes of pulling it off!

Arriving in the capital, he paid his respects to the Zhan brothers and then sent in his proposal of marriage. As he feared, they replied that they were postponing their decision until the results were out.

Jiren set his heart on gaining the highest honors and poured all of his efforts into the examination. As the proverb says, When a man's writing is good enough, the gods play fair. Jiren ranked high on the list of successful candidates, in the second honor group. Renewing his proposal, he assumed it would now be eagerly accepted; in fact he thought there was no longer any chance of failure. But the brothers replied: "There are three unmarried local candidates on the list, all of whom have proposed marriage. Father is at home, and we can't make the decision by ourselves, so we've sent him the three names and suggested he decide by lot."

Once again Jiren grew alarmed. What if he draws someone else's name? he asked himself. It's lucky I worked out a plan with his daughter for such an event! But if we're separated, we won't be able to coordinate our efforts. Without waiting for the election to the Hanlin Academy, he petitioned for leave to return home. There are two lines from *The West Chamber* that fit his situation perfectly, lines that I offer to the reader to sing in his place:

> For a painted eyebrow and a powdered cheek,
> He gave up the Hall of Jade and the Golden Horse.[14]

Driven by love, he sacrificed his chance of an Academy appointment and rushed home to urge his suit, confident of success. But as the proverb says, No matter how early you set off, someone is sure to have left before you. The

14. Written about 1300, *The West Chamber* is the most famous Chinese play. The lines, slightly misquoted, come from part 3, scene 1, where they are sung by the maid Hongniang. Jade Hall and Golden Horse refer to a hall of fame for eminent statesmen.

other suitors had packed and set off for home before the results were even posted, leaving this message for their friends to pass on to the Zhan brothers: "If we fail, no matter, but if we are lucky enough to succeed, we ask that in your letter home you commend us to your father and seek a marriage for one of us with his daughter." Both men were already there when Jiren arrived.

Each of the suitors sent matchmakers to plead his case as forcefully as possible, which threw Serena into a frenzy. As soon as she heard of Jiren's arrival, she told the matchmaker to urge him to "put his divine powers to work immediately to confirm our engagement. If I'm won by some ordinary mortal, I'll die in an unknown grave, and it will be no use coming and snatching my soul away."

Jiren was at a complete loss. All he could do was send a matchmaker over to plead his case as vigorously as possible. Knowing that Mr. Zhan was a snob who could be influenced only by questions of status, he sent the following message: "I passed in the second honor group and will soon receive a post. The other suitors have not yet been through the palace review, so even if they get appointments at the earliest possible date, they will still be three years behind me. If they receive posts in the capital, I'll be a whole tour of duty ahead. And if they place in the third group and are sent to the provinces, they won't catch up with me even if they put in a lifetime of service."

The other suitors had their own line of special pleading: "Someone who has passed the palace examination may not have received a post, but his rank is fixed once and for all. Moreover he failed to take part in the selection for the Academy, so the best he can hope for is an assistantship in one of the ministries. We haven't been through the palace review yet and may still end up in the top honor group.

What's more, we have another three years of study ahead of us, and there's little doubt that we'll get into the Academy. In either case we'll outrank him!''

Mr. Zhan did not reply to either plea. Because his sons' letter had recommended drawing lots, he so ruled, considering it more important to defer to them than to anyone else. He set a time for the drawing, at which the three names would be written on slips of paper and his daughter would pull out the winner, thus avoiding the controversy that bedevils these decisions.

Serena beamed. He's an immortal and with his godlike eyes knows every little move I make, she thought. When lots are being drawn in a matter as vital to him as this, how can he fail to use his magic and permit me to draw some other name? She sent him a message urging him to display his powers as soon as possible and meanwhile pulled herself together to await the lottery.

On the appointed day Mr. Zhan wrote out the names on slips and placed them in a golden vase. Next, as in court divination, he bowed four times to Heaven and Earth and four more times to his ancestors, after which he called upon Serena to do the same. When she had finished, he handed her a pair of jade chopsticks and told her to draw a slip from the vase.

The moment she received the chopsticks, Serena showed her sangfroid by picking a slip without a trace of timidity. But as bad luck would have it, instead of drawing the immortal, she drew a mere human being, a result so shocking to her that her eyebrows stood on end and her starry eyes flashed fire. Whatever happened to his supernatural powers? she asked herself.

At the height of her distress, her father announced: ''The choice is made,'' and told her to give thanks to the gods. But Serena was far too angry for that. She blamed the gods for their ineffectiveness and was in no mood to give them any thanks. Instead, with her native wit she improvised a plan. Kneeling down in front of her father, she appealed to him, a solemn look on her face: "There's something I wish to inform you of, Papa. I didn't dare tell you before, but if I don't do so now, I'm afraid my whole life will be ruined."

"There's nothing a child can't say in front of her parents. Come on, tell me about it."

Serena stood up. "Last night I dreamed of my late-lamented mother, who gave me this message: 'I understand three gentlemen have come to seek your hand. One of the three is your predestined mate, while the others have no affinity with you whatsoever.' I asked her which one she meant, but all she would say was that his surname was Qu. She told me to keep the prophecy in mind against the day it came true. Unfortunately I drew out someone else's name, and that's why I hesitate to give thanks to the gods." What she really meant was "I c-c-can't obey."[15]

Mr. Zhan thought for a moment. "Stuff and nonsense!" he declared. "If your mother has powers of this sort, why did she appear in your dream and not in mine? If this is true, she ought to have shown her powers at the drawing by helping this man rather than letting someone else be picked instead. It's a wicked lie, and I don't believe a word of it!"

"You may believe it or not as you wish, Papa. But I take Mother's orders very seriously, and I will *not* marry anyone who isn't surnamed Qu!"

15. Allusion to the story of an official who stuttered in refusing a direct order from the emperor. See *Han History* 42.

Mr. Zhan flew into a rage. "You disregard the orders of a living father and use your late mother's instructions to frustrate me! What makes it worse is the sheer absurdity of your story. How do I know you're not in love with him, that you haven't made the whole thing up? Very well then, *I* shall pray before her spirit tablet myself and ask her if it's true. If it is, she will have to send me a dream as soon as possible. But if three nights go by and I've had no such dream, your story will be an obvious fabrication, and not only will I reject this fellow Qu, I'll find out what's behind it and look into your disgraceful behavior." He stalked off, his eyes fixed firmly in front of him.

For Serena this humiliation came on top of the apprehension she already felt, and she was dreadfully upset. She sent the matchmaker to Jiren with a note of which the first part expressed her resentment and the second part took a final farewell.

But when Jiren tore it open and read it, he roared with laughter. "I *knew* this would happen!" he told the matchmaker. "I want you to go back and tell her that her father will have a change of heart within the next three days, I guarantee. This match will definitely be mine! I have a note for her, too, which I'll trouble you to deliver. Impress on her that she must follow the plan *exactly,* without a single mistake."

"Since you have such powers, why didn't you use them before to arrange your own marriage, rather than let her pick someone else?"

"That's just where my brilliance comes in! In the first place, I wanted to put her love to the test and see whether she would change her mind after picking someone else. Secondly, I was so annoyed with her father that I purposely used a little magic to fool him. And thirdly, immortals *have* to do the unpredictable thing, you know. If she'd picked me the first time, it would have been far too banal—boring in fact."

Still trusting in his powers, the matchmaker delivered the note. Serena was sobbing bitterly when she received it, but she had no sooner opened it than her tears turned to smiles and she began giving thanks to Heaven and Earth. "With this plan," she said, "there's nothing left to worry about!" But when the matchmaker asked her what plan she was talking about, she merely smiled and said nothing.

When the three days had passed, her father called her in and addressed her sternly: "I prayed to your mother for the truth and asked her to appear in my dream, but three days have passed without any response from her. Obviously your story is a pack of lies. But there must be a reason behind them. Come on, out with it!"

"Papa, *I* was the one who had the dream you asked for! Mother told me she wouldn't stoop to go near you while you were in bed with your concubine, so she came to me instead and gave me this message: 'Since your papa doesn't believe you, I'm going to give you a piece of evidence that will convince him. My only concern is that it will come as too great a shock to him.' That's why I didn't dare tell you before it became absolutely necessary. I was afraid I might shock you to death, Papa."

"What could possibly be so terrible? You'd better tell me now."

"Mother said that when you prayed, you not only spoke to her, you also burned a petition you had written. Is that so?"

Her father nodded. "Yes, that's right."

"Well, if you wish to know whether what I told you is true, just see if I get the words of the petition right.

Mother said that you wrote the petition without my knowledge and that you burned it as soon as you wrote it, and thus no one else saw it. She made me memorize it, so that if you asked I could repeat it to you as proof."

"I don't believe such a rigmarole! Are you telling me that you can repeat the text of my petition?"

"Not merely repeat it, but repeat it word perfect. If I get a single word wrong, what I told you will be a fabrication and you needn't believe any of it."

She opened her ruby lips and parted her jade-white teeth and, in a voice that echoed the warbling of swallows and the chanting of orioles, repeated the petition word for word. Her father, we need hardly say, shivered with fright.

"In the light of this," he said, after recovering his poise, "ghosts and spirits aren't fantasy after all, and marriage destinies really are preordained. Let us accept the match with the Qus."

That same day he gave instructions through a matchmaker that Jiren need not present his compliments but should at once choose an auspicious date for marriage into the Zhan family.

It so happened that the wedding took place in summer. The classroom where Serena had taught her pupils became her bridal chamber, and there the brilliant youth and the beautiful girl were united in marriage.

When she first approached her bridegroom, Serena was still in awe of him. Believing him to be an immortal, she did not dare behave too passionately. But after they had slept together until midnight and she had noted that he was full of the most ardent desire and quite devoid of any Taoist asceticism, and that his pillow talk was about lovemaking rather than the more ethereal pleasures, she realized that he was no immortal and insisted that he explain everything to her in detail. Having married her by deception, Jiren knew that he had played the fake immortal to a triumphant conclusion; if he failed to tell her the truth now but waited until she found him out, the consequences would be most unpleasant. So he told her the full story.

The explanation of the petition episode was as follows: When he heard that the choice was to be made by lot, Jiren spent his days and nights in a fever of anxiety about what to do. All day long he kept his eye glued to the telescope, alternately sighing and pleading with it: "You played the matchmaker to begin with. Now that you've got me into this fix, tell me, what am I going to do? I implore you to display your powers one more time and bring this extraordinary affair to a close. Don't give up halfway, or your remarkable achievements will be lost forever, and you'll never get the love and respect you so richly deserve."

He hung the telescope in his hall and bowed reverently before it, then took it up to the pagoda and kept his eye glued to it. When he saw Mr. Zhan in his hall grinding ink and writing something, he assumed it was another poem and decided to use the same trick he had tried on the daughter to hoodwink her father and scare him into accepting the suit. But when he looked at the document more closely, he realized that it was a petition to the dead.

No intelligent young man needs to be told any more than this. On reading the petition, Jiren realized what lay behind it, so he hastily copied it out, attached a note, and was about to send it off with a servant when he encountered the matchmaker and entrusted it to her instead. Who could ever have imagined that he would enjoy such a stroke of luck and pull off this remarkable coup?

By the time he had finished recounting all this to Serena, she was gasping with astonishment. "These events may spring from human ingenuity," she said, "but there is an element of Heavenly Will about them, too. Don't think of them as *entirely* contrived."

Next morning they arose and placed the magical icon in the tower as an object of worship. Every day they bowed down before it, and whenever some decision had to be made, they would consult it. By picking up the telescope and looking through it, they would always see something unusual, which they then treated as an oracle, and it never failed to produce results. From this example, it is clear that where the mind is concentrated, objects of clay and wood can work miracles. The worship of gods and buddhas means worshiping our own minds; it does not mean that gods and bodhisattvas really exist.

Of the girls in the household, Serena was the only one whose body Jiren had not had the pleasure of seeing before the wedding. The others had exposed themselves a year before, and there was no need for him to undress them now in order to know their innermost secrets. He flirted with them behind Serena's back, describing accurately what they were like below the waist, and the girls gave him a nickname, Master Thievish Eyes. Because they had already exposed their bodies to him, they also, needless to say, yielded up their essences as well. Jiren, who already possessed the queen of the flowers, gathered in the other blossoms too, which were of course the reason why he had become interested in this marriage in the first place; he did not confine his admiration to the peony and ignore the lotus flowers in their pond. It is clear from this case that women should not only refrain from exposing themselves in front of others, they should also refrain from nakedness in the privacy of empty rooms and secluded retreats. As the proverb says, Leaving your jewels out tempts the thief,

Irony!

painting your face tempts the lecher. But you can expose a pretty face and still retain your chastity, whereas if you expose your snow-white body, you can never be sure that one day that ice-pure chastity of yours may not be defiled.

*C*RITIQUE

The selfsame glass was used by other men for gazing at the scenery but by Jiren for picking out a beauty. Examples of the same kind of intelligence are to be found among the ancients. Storing up wood shavings to pave the ground or bamboo pieces to build a boat—cases such as these demonstrate an identical principle with regard to objects and the will to use them.[16] Jiren came up with a function for this object, in the light of which his official career must have been a notable one indeed. But when we consider the cases of voluptuaries throughout history, we see that this is the only quality of theirs that is worth emulating; apart from seduction and adultery, they lack remarkable talents. It is the same thing with thieves; they are clever enough about thievery, but not, unfortunately, about anything else.

16. These examples of ingenuity come from the biography of Tao Kan, *Jin History* 66.

CHAPTER 1

One man wins food and money by pulling off a coup;
Another loses silver and gold by relying on his wits.

Poem:

    Study the hills, if you're minded to aspire;
    Don't in the fetid lower reaches lie.
    Better to attain the heights and then turn back
    Than amid the sweetest waters foully die.
    The hills we need, as pillars to grind the waves;[1]
    Water cannot move a load of rock.
    Hang but a single painting on your wall;
    Its landscape will increase your virtues' stock.

This newly written poem urges each and every one of
us to aspire to higher things, not content ourselves with

1. The Grindstone Pillars are rocky islets in the middle of the Three
Gates Gorges of the Yellow River.

below us.[2] A man who aspires is like a mountain-endeavoring with each step to go higher while in ant fear of falling, and naturally he has to be bold and erprising. But as for the man who dwells in the depths, e chanced early in life to lose his balance and fall into a sink of iniquity, from which he ought to turn back and try to reform. On no account should he clasp the river to his bosom and renounce the hills, declaring: "I'm an unworthy sinner and, like the currents of the Three Gorges or the Mt. Lu waterfall as it gushes from its cavern, I doubt that I shall ever be able to turn back. I might as well let the water sweep me away into the deepest abyss and sink to the lowest level." Now, it may not be true that *all* men who do wicked things think in these terms, but unless they have the desire to turn back, they will inevitably arrive at this state. You must bear in mind that although the river never turns back, it still has the sea to end up in, but I very much doubt that there is any Peach Blossom Spring there for the wicked man who fails to repent. When he has exhausted the hills and waters, when his sins can get no worse nor his virtues any better, he will at last understand how deceptive the green waters are, and, when the Yellow Springs beckon, will regret that he has never met an upright man to stand like the Grindstone Pillars amidst the flood and inspire him to turn back.

A passage in the *Four Books* runs: "Even the wicked man, should he fast and cleanse himself, would be fit to offer sacrifices to God."[3] Now, to fast and cleanse means to

2. Cf. D. C. Lau, trans., *The Analects*, p. 128: "The gentleman gets through to what is above; the small man gets through to what is down below."

3. See D. C. Lau, trans., *Mencius* (London, Penguin Books, 1970), p. 133.

turn back. Why should a wicked man be allowed to sacrifice to God so long as he repents? I have a splendid illustration: Goodness is like sunshine and evil like rain. Suppose the sun has been out all day. When you see the moon and stars, you'll hardly think it cause for great celebration. But when you've had nothing but rain for days on end and are heartily sick of it, if the sun then breaks through, everyone will rejoice as if they'd seen the blessed skies. No one will blame the sun for coming out too late and shove it into the sea! That's why we don't find it odd when a good man does good; he has always done so, and we treat him the same way as we treat the sun that has been out all day—we're pleased, but not unduly pleased. But when a wicked man does good, we find it extraordinary; because he suddenly behaves like this after always behaving differently, his actions are like seeing the sun again after a long spell of rain. Not only do we befriend him, we embrace him. That is why, when wicked men repent, they are specially favored by God and find it easy to prosper. It's like the case of a thief or bandit who has just surrendered to the authorities; at his very first interview he is offered a position—unlike the aspiring man with no criminal record who has to wait for an examination year before he can even hope to rise.

There was a case recently of a slaughterer living next door to a devout Buddhist who observed all the dietary rules. One night a fire broke out that totally destroyed the Buddhist's house but left the tumbledown cottage next door—the slaughterer's—still standing. "The Way of Heaven is blind," said everyone. "The wrong person got the retribution." But on approaching the cottage they found a sheet of paper stuck up in front of the reception room. It contained a few columns of tiny characters:

HAVING SPENT HALF MY LIFE AS A SLAUGHTERER
AND INCURRED A HEAVY KARMIC BURDEN, I
HEREBY DECLARE BEFORE THE GODS THAT
BEGINNING ON SUCH-AND-SUCH A DAY I SHALL
CHANGE MY PROFESSION. I SWEAR NEVER AGAIN TO
KILL A LIVING THING. IF I BREAK MY VOW, MAY
HEAVEN AND EARTH DESTROY ME!

The crowd made a rapid calculation: The date on which the slaughterer took his vow was just three days before the fire.

"You no sooner repented than you got this reward!" they marveled. "But in that case why did the true believer who spent half his life improving his morals come off worse than you did?"

"There was a reason for it," replied the slaughterer. "According to what I've been told, a while ago the old fellow learned a marvelous counterfeiting technique by which one part of silver could be converted into ten parts that were indistinguishable from the real thing. As he grew more skillful at the process, he spent all his time behind closed doors working on his preparations, which is how the fire got started that burned his house down." The neighbors were deeply impressed.

As the proverb goes, One good deed covers up a multitude of sins, but in the light of this incident one sin also covers up a multitude of good deeds. "Repent" is evidently a word that those who do good must avoid at all costs but that those who do evil must embrace. To the good man repentance means evil, to the wicked man, good. The points of the compass differ, and in order to turn back travelers don't need to go from east to west or from north to south. Once they reverse themselves, they will be heading in a new direction.

The following romance tells of a confidence man who did repent and eventually reached the shore of Taoist salvation. He will serve as an example to all unworthy sinners, freeing them of the fallacy that their sins are too grievous to be forgiven and that they may as well continue on the wrong course.

In the Yongle reign[4] of the Ming dynasty there appeared a confidence man who was capable of the most sublime feats but whose name, place of birth, and physical likeness were impossible to determine. What little was known of him came from the accounts that poured in from all over the country—people in the east complaining about robbery and people in the west reporting fraud. No sooner was it rumored that this crooked genius had gone south than the same rogue would surface in the north. When his depredations began to hurt the public, warrants were posted for his arrest, but no concrete evidence ever came to light, and even if he'd been standing in front of them, people could not have laid a finger on him. When the officials themselves began to suffer, they dispatched constables to seize him, but no reliable clue ever turned up, and they could not have put him on the rack even if they had been able to catch him. Moreover, he knew how to disguise himself so thoroughly that someone he swindled one day was unable to recognize him the next. He was dubbed a demon of havoc, one who set the entire peaceful world on edge and forced people to take endless precautions. But the more precautions they took, the more trouble he

4. 1403–1424.

45

caused, and the more they worried, the more he patronized them. He continued his havoc for over thirty years, during which no one was able to catch and punish him, until one day the Thief Star withdrew from his horoscope and the Posthorse Star left the palace of his birth, and he contentedly settled down and reformed his ways. Then for the first time he revealed his name and place of birth and showed his true face in public, often telling of the things he had done in the hope that others might heed his example. Everyone near and far told anecdotes about his innumerable wicked deeds, anecdotes that have been passed down to the present day, with the result that we now know everything about him. Otherwise how could the author of this romance even begin his tale?

The confidence man in question came from Gao'an county in Zhaoqing prefecture in Guangdong and was named Bei Xi. He had no courtesy name, merely a sobriquet, Qurong. Why this one in particular? Because his father, a noted specialist in breaking and entering, made his living as a thief, and when people saw him in the vicinity, they would warn each other in code: "Bei Rong's here. Watch out, everybody!" The characters *bei* and *rong* combine to form *zei* (thief), and *bei* also happened to coincide with his surname.

When the son came into his inheritance, he felt a sudden desire for a better profession, declaring: "When a man of honor wants to make money, he ought to do it publicly, by open and aboveboard methods. Why operate under cover of darkness, sleeping all day and awake all night like a sneak thief or a cat burglar?" And so he gave up larceny for fraud and robbery for swindling and took up a new profession, remaining genial in public but turning deceitful in private. When people noticed that he was making a name for himself in a new field and enhancing the family's reputation, they bestowed on him the honorific Qurong, which, if the truth be told, was ironically intended. It may have differed from his father's nickname, but the first and last characters still combined to form the word "thief."

While he was still young, his parents warned him against the change of profession. "It's no simple matter making a living as a confidence man. You need to be just as shrewd, bold, and convincing as any of the heroes of old. Before you can trick people out of their money, you must have a wonderful degree of flexibility and a superhuman sense of anticipation. One mistake, and you're in trouble with the law. It can't *compare* as a profession with our family business, which we carry on at night when no one is looking and mistakes can be covered up. We beg you not to change but to continue in the old tradition."

But Qurong's mind was made up, and he refused to yield. "Mine is a god-given talent, not just the result of human effort. No matter who the hero is, he won't escape my trap, I'll guarantee you that."

"Let me give you a test," said his father. "If you can trick me into going downstairs, you'll be showing you have some ability."

Qurong shook his head. "If you were downstairs, I could trick you into coming up, but not the other way around."

"Very well," said his father, "I'll come down. Then we'll see what you have up your sleeve." Once downstairs, he invited his son to trick him into going up.

"But I've already tricked you into coming down," said Qurong. "Why do I need to do it all over again?"

Everyone knows this anecdote, which has been passed

down to the present day, but its hero has always been anonymous. Now for the first time his name can be revealed.

His parents swelled with pride. "He really *has* outdone his ancestors! One day he'll expand the business." Choosing a lucky day, they sent him out to pull off a small coup. They would be quite satisfied, they said, as long as he didn't fail altogether.

To his parents' surprise he was back within a few hours, followed by two porters bringing a banquet and several taels in presents. The banquet came with a full complement of wine tables, cups, chopsticks, and the like, all of silver inlaid with gold. Qurong handed the porters a few coins in delivery fees and sent them on their way.

Astonished, his parents asked why he had brought the banquet home.

"This isn't just any day," he replied. "It's my opening day! To pay up for a celebration and not be able to lick your chops over it—that would be hopelessly banal! Only if the whole thing came from someone else's pocket would it qualify as a brilliant coup. But why not sit down and let me explain it to you as we eat? You're bound to get a good laugh or two."

Delighted, his parents sat down and, wine cups in hand, listened to his account.

The banquet table had been prepared for a first meeting of the parties to a wedding; halfway through the celebrations the bride's family would send it to the groom's house. Well before that event, Bei Qurong had joined the crowd at the theatricals and noticed that in addition to the banquet table in use there was another table for display only. He guessed that after the banquet this other table would be sent to the groom's family and that servants would be needed to carry it over, and he came up with an idea. He knew that while the play was at its height the stewards of both houses would be rooted to the spot, oblivious to their duties. He also knew that this party was for male relatives only; not even the bride had come home for it. Disguising himself as a servant-boy of the groom's family, he intruded into the women's quarters, where a maid found him and asked which family he belonged to. "I'm a servant of the groom's family," he replied. "I came to the banquet with the master. The bride gave me a message for her ladyship but told me not to let the servants know, and that's why I've slipped in here like this. Please take me to see her."

The maid believed him and took him to the bride's mother.

"The new bride sends her respects," said Bei. "She begs you to take good care of your health and not miss her too much. And there's one other message which, although trivial in itself, touches on the family's honor. She hopes that you, as her mother, won't think she's being ridiculous by sending me here to tell you this, but she says the staff here are a greedy lot who are accustomed to stealing food and wine. When the banquet is being delivered, they're bound to exact a toll along the way and remove a few pieces from every dish. Although what they take isn't of any value, when the groom's mother sees the banquet she'll think it has already been started and that you are trying to insult her. Her young ladyship asks that when you send the banquet over, you get two reliable men to seal up the food containers and bring them to our house ahead of time. You mustn't tell the staff, in case they get up to their old tricks. And as for the men bringing it over, you don't need many; two should be ample. Give them the presentation cards to deliver, too; that would save a lot of fuss and bother."

The lady of the house, finding this advice only too plausible, followed it to the letter and sent the banquet off without telling her stewards.

As she did so, Bei stood beside her and whispered something in her ear, to give the porters the impression that he was a trusted member of the groom's household. Then, a little while after the banquet had left, he rushed out and quickly caught up with it. "Wait a moment!" he called. "Her ladyship says there's a lot of vegetables in a container that's been left behind. She told me to catch up with you and look after your loads while you rush back for it."

The servants hurried off. Once they were out of sight, Bei hired two new porters to carry the containers away. This explains why the banquet was brought home with no one in pursuit of it—and also why the news never leaked out. It was just the first of the exhilarating things he did as he began making his name.

His parents were full of praise and declared him nothing less than a wizard. From then on he would swindle someone here one day and someone there the next. His seven inaugural exploits all brought in modest gains, and he appointed his petty burglar of a father an emperor emeritus and would not allow him to work anymore. The whole family relied on Bei's nimble fingers for support, and they did better than just avoid starvation, too—they had meat and wine every day. Within a few years he was famous, and a number of young men were so impressed with his superior skill that they enrolled as his disciples. With a staff of his own he was able to expand his operations, and no place for a hundred miles around was safe from his scams. Notices were posted on every door:

INFORM THE AUTHORITIES
JOIN FORCES TO CATCH THE SWINDLER

A Huizhou pawnshop was situated just in front of the prefectural offices. The pawnbroker, an old hand of many years' experience who had never been swindled, was warned about Bei by his neighbors. "A con man has been active lately whose wizardry is simply out of this world. Everyone's on his guard. From now on you'll have to scrutinize each piece you accept in case you end up as his victim, too."

"He'd have to be superhuman to put one over on me," said the pawnbroker. "If he comes up against yours truly, I'll expose his little game and he won't be able to work his scams anymore."

It so happened that one of Bei's disciples was present when this remark was made and he duly reported it to his master. "Very well," commented Bei, "I'll just have to match wits with him."

One day while the pawnbroker was behind the counter, a customer brought in an ingot of gold weighing over ten ounces that he wanted to pawn for half its value. The pawnbroker examined it and concluded it was solid gold, so he weighed out fifty taels of silver and handed them over with the pawn ticket. The customer left.

A second customer was standing nearby with a few pieces of jewelry that he wanted to pawn. The pawnbroker examined them and rubbed their surfaces.

The customer smiled at this exaggerated concern. "Pawnbroker, these pieces of mine aren't worth very much, you know. Even if you made a mistake, your loss would be quite minimal. But that ingot you accepted just now—I suggest you to take a good, hard look at it, because it seems highly suspicious to me."

"It's pure gold with nothing bogus about it! Why do I need to look at it?"

"*I* can't tell whether it's bogus, but I do know the man who pawned it. He's a notorious crook who's never done an honest deal in his life."

His suspicions mounting, the pawnbroker took out the ingot and examined it once more, then handed it to the customer.

"Take a look at this gold. What's suspect about it?"

The customer took the ingot to the light and examined it, then burst out laughing. "A fine ingot of gold this is—worth all of eight taels of silver! Show it to the others. Let them examine it and see which of us has the better eye."

After rubbing the ingot and examining it, the other customers did find a flaw; the outside was genuine, but not the inside. It consisted of a gold skin weighing less than an ounce around a core of pure copper.

The pawnbroker was beside himself with anger. He wanted to give chase but didn't know where to go.

"He can't hide from your humble servant," said the customer. "If you'll promise me a reward, I'll guarantee to find him at once."

The pawnbroker hastily offered a reward and rushed off with the customer, taking the ingot with him. They came to a teahouse where the man who had pawned the ingot sat drinking tea with a few friends.

The customer pointed him out. "Go and seize him, then shout for the constables. Someone's bound to come to your aid. There's just one hitch though. You're badly outnumbered—one against four. If they wrench the ingot away from you, what evidence will you have against him?"

"You're absolutely right," said the pawnbroker, handing the ingot to the customer and asking him to remain outside. "Wait until I've called the constables and gotten my proof, then bring this in to back me up."

While the customer pocketed the ingot, the pawnbroker burst into the room, seized the man, and raised a hue and cry, at which a number of constables ran up and asked what the trouble was. When the pawnbroker explained, they asked to see his evidence. He shouted to the customer to bring it in, but there was no response, and when he went outside to look, the man had vanished.

"A perfectly good ingot of pure gold, and just because you're taken in by some con man you come and accuse me!" protested the customer. "There's nothing more to be said! I have the pawn ticket here, and I've not touched the money you paid me. Give me back my property this instant, or I'll take you to court." He handed the pawn ticket to the constables and asked them to recover the missing ingot for him.

The constables declared the pawnbroker at fault for being careless and letting himself be swindled; he would have to refund the value of the ingot or face indictment. The pawnbroker became so furious that his eyebrows shot straight up, but he could think of no way to extricate himself and grudgingly agreed to refund the money. He returned to his shop, weighed out a hundred taels of genuine silver, and got rid of his customer.

What was Bei's modus operandi? To demonstrate his powers, he had had two identical ingots made, one genuine, the other fake. The ingot that he pawned was the genuine one. He had arranged for a disciple to stand beside him with the other one and, after he left the shop, to let fall a sly remark or two to arouse the pawnbroker's suspicions. When the latter produced the original ingot, the disciple exchanged it for the other and handed the fake one back. As soon as the other customers discovered the flaw, the pawnbroker naturally begged the disciple to help him catch the swindler. The later developments were even easier to arrange; there was no longer any danger that the victim would escape the trap. But how would you rate this strategy of his? Novel and ingenious, wouldn't you agree?

At first Bei practiced locally, and his reputation, although great, was limited to Guangdong and Guangxi, but after the death of his parents there was nothing to hold him back. Taking his disciples with him, he flouted the law everywhere, and each of his exploits was more novel and ingenious than the one before. But let me wind up this account of his wicked deeds and start telling you about his repentance. The author's primary aim is to be found in the next few chapters. The events of this chapter are meant to serve as a warning rather than a stimulus.

CHAPTER 2

He acquires a host of enemies, and his evil deeds come to a head;
He distributes a fortune, and his goodness of heart emerges.

Bei toured the country with his disciples, stealing and swindling as he went, but he knew that ill-gotten gains cannot be kept for long, and if he couldn't save the money, he thought he might as well squander it. He patronized every famous courtesan and sophisticated catamite, handing out presents that ran into hundreds of taels and never calculating his bordello fees in tens or his tips in singles, and as a result he won acclaim as the leading patron of the pleasure quarters. But because he took care to change his name when he arrived in a new town, the courtesans were wasting their time if they fell in love with him. Once he left town he was untraceable.

His travels continued for several years, during which he visited most of the capitals, all except the two national capitals, Beijing and Nanjing. If the imperial seat can't boast a miracle-working con artist among its residents, he thought, it can hardly qualify as a national capital! I'll just have to go up there and confer a little luster on the court. Besides, I'm tired of swindling ordinary people. The officials are the one class I've never conned, and I mustn't let them off. Even if those in the capital have no money and my take doesn't amount to much, so long as I can wangle a few letters of introduction out of them and travel about the country as an impostor, it should open people's eyes.

He packed his bags, hired the largest available boat, and set sail for Beijing. Nanjing's turn would come later.

A writing-brush salesman from Huzhou was looking for a passage to Beijing, but Bei's disciples, noting that his purse was empty and that he had no goods worth cheating him out of, did not want to take him. "But there's no one in the world with *nothing* to his name," protested Bei, "just as there's nothing in the world that needs to be thrown away. If you cheat a beggar out of the rags on his back, they'll come in handy some day when you're on the run yourself. So long as we can get this man on board and con him, there'll come a time when he can be put to use."

Inviting the salesman on board, Bei regaled him with

the finest wine and food. The salesman asked what business he had in Beijing and where he would be staying, and Bei, making free with the name of a certain prominent official, replied that he would be going straight to his father's offices.

"So you're the young master!" exclaimed the salesman. "Your esteemed father is a customer of mine; in fact he gets all his brushes from me. I'll certainly be visiting his offices to sell my goods and I'll call on you at the same time, if I may."

"Excellent!" said Bei. "But in that case you'll be selling brushes to other officials besides my father. I expect all the officials at the higher levels of government use your invaluable products and that you'll be distributing them everywhere?"

"Of course."

"To whom, exactly? I'd be interested to know."

The salesman took out a notebook giving the names of all his customers. He also produced invoices showing that so-and-so had ordered so many packets of brushes of such-and-such a type at the agreed price of so many taels. Every item was set forth clearly, to aid in distribution. Bei stored all this information away in his memory.

A couple of days later, he brought the subject up again. "It occurs to me that traveling to Beijing is so expensive a proposition that you might as well buy a few extra boxes of brushes while you're at it. Why make life harder for yourself by bringing so few?"

"My capital's so limited that I can't afford any more."

"What a pity we didn't meet before! If I were still at home, I'd have plenty of funds and could easily have lent you a few hundred taels. You could have purchased more goods, brought them to the capital, and paid me back out of the proceeds. Simple!"

This remark awakened the salesman's acquisitive instincts. All that night he tossed and turned, excited at the prospect.

Next morning he went to see Bei. "What you said last night, sir, makes a great deal of sense. It occurs to me that we're not *very* far from your home even now. If you would be kind enough to write me a letter, I'd have time to go there, collect the funds, buy a few more boxes of the best brushes, and rush them to the capital. In the meantime I'd like to ask whether you could take these goods with you to the capital and have one of your servants deliver them for me. I'd collect the money when I arrived."

Bei knew that the salesman had fallen into his trap and magnanimously agreed. He wrote out an order instructing his chief steward promptly and without fail to hand over a number of fifty-tael ingots to a certain salesman for the purchase of goods to be sold in the capital. The salesman took the order and departed, thanking Bei profusely as he left.

On arriving in the capital, Bei acted the part of a salesman and visited all of the officials on his list to deliver brushes. "I am his younger brother," he explained. "He's too ill to travel himself but was afraid you might be waiting for the brushes and has sent me on ahead with them. Please look them over and name a price. If you find it convenient to pay now, just give me the money and I'll take it back to him so that he can meet his medical expenses. Otherwise, please wait until he comes to collect it himself. There's just one request I'd like to make of you. My brother says business has been slack for years and he can't make a living from Beijing alone but would like to add Nanjing to his route. If you have any protégés, classmates, relatives, or friends along the way from Beijing to Nanjing, he would greatly appreciate a few letters of introduction. Recommending a man's brushes is a refined thing to do, not in doubtful taste at all, and I hope you gentlemen won't decline."

So convincingly did he speak that the officials assumed he had no ulterior motive and wrote out their letters of recommendation and also paid up the money they owed. The letters opened with the usual formalities and went on to talk of personal matters, the brushes being mentioned only in a postscript.

But whether the recipients actually bought any brushes was a matter of supreme indifference to Bei, for "the Old Tippler's mind was on something other than the wine."[5] All he wanted was to know how to address his hosts on visiting cards and what to mention in letters; armed with that information, he could write his own letters of introduction. As for the writing, that was no problem; he could imitate anybody's hand.

Once he had left the city a few miles behind him, he began acting the part of itinerant patronage-seeker and at each place on the route south collected a gift. Since he had the formal greetings and the confidences down pat, his hosts trusted him implicitly, their only fear being that their hospitality might not be sufficiently warm. They gave him money as well as gifts—and also presents for the officials from whom he had brought letters of introduction; it was never just a single item that he received. Nor did Bei

5. A common expression drawn from Ouyang Xiu's "The Old Tippler's Pavilion."

confine himself to patronage-seeking. Wherever there was a service to be performed or money to be made along the way, he leaped at the opportunity.

One day he noticed a number of boats plastered with signs in bold characters:

THE CLERKS, RUNNERS, AND OTHER PERSONNEL
OF THIS OFFICE AND CIRCUIT JOIN IN WELCOMING
YOUR HONOR TO YOUR NEW POST.

Bei at once retraced his journey ten miles and had a printing-block engraved with the name and rank of the official in question. After running off a number of copies and pasting them outside the cabin and along the railings as well as on his cases, he sailed back in the direction he had come.

The clerks and runners assumed it was their new superior's boat and came on board to greet him. Accepting their greetings, Bei opened the dispatch case they had brought on board and stamped the date on the documents it contained. Needless to say, the staff had all brought presents, which they handed over on meeting him, and Bei put their contributions aside as first-meeting money.

A day or two later he gathered the staff in his cabin for some gentle advice. "I'd like a private word with you all. I want you to be absolutely loyal to me and not betray the trust I am going to place in you."

The clerks and runners knelt down before him and asked humbly for his instructions.

"The day I left the capital I took out an emergency loan, telling the creditor that I would collect the money and repay him within three days of taking up office. He's on my heels right now. Now, I don't imagine there's any money available when one first arrives in a post. What complicates matters is that once he arrives, he's bound to make a public issue of the loan. The only good solution would be to find the sum before he arrives and get rid of him. Many hands make light work, as they say. I'm afraid I'll have to trouble you all to chip in and relieve me of this burden. Once I'm in office, I'll find ways to repay you."

The staff were only too eager to ingratiate themselves with their new superior and readily agreed. They scurried about and within three days had brought him the money, vying with each other as to who could contribute the most—a windfall for Bei.

In the dead of night he put the money in a box, lowered it gently into the river, then fled ashore and disappeared. After lying low for a day or two to assure himself that the escort boats were far away, he told his disciples to dive in and fish out the money. Another coup for Bei.

In Nanjing he counted up his money, which ran into the tens of thousands. If you have this much money and don't distribute any of it, he thought, you're bound to bring disaster upon yourself. I'd better find a few good deeds to perform: first, to stop the money from plaguing me; secondly, to cover up my sins; and thirdly, to let people get some benefit from my scams. The proverb puts it in a nutshell, Cure your ills while your luck holds. How can I be sure that my success will last all my life and that I'll never have a setback? If the Thief Star recedes from my destiny and my swindling days are over, I'll never be able to *steal* my way to virtue! He resolved then and there to cease his wicked deeds and instead spent his days wandering the streets—a man on the lookout for something to do.

One day he arose early, ate his breakfast, and was strolling down the street when he found himself surrounded by four or five burly men. "We've been after you for ages," they said. "Where have you sprung from this time? Anyway, now that we've got you, we're not about to let you go. You'll have to pay a little visit first." They dragged him off.

When he asked why, they said only: "When you meet your enemy, you'll know."

Bei was alarmed. From the look of things, they must be constables, he thought, and the enemy they mention must be some victim of mine who has caught me and is taking me to the authorities. In a whole lifetime of wrongdoing I've not suffered the least misfortune. How come the moment I want to mend my ways my old misdeeds come to light and I'm dragged off and put to death?

Utterly bewildered, he found himself taken away and locked in an empty room. The men then left to summon his enemy, so that he could meet his match, as they put it.

Bei had just thought up a trick escape plan when there came a rap on the door and a crowd of people surged in—but a crowd of beneficiaries, not victims. They were the courtesans he had once patronized; after moving to Nanjing, they had become famous in the pleasure quarter. Longing for his company, they had told their servants not to let him get away if ever they ran into him. The "enemy" the servants had mentioned was not the kind of enemy who demands your money or your life, but an enemy in the sense of "beloved enemy." And the "match" of "meet your match" implied marriage rather than a coup de grâce.

The women were smiling gaily as they approached to offer their greetings, but after one look at him they turned away in fright, as if he were a total stranger, and stood a little way off in small groups, whispering to one another, with no sign of affection on their faces. Why? Because Bei carried a marvelous preparation with him at all times, and it was the work of a moment to disguise himself. When the men dragged him away and locked him up, he thought disaster had finally struck and seized his chance to alter his appearance after they left, touching up his face to suggest a combination of theatrical roles, something between a minor character, a clown, and a villain. His figure still looked the same, but his face had been drastically altered, and naturally the women were perplexed. While one said he looked a bit like Bei, another denied it. A third said: "He never used to have a scar on his face. Where did he get this purple blotch all of a sudden?" A fourth put in: "He never had a mole beside his eye. Why does he have this black mark?" "His complexion used to be soft with a hint of toughness. Now it's plain ugly with a touch of charm," said a fifth. They whispered together, utterly mystified.

Although Bei said nothing, these thoughts were running through his mind: How different my line of business is from a merchant's! What the merchant fears most is being taken advantage of by strangers; the more people he knows, the safer he feels. But what I fear most is being taken advantage of by acquaintances. Now that these prostitutes have recognized me, they'll spread the news, which will be bad for me. They may not be my victims, but I'd just as soon they didn't know who I am.

In an altered voice he began questioning them. "What do you mean by dragging me here? Why are you turning your backs on me?"

"We have a friend who looks much like you," they replied. "It's years since we've seen him, and because we miss him terribly, we told our servants to keep an eye out for him. When they dragged you in here, we were looking forward to a reunion, but instead we find ourselves in the presence of a total stranger, which is why we're so hesitant about approaching you."

"What is so wonderful about your friend that makes you miss him like this?"

"He was not only generous, he was considerate as well. He gave us ever so many gifts, and whenever we look at one of them we miss him. That's why we can't get him out of our minds."

As they explained, one young girl began to weep. She had concluded that this was not the man she loved and that it was no use chatting to him, so she walked away, hiding her tears.

These tears of hers will generate a wondrous tale that will last a thousand years. A poem bears witness:

A whore can always fake her sadness;
No grief she feels, although her tears pour.
But Mistress Su felt lost and lonely;
Her tears rose from the heart's core.

CHAPTER 3

A single brushstroke is added by divine intervention;
Twin temples are built by a brilliant trick.

The courtesans Bei had patronized numbered in the thousands, far too many for him to remember them all, and although this girl looked somewhat familiar, he could not think of her name. But when he saw her trying to hide her tears as she left the room, he knew there must be a reason and asked what her name was, where she was from, and how she became a prostitute. He found that there was good justification for her tears. Her name was Su Yiniang, and she had been an unregistered prostitute in Suzhou. Her husband was a wastrel, a true habitué of the lower depths who, after squandering the family property, had forced his wife into prostitution. Her first customer had been Bei Qurong, who was struck by her decorous manner, so unlike that of a prostitute, and also by the fact that she seemed too shy for her role. On asking her about her background, he learned that she had been driven into prostitution by poverty, nothing else. He slept with her only one night but gave her several hundred taels and told her to lock her door and take no more clients, but her husband gambled away the money within a couple of months and sold her to a brothel, where she could no longer work in private but had to receive her clients in public. And so she began to think fondly of her lover and wept for him constantly. On hearing that he had been found, she was beside herself with joy and came skipping along to see him, but now that she knew the man was not Bei—the faint resemblance serving only to stir up cruel memories—she began to cry. If she stayed a moment longer, she feared, she would break down completely, so she left the room choking back her tears.

Bei was overwhelmed with pity. Using a clever remark or two he extricated himself from the other women and, after preparing a large number of presents, paid a call on her. At sight of him she burst out weeping, but he feigned ignorance and asked the reason. She told him her story and began sobbing inconsolably.

"Why are you so determined to find him? You can tell *me*. Is he the only one in the world capable of a good deed? Is there no one else as free with his money?"

"I had two things in mind," she said. "First, he slept with me only one night but lavished a great deal of money on me, getting so much less than he gave that I want to make it up to him by allowing him to enjoy himself to the full. Secondly, I was forced to become a prostitute, and since he's a man of honor, he may buy me out. *That's* why I think of him all the time, why I can't forget him!"

"Making it up to him for that night may not be possible, but buying you out should be easy enough. I have a little money myself, enough to see to that anyway. But there's one problem in my case. I'm constantly on the road, here today and gone tomorrow, with no fixed address, and I'd find it very awkward to keep a wife or concubine. The best I can do for you is buy you out and return you to your former master."[6]

"If I'm returned to *him,* I'm sure to fall back into the fiery pit. It will be just one more dead end. My real desire is to spend the rest of my days with you, but if that's impossible, the kindest thing you could do for me would be to find some quiet nunnery where I can be tonsured as a nun and take my vows in the faith."

"I'm afraid that may be just a pretext on your part. If you really have 'the courage to pull back' and can give up this world in order to reach salvation's shore, I'll see that you are back in decent society tomorrow and tonsured as a nun the day after. I'll not only pay your living costs and religious expenses, I'll even build you a Tathagata prayer chamber, a Tutelary Gods meditation area, a Four Vajra gate, and an Eighteen Arhat contemplation hall. Provided you hold true to your vows and don't develop any worldly

6. The text alludes to the rescuers of the heroines in two Tang dynasty tales.

longings or betray your desire to reform but become a good nun and a true bodhisattva, my rescue will have been worthwhile. Now, can you promise me that?"

"I'll swear an oath here and now: Should I fail to persevere and, after becoming a nun, develop any worldly desires, let me be struck down by disaster and thrown into the deepest pit of Hell." After swearing the oath, she withdrew to her room and did not come out for some time.

Bei waited, thinking she had gone to relieve herself. But when she reappeared, a vivacious beauty had been transformed into a flesh-and-blood bodhisattva. She had shorn her jet-black tresses and cloud-puffs and slashed her scented, peachlike cheeks to show that she had burned her bridges and would never go back.

Bei shivered in fright. He was about to say something when the madam and her husband burst in, screaming that Bei had enticed Su Yiniang into the Buddhist order to swindle them, close down their business, and destroy their livelihood. They seized him and began a life-and-death struggle.

"Your business, your livelihood—that's just *money*!" cried Bei. "I'm not exaggerating when I tell you that I have all the money in the world and could come up with any amount you care to name. If you insist on taking me to court, I daresay I could send both of you to your deaths, but I assure you that you'll never succeed in ruining me. You'd be far better off doing a good deed by allowing her to join the order. Let me find some money and pay you back the purchase price. That would be fair."

When they insisted on the purchase price plus gifts, Bei paid the entire amount and took Mistress Su off to his lodgings. That night they avoided even the appearance of impropriety by not sleeping in the same bed but "holding a candle and waiting for dawn."

The next day Bei asked a few brokers—*white ants,* as they are called because they help people buy and sell houses and live off the commissions—to find him an extra large house to convert into a nunnery. He put no limit on the price, but one important consideration was that the house be big enough to convert into two entirely separate dwellings.

Within a few days several brokers reported back: "There's a certain distinguished family who own two very quiet and pleasant garden houses that are entirely separate but form a single unit to the outside. There's also a good deal of extra land there to build a nunnery on. They want five thousand in cash and won't settle for a penny less." Bei went with the brokers to inspect the property, which proved to be a splendid one, and closed the deal at the asking price.

After converting one part into a nunnery, he had a few buddha statues made and asked Mistress Su to move in and begin observing religious discipline. He also chose a name in religion for her, Pure Lotus, likening her to a lotus blossom because she had joined the order from a brothel unsullied by all the filth around her.

The other part he left as it was, intending to use it as a pied-à-terre on his frequent visits to town. Attached to it was a tall building in a very secluded position that was surrounded by double walls—the ideal place in which to store the things he stole. Here no one would find them, and the building would serve as his Treasure Bowl.[7] It had

7. Owned by the early-Ming Croesus, Shen Wansan.

a weatherbeaten name tablet, Return-to-Rest Hall, which the previous owner, an official who had resigned from office, had put up to signify that he was returning home for good.

By a strange coincidence, this very day one of those block characters sprang an odd trick of its own; the character for *rest* suddenly acquired an extra stroke, turning the name into Return-to-Right Hall.[8] When Bei inspected the property, the name had read Return-to-Rest, but when, after choosing an auspicious day, he moved in, he looked up and noticed a tiny change that made all the difference in the world. It now bore an entirely different meaning.

Right is the opposite of wrong, he mused. If I don't change my wrongful thinking, I'll find it hard to get back on the right path. Perhaps it's a miracle sent by the gods? After seeing me do one good deed, perhaps they wanted me to repent and added the extra stroke as an inducement.

On closer inspection he found that the added stroke differed from the others; they had been chiseled into the wood, but this one was raised above it. And it wasn't black or even dark, but of an entirely different color. Fetching a ladder, Bei climbed up to examine it and discovered that the stroke was merely damp clay freshly deposited by the swallows. Birds and beasts are ignorant creatures who couldn't possibly have added that stroke by themselves, he thought. Obviously the gods of Heaven and Earth must be behind it.

From that point on he ceased his wrongful thoughts and tried to emulate Mistress Su in abandoning worldly desires and seeking refuge in religion. Because his feats

8. A stroke across the top of the character for *rest* turns it into the character for *right*.

resembled those of an immortal in that ordinary folk couldn't figure them out, he concluded that Taoism would be easier than Buddhism and chose what came to him most naturally. He converted his building into a Taoist chapel, and he and Pure Lotus pursued their separate vocations, seeking to return together as immortal and buddha, respectively. As his Taoist name he took Return-to-Right; since the gods had given it to him, he thought, it would serve as a constant reminder to avoid any wrongful thoughts.

One day he put forward a new plan. "I propose to turn the site into a monastery, and to do the job properly I'm thinking of building two temples, one to serve the Three Purities and the other the Three Treasures.[9] Otherwise you'll have your Guanyin gallery and Arhat hall but no statues of Tathagata or Sakyamuni, and how would that look? My chapel is in even worse state; it's cramped and dilapidated, and still only in the early stages of conversion."

"Temples like that will cost you thousands," said Pure Lotus, "and now that you've become a priest you've lost your chance to make any money. Even if you do have some savings, you'll need them for the future. You can't go throwing money about the way you used to do."

"Never mind. Let me try a little magic and see if I can change a few hearts. I guarantee that within a year a donor will appear who will provide all the funds we need, so that I won't have to contribute either money or effort. *That* will show you what superior magic I have!"

"But you're just setting out to become an immortal and haven't even attained the Tao yet! What magic do you

9. The Three Purities or Pure Ones are the supreme gods of Taoism. The Three Treasures are the three images in the main halls of Buddhist monasteries, representing Sakyamuni, Bhaisajya, and Amitabha.

have that could possibly change people's hearts and get them to contribute so readily?"

"Don't bother your head about it. I'm leaving for home now to see to my parents' funerals and won't be back until this time next year. But I guarantee that by the time I return the temples will be built and the statues of the Three Purities and Three Treasures handsomely finished, all ready for me to step into the prior's job."

Pure Lotus failed to grasp his meaning and took his promises for bragging. A few days later he declared that the statue of one of the Eighteen Arhats had been poorly finished and that he needed to call in a noted sculptor to redo it. Although Pure Lotus urged him to be satisfied with the statue as it was, he insisted on replacing it. He then departed, taking all his disciples with him save one, whom he left behind to look after the buildings.

Pure Lotus had been alone in her chapel for six months when suddenly an official and a merchant arrived together, both of them intent on good works. The official said he had come from Huguang with over a thousand taels to build a temple in which to install the Three Purities, while the merchant said he came from Shanxi with a similar amount for a Buddhist temple to honor the Three Treasures.

How did these benefactors hear of this good cause and suddenly decide on their acts of charity? Why did Return-to-Right's magic prove so superior? Read the next chapter and find out.

CHAPTER 4

Blessed with uncanny luck, a swindler gains success;
Falling for a crafty ploy, benefactors win good fortune.

A flabbergasted Pure Lotus asked the official and the merchant how the idea for their acts of charity had occurred to them. Moreover Huguang and Shanxi were so far apart; without coordinating their visits how could they have arrived on the same day? There had to be a reason.

"An extraordinary thing happened to me," began the official, "which will simply amaze you. I've always been devoted to the immortals and spend all my time studying longevity practices. My devotion moved the Highest Purity, and a true immortal came down to earth and delivered a personal message to me: 'A monastery has recently been established in Nanjing,' he said. 'It is complete except for a temple. The prior is a true immortal who has been sent down to Earth but will soon ascend to Heaven again. Since you are a devotee of the Tao, you should go at once and see to this noble deed. Whether or not you attain eternal life may very well depend on this man.' Awestruck, I asked him to give me a timetable for the construction. He gave me dates for starting, getting up the frame, and finishing the work. The day it was finished the prior would put in an appearance. My meeting with him was predestined and would ensure me of the rewards of enlightenment. That's why I was so punctual. I didn't dare miss the heavenly deadline."

It was pure coincidence that the merchant had arrived together with the official, for the two men had never met. By the time the official had finished speaking, the merchant was deeply suspicious and questioned him closely. "Im-

71

mortals are just figments of the imagination, you know. You need to have some proof before giving them any credence. How do you know he was a true immortal from Heaven? Why couldn't it have been someone from here who wanted you to build a temple for him and made up the whole rigmarole?"

"Do you suppose I'd have believed him without proof?" replied the official. "I saw and heard such miraculous things that I concluded he was a true immortal and didn't dare mistrust him."

"What was it you saw and heard?" asked the merchant. "Give me some idea."

"The first time he visited he claimed to be a true immortal from Heaven. My young servant was incredulous and replied that he was talking nonsense and that I would not even be informed of the visit. At that point the man wrote a few characters on the gate in a large hand:

RESPECTFUL GREETINGS FROM
THE TAOIST WHO TURNED BACK

"Before he left, he told my servant: 'I'm an old friend of your master's, and when he sees this visiting card of mine, he'll remember. I'll be back to see him tomorrow at the same time. He'll come out and see me anyway, even if you don't pass on the message, so it's no use trying to keep me away.' My servants waited until he had gone, then fetched a bowl of hot water and began scrubbing the gate, but no matter how hard they worked, they could not scrub the message off, at which point they told me. I was incredulous too, of course, but I went out and watched them scrubbing and found that they were telling the truth. I called in a carpenter to shave the characters off with his plane, but, incredibly, the message was still there after he had planed off the top layer of wood. And it was still there when he took the next layer off. Even when he got right through to the other side, it was still visible. At that stage I began to believe just a little. I knew that The Taoist Who Turned Back was the sobriquet of Lü Dongbin,[10] and I told my servant: 'If he comes back tomorrow, don't turn him away. I definitely want to see him.'

"He did return the next day, and as I rushed out to welcome him, I noticed that he carried on his back a priceless sword that was exceedingly sharp and flashed in the sunlight. At his waist was a miniature calabash about three inches wide and an inch deep. While he was still some way off, I told him: 'If you're a true immortal, please take off your sword and lay it down so that we can greet each other. How do I know you're not some hired assassin, armed with a naked weapon as you are? No matter how much I wanted to welcome you, I wouldn't dare.' "

"He took off the sword as calmly as you please but didn't lay it on the table or hand it to anyone. Instead he slowly inserted it into the calabash. Within minutes that whole three-foot blade had vanished into thin air! All that remained was a sword-hilt sticking out of the mouth of the calabash like the handle of a pot or case. Now, I ask you, on seeing that kind of thing, how could I help but be convinced? What strengthened my conviction was that none of the requests he made was in the least self-interested. He wouldn't be handling the money himself, but wanted *me* to oversee the building and install the Three Purities—a work of charity that I could actually watch as it took shape. How could I refuse such an offer?"

10. One of the Eight Immortals of Taoism.

He turned to the merchant. "And what was it *you* saw that brought you here? Did you have any proof?"

"Certainly I had proof. An abbot from this monastery visited my town to seek alms and sat meditating outside my door all day long, not saying a word. All he had was a blackboard upside down in front of him, on which a few columns of characters were written:

ALMS SOLICITED FOR CONSTRUCTION OF LARGE
TEMPLE. SINGLE DONOR SOUGHT. MONEY WILL NOT
BE HANDLED BY SUPPLICANT. INSTEAD DONOR IS
REQUESTED TO GO AND OVERSEE BUILDING
HIMSELF. THE WORK OF MERIT WILL APPEAR
BEFORE YOUR EYES, BUT ITS REWARDS NEED NOT
WAIT UNTIL AFTER YOUR DEATH.

"When he had sat there a long time without saying a word or even changing his expression, it occurred to me he must be a Zen priest, so I asked him what treasure mountain he was from, and he mentioned this place. Now, I'm quite well off, but I have no son, and I'd made quite a name for myself as a philanthropist. I noted that the priest wasn't soliciting alms for himself but merely to build a temple, and when I heard that the work would be something I could watch as it went up, I signed the contribution book and sent him on ahead. Before he left, he gave me a schedule for beginning, getting the frame up, and completing the job that was *identical* to yours. Surely this abbot can't have *connived* with the immortal? Let's ask him to come out and clear the matter up for us."

"But no priest from this monastery has *ever* gone out soliciting!" protested Pure Lotus. "Perhaps he mentioned some other place and you got it wrong, venerable sir? Since this other gentleman met a true immortal who wanted him to perform a charitable work, naturally I welcome such magnificent generosity. But as for your gift, venerable sir, it was not solicited by this monastery, and I wouldn't dare take it under false pretenses. Moreover, when a nun has a temple built, it's up to *her* to solicit funds. She doesn't delegate the responsibility to a priest! A holy place oughtn't to have any shadow of suspicion over it, so I cannot honor your intention. May I suggest, venerable sir, that you take your money and make inquiries elsewhere?"

The merchant was utterly confused. "But what he said fits this place so *perfectly*! How can it be wrong?" He turned to the official for advice.

"Since you had the impulse to do good, you shouldn't stop now," said the official. "Even if the request did not come from him, even if you were doing this against your own will, wouldn't it still amount to worshipping Buddha?"

The merchant agreed, and the two men spent the night together. Next morning they walked over the lot to choose a building site and estimate the materials needed. But then they came to a certain place, noticed a particular statue, and removed an object from it that shook them to the core. So startled was the merchant that his hair stood on end and he began mumbling the following words over and over:

Prithee cease thy hustle and bustle;
Lift up thine eyes and see the gods.

Where do you suppose he was when he received this shock? Which statue was it that he saw? And what was the object that so alarmed him? Of the eighteen statues in the Arhat Hall there was one that was the image of the abbot who had solicited alms. When he saw it from a distance, the merchant was agog, and the closer he drew, the closer the resemblance became. The statue held a book in its arms that resembled the subscription book he had signed. When he took it down and looked at it, he found that, although made of potter's clay, it held a strip of red paper with someone's name on it in large characters—*in his own handwriting!* Wouldn't you expect him to be astonished—and convinced—by this fact?

"In the light of this," said the merchant, "the immortal must have been a true immortal and the buddha a true buddha. You and I are lucky enough to have our destinies entwined with a buddha and an immortal. Provided we see this temple through to completion, our reward is assured." Impressed by this evidence, the official was also more in awe than ever.

Choosing a date for the groundbreaking, they pressed ahead with the work by day and by night and managed to finish before the deadline. On the specified date both temples were complete and the statues installed.

Just as everything was finished, a holy man appeared. The merchant and official noticed that he wafted along like an immortal with a gait unlike that of a human being.

"Who *is* this brother in religion?" they asked.

"He's the prior of our monastery, whose religious name is Return-to-Right. He has just come back from his parents' funerals to devote himself to the study of the Tao."

The official at once bent his head and bowed four times before him as a true immortal. Without daring to seem forward, he asked the immortal to choose a name in religion for him and to accept him as a disciple so that, on returning home, he might continue to pay him homage. Return-to-Right granted both requests.

For his part the merchant did reverence to Pure Lotus as a living buddha and asked her for a name in religion for future use. If Buddha blessed him with a son, the son would be given this name, as if in attendance on her lotus throne, so that he might enjoy a long and fortunate life. Pure Lotus also granted the request.

She and Return-to-Right prepared vegetarian dishes for their guests and entertained them for several days before seeing them on their way.

This Buddhist nun and Taoist priest now devoted themselves to their religious disciplines and in less than ten years had achieved success. As the proverb so aptly puts it, A prodigal son who repents is a pearl beyond price. Anyone who takes the wrong turn but then regains the true path is in a different class altogether from someone who has behaved properly all his life. "Once he sees the light, he never strays again," as they say. He doesn't repent a second time and resume his wicked behavior.

Separated only by a wall, Pure Lotus and Return-to-Right practiced their religions for ten years, and not a soul knew that this Taoist brother was a former confidence man. But after seeing the light, he no longer wished to deceive anyone and freely admitted his ugly behavior. People learned that his past had been more sordid than any prostitute's. It was his good luck to repent early in life, before he fell foul of the law, for whenever we reform, the bad luck in store for us also changes for the better.

"You've spoken about the things you did in the past," said Pure Lotus, "and I already know most of them. The one thing I'm still not clear about is how the temple got built. Six months before you were sure that someone would contribute the funds, and you were right. Why? You couldn't have possessed magical powers of that sort while still only in training to be an immortal!"

"To be perfectly frank," said Bei, "that episode belonged to my old life as a confidence man. The Thief Star had begun to recede, although it hadn't quite left the palace of my birth, and my fate was about to turn, but somehow I still pulled off a couple of jobs and conned two donors into contributing. Fortunately both men could afford it, and the project I tricked them into was a good one, so I don't feel too guilty about it. Otherwise I'd have been like a Feng Fu who makes a fool of himself by failing to kill the tiger and then has to endure a lifetime of ridicule as well."[11]

"What method did you use?" asked Pure Lotus. "Don't tell me a confidence man has the power to make writing penetrate a gate, cause a tiny calabash to swallow a three-foot sword, order the gods about, and send an arhat off to solicit alms!"

"There's an explanation for each trick. They may *seem* fantastic, but once explained they're worthless. Every thief has a ploy or two to baffle the public with, and I like to feel that my intelligence is several times greater than a thief's. I wanted to build the temples but begrudged spending my own money, so I came up with an idea for tricking others into donating. I knew that the official was a devout believer in the immortals and that the merchant had always been ready to donate, so I laid a trap for them. I took two disciples with me, one dressed as an immortal, the other as an arhat, and sent them to Huguang and Shanxi, respectively, to act out their roles, while I went home to see to my parents' funerals. What a surprise! The gods came to my

11. Feng Fu was a tiger hunter who, after appointment as an officer, killed another tiger and forfeited the respect of his peers. (Apparently it was now beneath him.) See D. C. Lau, trans., *Mencius*, p. 198.

aid and, by the time I got back, had carried out my clever little scheme for me—a case of 'When a man wants to do good, Heaven comes to his aid.' Heaven does half the work and man the rest; it can't all be ascribed to trickery."

He went on to reveal the hitherto secret details— enough to make anyone double up with laughter. The message on the gate was written in turtle urine, a substance that penetrates through wood and resists all efforts to scrub or plane it off. The immortal's sword was hollow and made of lead and tin. The calabash had been filled with quicksilver, which dissolves those metals on contact, so the sword-blade vanished soon after it entered.[12] As for the statue of the arhat, that was a likeness of the disciple whom Bei had sent to Shanxi. It was with this plan in mind that he had insisted on having the statue redone before he left. After the subscription book was signed, it was sent back to the monastery, where Bei had told the custodian to wrap it in a little clay and tuck it inside the arhat's clothes. When the merchant saw it, he was convinced beyond the shadow of a doubt and went ahead with his charity.

By this time Pure Lotus was agog with amazement; again and again she marveled at his ingenuity. But if he was so clever, she protested, why hadn't he pursued an honorable career? Had he applied his superb talents to military strategy, he would surely have become a second Chen Ping or Zhuge Liang and made vast contributions to the court.[13] Why had he so abused his natural gifts?

Obviously, formal qualifications should not be rigidly

12. In Chinese alchemy, mercury amalgamates easily with other metals, particularly lead. That may be the reasoning behind this episode.

13. Famous strategists of the Han and Three Kingdoms periods, respectively.

adhered to in making appointments. Heroes are to be found among bandits and burglars, too, just as gallant men exist among bird mimics and sneak thieves.[14] And when a wicked man repents, he benefits not only himself but the court and society as well.

Eventually both Return-to-Right and Pure Lotus garnered the fruits of enlightenment, one soaring aloft while the other was translated in the lotus position. The only thing we don't know is where they are installed in the Eastern and Western Heavens and what ranks of immortal and bodhisattva they hold. (Somewhere in the middle, I should think.) The strangest thing of all was that after returning home from building the temple the Shanxi merchant had three sons in quick succession. And the official from Huguang did learn the art of nurturing his health and lived on into his nineties before dying of natural causes. Analyze these cases as you will, it is hard to come up with an explanation. What does emerge is that those who do good deeds will eventually receive blessings so long as they throw themselves wholeheartedly into their charity. There is no need to ask whether the one soliciting the alms is genuine—or even whether he exists. Not only does the swindler's victim earn the same moral credit as the man who feigns ignorance, even the victim of a robbery finds his bad luck offset by blessings. If there were no wealthy people in the world, who would provide for the cold and hungry? When all is said and done, the only difference between losing your money to robbers and giving it away to charity is that the first action is involuntary and the second intentional.

14. The archetypal feudal lord, the Lord of Mengchang, had retainers of various kinds, including a bird mimic and a sneak thief. See *Shi ji* 75.

CRITIQUE

Bei's career forms the main text of this story, its first few passages being merely a prologue. The excellence of the main text goes without saying, but the prologue also offers innumerable delights to the mind and eye. Hills and waters form a striking analogy, which is followed by one of rain and sunshine. They make a striking simile, which is followed by the change of heart. A change of heart signifies repentance, plumbing the ultimate mystery, after which there is no further obliqueness. Instead we have the passage about journeys—an even finer illustration. In all this there is no thought that fails to attain the heights, no word that fails to reach the depths. I cannot *imagine* how Liweng's[15] mind became so brilliant!

However, a man may make his mind brilliant without being able to make his mouth brilliant as well, or he may be able to make his mouth brilliant but not his hand, in which case, even if he has superb arguments and remarkable ideas, he will have no way to get them down on paper. As a result it is far easier to find a lively man than a lively book—because Heaven has ways of limiting their number. Contemporary authors may or may not have Liweng's mind, but even if they do, they cannot possess his brilliant mouth and hand as well, and I advise them, after reading *Twelve Lou,* to lay down their writing-brushes. If they insist on imitating him, to have any hope of following in his footsteps, they will have to summon the Five Titans into their minds to open up apertures everywhere and confer real brilliance on them—and then have the Five emerge and refashion their mouths and their hands.

15. Liweng is Li Yu's best-known name.

*H*OUSE *O*F *G*ATHERED *R*EFINEMENTS

CHAPTER 1

The flower-seller won't sell flowers from the rear
*   courtyard,*
While the customer is accustomed to buying priceless
*   treasures.*

Poem:
> Could this be a vision of Heyang county?
> Or the Quarter of Tattered Brocade?[1]
> When bought, the flowers were just in bud;
> Now sold, their scent has stayed.
> A swarm of bees! The market scene's
> As busy as a butterfly's wing.
> Grudge not the cost, my lords—all is
> For sale but the beauty of spring.

1. When Pan Yue (247–300) administered Heyang county, he planted flowering peaches everywhere. The Quarter was a country retreat of Pei Du (765–839) that contained a hundred apricot trees.

This poem was written twenty years ago by the Romancer Who Awakens the World.[2] At the time I was buying flowers in the market below Tiger Mound,[3] and I lingered there, among its riot of colors and profusion of scents, unable to tear myself away. An old man, more interested in collecting memorable lines than in making profits, handed me brush and ink and asked me to write a poem for him, which is how I came to write this on his whitewashed wall.

A market is the most vulgar of places, while flowers are supposedly the most refined of objects. And yet, incongruous as the terms *vulgar* and *refined* may be, these flower-sellers not only make good money, they also enjoy a tranquil life, which is why they are the object of such envy in my poem. But flower-selling is not the only enviable trade. I know of two others. And what might they be, you ask? Bookshops and incense shops—which, together with flower shops, are known as the "three refined trades among the vulgar."

People who open these shops do so for karmic reasons; they open them, not because they just happened to learn the trade, but because their last existences were spent as insects or animals. What kinds of insects and animals? Florists were bees, booksellers were bookworms, and the men who run incense shops were musk deer.

But there is one other trade that is the most refined of all, so why is it not at the top of my list? Those who run antique shops are known as the connoisseurs of the marketplace, and since they pass themselves off as cultivated men,

2. One of Li Yu's fiction-writing pen names. The poem is found in his *Independent Words* 5. The third line differs.
3. A resort outside Suzhou.

oughtn't they to be listed *before* the three trades I have mentioned? But because antique shops sell books, flowers, and perfumes together with their antiques, the owners are reluctant to consider great literature, rare flowers, and exotic perfumes as if they were new products. Nevertheless, for all their protestations, both the vulgarity *and* the refinement of business resides in these men.

There are cases in which the business is the essence of refinement but the merchants are the height of vulgarity. These merchants spend their lives among books, flowers, and incense and not only fail to appreciate them, they loathe the smell of flowers and incense and are bored to death by the classics and histories. Are they not somehow *involved* with these objects against their will? They, too, must have been insects or animals in a previous existence and now find themselves in their present state because their physical form has changed but not their temperament. Bees know only how to plunder flowers, not how to appreciate them, and toil their lives away for the benefit of others. Bookworms know only how to devour books, not how to understand them, and grow old and die in graves of half-eaten volumes. The musk deer is full of scent, of which the deer itself is completely oblivious. It may have a richly perfumed navel and scrotum for others' pleasure, but to the deer its scent is a burden. Such merchants are not the refined among the vulgar, but the vulgar among the refined.

I shall now tell of a few people who did manage to change themselves completely and appreciate these things, and who supposed that they had hung out their shingles in a genteel business where customers would patronize them. But there was just one problem. They also had another shingle, signifying physical beauty, which should never be displayed, lest it lead to trouble. I respectfully urge all handsome young shopkeepers to take caution as their watchword.

During the Jiajing reign[4] of the Ming dynasty there lived in Wanping county of Shuntian prefecture two young men, Jin Jongyu and Liu Minshu, who were fellow students as well as good friends. They were far too distracted by a variety of arts and pastimes to devote themselves to full-time study, so neither succeeded in the examinations, and on reaching their twenties they gave up their studies for careers in business.

They had an even younger friend, Quan Ruxiu, who came from Yangzhou and whose face and figure rivaled He Yan's and Shen Yue's for beauty.[5] Male though Quan was, his looks surpassed those of the most gorgeous women. He carried on a rear courtyard relationship[6] with both Jin and Liu who, treasuring their friendship, managed to avoid any jealousy over him. Indeed they did more than avoid jealousy, they used him as a means toward a closer physical bonding themselves. For all people knew, two young men had taken on a third, but the truth was that all three had coalesced.

"We're all well educated," they said, discussing their future. "We've given up our studies but have still to choose a specialty. Only if we select some genteel trade will we be able to keep our status as cultivated men." In reviewing all thirty-six occupations, they found few that appealed to them. Books, incense, flowers, and antiques were the only ones to meet with general approval, so they decided to start

4. 1522–1566.
5. Household words for male beauty.
6. Euphemism for anal intercourse.

a business that would combine all four products. Renting a three-unit shop on West Riverbank, they knocked the units into one and in the middle installed a bookshop run by Jin, on the left an incense shop run by Quan, and on the right a flower shop—to which was attached an antiques section—run by Liu.

At the rear stood a tall building to which they gave the name House of Gathered Refinements. The superb quality of its design and the tastefulness of its furnishings go without saying. On balmy, moonlit evenings they would gather in this building, and there would be music and singing of consummate artistry that ravished the senses of all who listened. There was no rare or remarkable book they failed to enjoy there, nor any strange incense, nor any exotic species of plant or flower. They would touch no antique after the Han, nor hang on their walls any painting later than the Song. And when they had finished enjoying a piece, they would sell it, and the longer it had been in their possession, the higher would be the price that they asked— as if the world should foot the bill for the pleasures of these artistic connoisseurs.

Jin and Liu had wives who lived elsewhere, while Quan, who was single, lived in the shop as wife to both men, who stayed with him on alternate nights, nominally to look after the shop but actually to enjoy the pleasures of the rear courtyard. By day they made their money, by night they took their pleasure. Where else in the world would you find two such heavenly immortals? There was not a single young man in the capital who did not admire and envy them—admire the serenity of their lives, envy their rare delights.

They ran their business differently from other shop-keepers. Although their aim was always to make a profit, they observed a certain style in the way they did it. There were three conditions under which they wouldn't buy and three more under which they wouldn't sell. When wouldn't they buy? When the goods were inferior, fake, or of suspicious origin. "These are high-class businesses," they would say, "and if you stock inferior or fake goods, you'll not only ruin your reputation, you'll drive people away, with unpleasant consequences. As for goods of suspicious origin, whether stolen by thieves or servants, although the prices are tempting, there's not much money to be made from them, and the legal trouble they may involve you in will cost you your reputation as well as your investment. Putting your head in a noose—that's not what a man of refinement or a connoisseur would do!" By imposing these conditions on themselves, they avoided any risk of disgrace.

What of the conditions under which they wouldn't sell? They wouldn't sell at too low or too high a price, or if the customer had any doubts. "Genuine goods at honest prices" may have been just a slogan for other shopkeepers, but they took it seriously. Although their prices were not fixed, they would discount no more than ten or twenty percent. Not only would they refuse to go higher, if someone they knew offered them the nominal price, they would weigh out the discount and return it, to demonstrate their honesty. Sometimes a customer they had not dealt with before would wrongly identify an article and suspect it to be a fake, and in such a case, even though the money had already changed hands, they would decline to complete the sale, explaining: "What's the point of paying out your money and getting nothing but doubt and suspicion in exchange? You'd be better off trying somewhere else."

They never deviated from these rules. When the shop

first opened, business was slow, but it picked up steadily until the premises could no longer hold all the customers. From commoners to officials, from officials to mandarins, no class failed to patronize them. So famous did they become that even the emperor's own palace women, if they wanted a famous flower or an exotic incense, would send a eunuch over to the House of Gathered Refinements to buy it.

Whenever a mandarin or an official visited them, the owners would invite him upstairs to sit down, and only after serving him tea would they fetch the goods he was interested in. When the patrons noted how elegantly the room was furnished and how cultivated the owners were, they would make an exception and treat them differently from other shopkeepers. Some patrons would leave them standing while they chatted, while others would ask them to sit down. Generally speaking, Jin and Liu were more often left standing, while Quan, although a commoner, was treated as if he were an officeholder and regularly asked to sit and chat. Why was that? Because he was young and had a lovely face, and presumably the officials were no sticklers for morality but enjoyed a homosexual affair on occasion. Whenever Quan joined them, they would have loved to make their laps into easy chairs and clasp him to their bosoms. How could they bear to leave him standing at a distance? Which explains why he sat far more often than he stood.

At the time in question, Grand Secretary Yan Song's son, Yan Shifan, whose sobriquet was Donglou, served as a Hanlin compiler and enjoyed immense power.[7] One day

7. Yan Song (1480–1565) and his son Yan Shifan (1513–1565) have been recorded in history as abominable tyrants.

89

as he sat in the court anteroom chatting about painting and antiques with his colleagues, they began praising the objects in the House of Gathered Refinements as uniformly exquisite. And not only were the objects of high quality, they said, the shopkeepers were quite cultured themselves. At this point one or two of Yan's colleagues volunteered: "The most delightful is the youngest, who is sweetness and innocence itself. With him sitting opposite, you've got your rare incense, your exotic blooms, your antiques, your books right there in front of you. Why bother to look at anything else?"

"If they're running short of pretty boys on Lotus Seed Lane, do we have to go *behind the counter* for them?" asked Yan. "I simply don't believe you can find a beauty like that in the marketplace!"

"Words alone won't convince you. If you're at all interested, why don't we go and see him?"

"Very well, let's go over as soon as court's out."

This suggestion prompted his colleagues to send word to the shop. They had two motives in mind. In the first place they wanted to curry favor with the great man; if he approved of their choice, it would show that they shared his tastes. And secondly, they wanted to ingratiate themselves with the shopkeepers by informing them that a Very Important Person was on his way over and giving them time to get ready. If the shopkeepers could satisfy this customer, he would be worth as much to them as dozens of other officials, and the profits would be considerable. When *they* went shopping there, a little something would surely be knocked off the price. So they told their servants to deliver the following message: "His Honor Yan is coming to inspect your wares, and you ought to make some preparations. He's different from other officials; you can't afford to slight him. Not only must the tea be of the finest quality, even the person who serves it and keeps him company ought to spruce himself up and appear well groomed and smartly turned out. If His Honor consents to say one word of approval, this will be your lucky day! The Yan household on its own is worth at least half as much as the palace. And not only will you make money, you'll find it quite easy to land an official post."

Jin and Liu were alarmed. "Seeing to the tea—that's our job. But why this talk about the person who keeps him company? Why should *he* have to spruce himself up? He's not some official's pet doorman or singing-boy! When officials go upstairs and have no one else to talk to, we send him up to list what we have in stock and discuss prices. By now it's evidently become *de rigueur,* and they *expect* to see him! From what they say in their message, it's obviously him, not our goods, that they're interested in. I imagine those officials gave old man Yan a glowing account to tempt him here—worshipping Buddha with borrowed flowers, as it were. But this old man is different from others; he's bold and ruthless, and if he likes what he sees, he won't be content to scratch the itch through his boot, he'll do his damndest to fool around with the lad. We may not be jealous of each other, but we'll certainly be jealous of an outsider!"

After talking it over privately, they called Quan in and asked him to decide.

"I don't see any problem," he said. "Let me leave before he gets here, then just tell him I've gone out. Officials get carried away and boast about their pleasures in front of their colleagues, that's all. He'll hardly go so far as to arrest me!"

"You're right," said Jin and Liu, hiding him away and getting on with their preparations.

Within a matter of minutes Yan swept in followed by several officials. They were escorted by a squad of fierce-looking servants.

Entering the shop, Yan cast an eye all around and, seeing no young man there, assumed he had gone upstairs. When he arrived upstairs and still saw no sign of him, he asked his entourage.

"He'll be out in a moment," they replied. "When *we* visit, he always comes and keeps us company. Now that his lucky star has descended from Heaven, he's hardly going to run away!"

Yan was a master of intrigue, an exceptionally shrewd man, and he realized that the shopkeepers must have been tipped off about his visit and have packed Quan off somewhere else. "In my opinion," he said, "he certainly won't be out to see me today."

We gave them notice, his colleagues thought. We didn't just drop in on an impulse. He must want to expand the business. He *can't* have run away! It never occurred to them that extraordinary men might also be found in the marketplace, men who, unlike officials, value friendship over status and would sooner antagonize a powerful official than a friend.

Yan's colleagues were confident enough to suggest a wager: "If he doesn't show up, we'll treat you to a banquet. Let's bet on it." Yan accepted the bet, and they waited for Quan to bring the tea.

Unfortunately the tea, when it came, was brought by an elderly hunchback instead of the young shopkeeper. Asked where the young master was, the servant replied:

"He didn't realize you gentlemen would be honoring us with a visit today and went out."

Their faces dropped. "His Honor Yan is not just another customer, you know. It's terribly hard to get an interview with him. Hurry up and find your master, lest he spoil the whole occasion." The servant departed.

After a short wait Jin and Liu came upstairs and saluted. "What sort of things would Your Honor like to see? We'll be happy to bring them up."

"I'd like to see everything you have, no matter what the kind. But bring only your choicest, most expensive pieces, the ones no one else can afford."

The two shopkeepers flew downstairs and gathered up their most valuable antiques, their most exotic flowers and perfumes, plus a book catalogue or two, and brought them up and set them before Yan.

Yan's aim had been to see Quan, not buy anything, but now, although furious at the youth's absence, he betrayed no hint of anger. Instead he set aside all of the most valuable pieces, praising them as he did so. No mention of the youth escaped his lips.

"I'd like to buy all of these," he said, after making his selection. "I understand that your prices are not completely dishonest. Let me take these pieces with me, and I'll pay you when I receive your invoice with the net cost."

Jin and Liu had been afraid that Yan, having come on Quan's account, would not leave without him but would insist on waiting, and they knew they would be sorely embarrassed as time dragged on. So when Yan wished to leave promptly and with no sign of irritation after buying a great quantity of goods, they felt particularly grateful and quickly agreed. "Our only concern was that Your Honor might not want them. By all means take them with you."

Yan ordered his servants to bring the items, and they followed him out of the shop with the goods stuffed in their pockets or slung over their shoulders. Stepping into his sedan chair, Yan apologized once more and then was borne merrily away.

His companions, however, were chagrined, not so much because they had lost their bet and would have to stand treat, as because they feared Yan's displeasure. They had miscalculated in this trivial matter, and he would be less inclined to entrust them with more important things in the future. Such is generally the way with those who are overly concerned about their own advancement.

Having brought his tale this far, the author must pause for a moment; the next episode is too long to be told without a break.

CHAPTER 2

In protecting the rear, they lose the front;
By joining a benefactor, he meets a nemesis.

Jin and Liu waited until Yan and his entourage had left the premises before making out the invoice, which came to exactly a thousand taels. They were reluctant to collect the money at once and delivered the invoice only after five days had passed. At the Yan mansion a steward accepted it and soon returned with the message: "His Honor has taken note of it."

Jin and Liu were well aware that the official mentality differed from that of other people—officials were quick to take goods but slow to pay for them—and concluded they would not succeed at the first attempt and might as well go home. A few days later they tried again and received the same answer. From then on they took turns going every few days but were never offered a single tael, not even a cup of tea. The very words they received were doled out like precious gems. Nothing was ever added to the *has taken note* formula.

You have to give money to get money, they thought. Collecting from officials is like alchemy: You can't start the reaction with nothing, you must seed it with a little silver. Unless we leave a package at the gate, his people will never put themselves out!

They weighed out five taels and gave them to the steward in charge, urging him to do his best to transmit their message. They even promised him a commission; if the payment were made in full, they would set aside ten percent as a gratuity. When the steward realized that they knew the ropes, he offered them his candid opinion.

"You two will never be able to collect your money like this. I understand there's another shopkeeper who's young and good-looking and that His Honor has heard about him but not yet seen him. Well, His Honor intends to keep these goods of yours in hock to persuade the young man to visit here. Provided he comes, the money will be paid. Look, you two are shrewd enough. Why throw the key away and try picking the lock with a piece of wire? What happens if you break the spring?"

Jin and Liu felt as if they were awakening from a dream. In a cold sweat, they stepped aside to talk the matter over: "We've been too clever for our own good. If we'd let him see Quan that day, perhaps he wouldn't have taken our things. But who would have imagined that goods would spell disaster?[8] To get *them* back we have to sacrifice *him,* and vice versa. We'll have to give up one or the other, but which should it be?"

After a moment's thought, they came to a firm conclusion: "A thousand taels is far easier to come by than genuine beauty. Let's give up the goods."

They turned back to the steward. "That assistant of ours is just a boy," they said. "He comes from an old family who have sent him to us to learn the business. He's never even been allowed out—we're afraid his parents might worry. Whether or not His Honor pays us, we aren't going to hand over someone else's child for money! Besides, we put up the capital for those goods and deserve to get a return on it. We shan't be back again. If by some fluke the money does become available, please let us know and we'll come for it."

The steward laughed. "Tell me, gentlemen," he said, "are you going to keep your shop open now that you've decided not to collect the money?"

"Of course. Why not?"

"*What!* You own a shop here in the capital, so how can you be so ignorant of who holds power? As the proverb says, The poor and humble are no match for the rich and powerful. If you don't collect the money, it'll be a clear sign of your hatred and contempt. Is he a customer you can afford to hate and insult? If he wanted to sleep with your wives, I could understand it. Naturally you'd risk anything to stop him. But all we're talking about here is a friend of yours. Taking him along for the master's appreciation is like sending him an antique or a painting; even if it comes back a little the worse for wear, it will still not have lost all

8. A pun: the words for *goods* and *disaster* are both pronounced *huo*.

its value. Why give up thousands of taels for a cup of vinegar? What's more, after you've given up the money, other things will start happening to you; you'll never feel quite secure again. I strongly advise you against a course of action that spells nothing but trouble."

The partners began to regret what they had done and told the steward that they fully agreed with him.

Once home, they wept in front of Quan, then told him the heart-breaking news and asked him to go with them to collect the money. He firmly refused. "If a virtuous woman won't take a second husband, how can a loyal man take a third master? Apart from you two, I shall *never* consort with anyone else. I'd rather have the cost of those goods chalked up to my account than do anything so disgraceful!"

Jin and Liu impressed on him the dangers they ran. "If you don't go, not only will we lose our money, it will be very difficult to keep the shop open. We're bound to be hit by some disaster or other."

Firm as Quan's resolve was, it could not withstand his partners' pleading. He had no choice but to consent and accompany them to the Yan mansion.

The steward at the gate was delighted to see them and rushed inside to report. Yan at once ordered them admitted, and Jin and Liu saw Quan as far as the inner gate before turning back.

Meeting Quan for the first time, Yan examined him from head to foot and concluded to his vast satisfaction that this was indeed the most beautiful boy in the entire city. "You're a young man of taste and I'm a lover of art, so why did you hide from me that day when the other two were willing to meet me?"

"I happened to be out when you visited. I would never dare hide from Your Honor!"

"I've been told that you play various instruments exquisitely and that you're also an expert at tending flowers and arranging antiques. As for burning incense and making tea, that's your forte and there's no need to test you. I need someone to keep me company in my library and would like to prevail on you to come and live here as my external concubine. It would save me the trouble of engaging a companion, which would be a great boon. Are you agreeable?"

"My parents are both elderly, and since we're a poor family, I shall need to earn some money to support them. I'm afraid I couldn't leave them for very long at a time."

"But I understand you're an *orphan!* Why are you trying to deceive me? You're so thick with those two scoundrels that you can't bear to part with them. That's why you're making these excuses! Do you mean to say that an official like me isn't worth as much as two shopkeepers? They managed to hire you all right. You think *I* don't have the means?"

"Those two are my sworn brothers as well as my colleagues, and there has never been anything improper about our relationship. Your Honor should not be so suspicious."

Yan knew this was untrue but took no notice. I still haven't won him over, he reflected, and he doesn't feel any affection for me yet. Why would he abandon his old friends to consort with me? He kept Quan in his library and spent the next three nights with him.

Yan was devoted to homosexual affairs, and there was not a single attractive catamite in the city of Beijing who had escaped him. Even his subordinates, qualified officials though they were, if they were young and good-looking and willing to mount the stage, would be shown excep-tional favor and invited to a rendezvous in the rear court-yard. With such wide experience, he was naturally a connoisseur, and when he saw that Quan's skin was as smooth as butter and his rump whiter than snow—virginal, despite the two husbands—he fell madly in love with him and insisted that he stay.

In the course of the next three nights he used a vast amount of cajolery to win Quan's favor by the soft and gentle approach. But the young man proved himself a veteran campaigner. So confident was he in his adamant refusal that blandishments fit to call down flowers from Heaven had no effect whatsoever.[9] To every approach he had a reply, to every proposition an excuse. Unable to persuade him, Yan had to send him away—at least for the present. On the fourth day he had the goods brought before him and looked them over once more, then chose a few of the best pieces for himself and sent the rest back. In addition to the cost of the pieces that he kept, he paid Quan twelve taels in personal compensation.

Quan could scarcely refuse. He tucked the money in his sleeve and, as he went out the gate, he handed it to Yan's servants. He was ashamed to betray his friends by accepting it.[10]

On meeting Jin and Liu, he was indeed overcome with shame, and his only thought was to kill himself. His part-ners had to plead with him again and again before he reluctantly agreed to go on living. Afterwards, whenever he saw Yan's sedan chair passing by, he would duck out of

9. Expression originating in Buddhist myth for blandishments or verbal exaggerations.
10. The text alludes to the Shang dynasty loyalists Bo Yi and Shu Qi.

sight lest Yan come in and molest him again. From time to time Yan would send an invitation, but Quan always declined on the grounds of illness. After he had done this a number of times, he felt he could hardly refuse anymore, so he chose a day when he knew Yan was out to go and sign the visitor's book. In doing so he was clearly treating Yan the way Confucius had treated the usurper Yang Hu.

Yan was furious. An eminent man like me, one whose lieutenants staff the court, a man who can get anyone he wants—why, not even a raving beauty, the daughter of a multimillionaire, would dare refuse me if I wanted to marry her! And yet this orphaned nancy-boy from a commoner's family has the nerve to snub me when I make an overture! It's the fault of those two rogues, who have gotten him so firmly hooked that he won't change, but I'm still furious about it. I shall have to think of some way to entice him here. There's just one snag. With a handsome youth like that in the household, my concubines are inevitably going to be attracted. Even if nothing happens, they're bound to make invidious comparisons and I'll look older and uglier than I really am. I shall need to find the perfect solution before inviting him here, if I'm to get any permanent advantage. But although he thought long and hard, nothing came to mind.

At that time a eunuch named Sha Yucheng enjoyed great power. From his position inside the palace he had colluded with the Yans in a variety of nefarious schemes, and like them he stood high in the Emperor's favor. A chronic asthmatic, he had returned home at nine o'clock that day to rest, after attending the levee. Although he held the title of palace eunuch, Sha was no different from an official. He had begun his career as an art connoisseur and had a keen appreciation of plants and antiques. No matter how hard Yan Shifan worked to earn a connoisseur's reputation, he was a rank impostor in comparison with the eunuch.

One day Yan paid a call on Sha and found him arranging his *objets d'art* and watering his plants, not doing the work himself but shouting orders at his staff. Despite the stream of orders, he seemed quite unruffled.

Yan made a gesture of help, then commented: "These things were meant to bring us pleasure. If they involve us in this much effort, they're nothing but a burden."

"When your boys can't be relied on, you have to see to things yourself," replied the eunuch. "I've been trying to find a suitable boy for years. If Your Honor has any conscientious lads who are knowledgeable about these matters, I'd be greatly obliged if you'd let me have one."

This remark brought back all of Yan's previous concerns, and with them came a plan.

"My boys are even more hopeless than yours, I'm afraid. However the city has recently produced a young connoisseur who's not only very knowledgeable but also a brilliant musician and chess-master. Many officials have been after him as a page-boy, so far without success. But I suppose he might come if *you* were to invite him. There's just one problem with the lad. He's past puberty and now thinks of nothing but girls, so even if you do manage to get him, you won't be able to keep him for long. The only solution would be to remove his desire to leave by doing what was done to you: castrating him."

"That's no problem," said the eunuch. "I'll get him in here with a trick I know. If he's willing to be castrated, fine. If he isn't, I'll get him drunk on drugged wine and gently relieve him of his privates. He may not be willing to serve as a eunuch after he comes to, but he certainly won't be able to grow them back again!"

Delighted, Yan urged him to put the plan into operation as soon as possible, lest someone else get the boy first. Before leaving he offered another suggestion: "While Your Grace has a use for him, this question won't arise. But if the time should come when you pass on and have no further need of him, I hope you'll see to it that he's returned to his sponsor. Whatever you do, don't let him go to anyone else."

"Of course! An invalid like me—how many years do I have, anyway? And a eunuch is hardly going to have any sons to inherit his property. By all means come along and claim the lad."

This was the whole point of Yan's stratagem. He had calculated that an invalid like Sha would have only a few years to live and that the boy would come his way at the eunuch's death. His aims—to avenge Quan's snub and also work out a long-term arrangement—would be fulfilled by proxy. When Sha guessed what was on his mind, Yan burst into laughter, after which they enjoyed a few drinks together and parted.

Next day Eunuch Sha sent a servant to summon Quan: "A while ago I bought some bonsai from you that have not been pruned and have grown rather straggly. The youngest partner is requested to come and restore them. In addition, the palace has placed an order, mainly for creams, perfumes, and the like, and I want to have him take it away and check off the items."

Jin and Liu promptly accepted and told Quan to go to the palace at once. Since Sha was a eunuch, they assumed there was no reason for suspicion, even if he kept Quan overnight. Moreover, having offended Yan Shifan, they were afraid of his retaliation and thought that Sha, who was on good terms with Yan, might come to their rescue in an emergency. This is why they accepted so promptly, their only concern being that Quan might not perform his duties well enough.

Quan accompanied the servant to the palace, where he paid his respects to Sha and chatted briefly before asking the eunuch's wishes.

"Seeing to the plants and checking the order for the palace—that's the least of it. I've long heard of your great reputation but never had the pleasure of meeting you, so I want this visit to pave the way for a friendship between us. I'm told you're a specialist in the arts, particularly music—in fact that you're the most accomplished artist in the capital. On your visit today I'd like you to demonstrate all of your talents and not stint on the things you have to teach me."

Quan, who had come there to cultivate the eunuch's friendship, did not scruple to use this opportunity to win his way into the eunuch's favor and gain his protection. He not only ignored all modesty, he even exaggerated his accomplishments, lest, by confessing to a single field in which he was not proficient, he forfeit the chance of another invitation. Eunuch Sha was delighted to hear the claims. He ordered his boys to bring out a variety of musical instruments and set them in front of Quan on a mat. He then asked his visitor to demonstrate his talents while joining in the drinking. Quan obeyed scrupulously, pouring all his skill into the performance.

Young Yan certainly knew what he was talking about, thought Eunuch Sha as he listened. A boy with these gifts will never agree to serve me unless I castrate him. But rather than ask him, in which case he'd probably refuse, I'd better act on my own.

He winked at one of his servants, who brought in some drugged wine and filled the young man's cup with it. Soon after drinking it, Quan began to grow limp. His head lolled forward and he slumped in the easy chair like an unwakable Chen Tuan.[11] Eunuch Sha roared with laughter. "Come on, lads! Go to it!" he called. Before the drinking began, he had hidden the castrators behind the ornamental rock. They now came forward, pulled off the boy's trousers, gripped his genitals, and with a light, deft cut sliced them off and threw them on the ground for the Pekinese dog. After some watery blood had oozed out, they applied styptic powder to the wound on a hot compress, wiped away all traces of blood, and pulled Quan's trousers on again as if they had never been off.

After sleeping for an hour, Quan awoke with a start, but although he felt some pain, he was still under the influence of the drug and did not know where the pain came from. With a conscious effort he focused his gaze on Eunuch Sha.

"I'm afraid I drank too much and took liberties that offended Your Grace."

"You look a little tired," said Eunuch Sha. "You'd better go into the library and rest."

"Just what I feel like doing."

Eunuch Sha told his staff to help Quan into the library where, because of the lingering effects of the drug, he fell asleep as soon as his head touched the pillow.

We do not know when he will awaken from his long

11. Chen Tuan was a legendary Taoist figure who could sleep for years at a time.

sleep and what despair he will feel. Having read this far, gentle readers, are you able to steel your hearts and feel no pain on behalf of the little shopkeeper?

CHAPTER 3

The great man loses power, and his skull makes up
for genitalia;
The castrato takes revenge, and his urine compensates
for spittle.

In the ivory-inlaid bed Quan slept on and on, dead to the world. He slept until after midnight, when the effects of the drug wore off and his wound began to ache. Awakening with a cry of pain, he felt his body all over—something was missing! Then, as he touched the place where it had been, the pain grew unbearable. He ran the events of the previous day through his mind and suddenly awoke to the truth: the benefactor he had allied himself with had turned out to be his enemy! And his own flaunting of his talents had been the cause of his undoing! At this thought he could not help wailing and sobbing, which he continued from three o'clock until dawn.

At nine o'clock two junior eunuchs came in and offered their congratulations. "From now on you belong to His Majesty's household, and no official has any authority over you! No man will ever dare harass you again!"

But their congratulations only made Quan feel worse. He had lost all chance of ever taking a wife. Worse still, he would have to part from his husbands and could never rejoin them in marriage.

At the height of his anguish another eunuch entered, this time with a summons: "His Grace has arisen. Come and make your kowtows."

"But I'm a guest in this house. Why should I kowtow?"

"Now that you've been castrated, you come under his control. *Of course* you have to kowtow!" All three eunuchs left the room.

Even if I don't kowtow, I'll still have to take leave of him in order to get out of here, thought Quan. If I totally ignore him, he'll never let me go!

Clambering out of bed, he hobbled painfully, step by step, out of the library and into Eunuch Sha's presence. He was just going to bow when the eunuch, whose stern expression and tone were vastly different from the day before, forbade him. "Your wound hasn't healed yet, so you'd better omit the kowtows for the present. Come back and pay your respects in five days' time. With effect from today, I'm putting you in charge of the library; all the antiques and books will be in your care. I'm also assigning you two boys to help with the plants and trees. If you're willing to give me loyal service, naturally I'll show you special favor. But if you fall short in any respect, you need expect no mercy. Someone who's been castrated can only join us eunuchs here. There's no escape for him, not even to Heaven itself!"

A shiver of fear ran through Quan as he bent at the waist and pleaded: "Now that I've been castrated, of course I wish to serve Your Grace. But I can hardly perform my duties before the wound heals. I beseech Your Grace to grant me a few days' leave in which to go home and recuperate. There'll be time enough to come back and take up my duties after I'm better."

"Very well, I'll allow you ten days to recuperate." He gave an order to his servants: "Boys, escort him out of the palace and deliver him to the owners of the House of Gathered Refinements. Tell those clerks to take good care of him. If they let him die, I might want more than just their penises in compensation." The eunuchs saluted and began helping Quan out of the gate.

Jin and Liu had exulted when Quan received the call from Eunuch Sha. They hoped he would stay a few extra days and reveal more of his talents for the eunuch's appreciation, so that all three of them might enjoy protection. When Quan did not return, they felt quite easy in their minds and never went to meet him—the opposite of their attitude during his visit to Yan, when they slept not a wink the whole three nights. On that occasion they could scarcely wait for dawn to harness up their donkeys, or for evening to light their torches. The reason, of course, was that Eunuch Sha lacked even a weapon to hunt with, while Yan was armed with the panoply of war. Strangely enough, however, when they had agonized over imminent disaster, only the rearguard perished, while now that they felt confident of smooth sailing, the entire vanguard was lost at sea.

When they saw a group of junior eunuchs helping Quan in the door, his face the picture of misery and his flesh drained of color, they assumed he had been unable to hold his liquor and needed help in getting home after a night away. Little did they realize that Quan's sexual fortunes had run out and that his hopes of marriage were dashed forever. He blurted out the story of his castration and then broke down, so affecting his lovers that they wept, too, and practically drowned in their tears. The eunuchs who had escorted Quan grew impatient and pressed Jin and Liu for a guarantee that they could take back to His Grace. Needless to say, if the slightest mishap occurred, the victim's relatives would have to pay for it with their lives.

Terrified of becoming involved, Jin and Liu at first refused to sign. The eunuchs began pulling Quan away, intending to take him back, at which point the two men had no choice but to write out a pledge: "If we should be guilty of any oversight, we are prepared to answer for it with our lives."

After seeing off the escorts, Jin and Liu began sobbing again. They searched far and wide for capable doctors and eventually got the wound to heal. Their main concern during those days was to save Quan's life, and they had no time to think of their own pleasure. Then just as Quan's wound healed and they were about to express their old love for him in a final farewell, a group of eunuchs came bustling in.

"Your time's up," they declared. "Hurry back to the palace and take up your duties. If you're just a few minutes late, we'll have to bring in the people who signed the pledge, and they may find themselves castrated too."

Jin and Liu were scared out of their wits. With tears in their eyes, they saw Quan to the gate.

Back in the palace, Quan realized that, castrated as he was, he had no chance of escape and would have to knuckle under and serve the eunuch. Perhaps, who knows, it was in his destiny to become a powerful eunuch himself; promotion might come his way. So he threw himself unstintingly into his duties, and Eunuch Sha was delighted with him and treated him as his own son.

At first Quan was ignorant of how he came to be castrated, but on questioning his colleagues he learned that the master intriguer himself was responsible. Consumed with hatred and eager for revenge, he still feared that if he told anyone and it came to Yan's ears, not only would his own life be in danger, but his two lovers would be implicated and lose *their* lives too, and so he feigned complete ignorance.

Whenever Yan paid Sha a visit, Quan would try to ingratiate himself. "My work kept me so busy before that I couldn't visit you very often," he told Yan. "But now that I'm here, it's just as if I were living in Your Honor's own mansion; if there is anything you need me for, just send for me. So long as His Grace is prepared to let me go, I'll be happy to spend two days in every three with you."

Yan was delighted. He often asked Quan to keep him company on the pretext that his plants and trees needed attention. Eunuch Sha, lacking genitals, had no need of him at night and was always ready to share him with a kindred spirit.

Once inside Yan's mansion, Quan set to work as a spy. Anything Yan did or said that conflicted with the court's interests or harmed the nation was jotted down in a notebook for future reference.

A few months after Quan's castration, Eunuch Sha suffered an unusually severe attack of asthma. His condition steadily worsened until, a year later, he collapsed and died. On his deathbed he fulfilled his promise and presented Quan to Yan.

Quan was even more pleased to find himself in his enemy's sole employ and in less than a year had ferreted out every offense for which father and son had been responsible.

It so happened that the Yans' crimes had come to a head and were about to be revealed. On the very day that Quan finished his investigations, trouble broke out.

When Yang Jisheng[12] submitted a memorial condemning Yan Song's "ten crimes and five evils," the emperor disregarded it and even had Yang executed, a decision that all loyal officials protested, some by seeking to resign, others by impeaching Yan. The emperor's only recourse was to a temporary display of authority; he ordered Yan Song to resign and sentenced his son Yan Shifan, his grandson Yan Gu, and others to exile in a malaria-ridden part of the country. He did so to remove the Yans from the scene in the face of mounting criticism, but he fully intended to reinstate them as soon as the furor had died down. However he was foiled in this covert intention of his by the most junior of his loyal aides. Not only did the Yans fail to get reinstated, they were displayed as criminals in the marketplace—a sight to warm the heart.

After Yan Shifan was exiled, the members of his staff were placed in the custody of the prefectural and county offices to await the disposition of the case, when they would either become government property or be returned to their original masters. As the roll was called, Quan cried out in a ringing voice: "I'm not one of Yan Shifan's servant-boys, I'm a eunuch on the staff of the Sha household. At the time of His Grace's death, I ought to have been presented to court, not handed over to a private individual! I beseech Your Honor to lose no time in drawing up a recommendation that I appear before His Majesty to explain the circumstances. If Your Honor tries to hush the matter up, I fear that when the truth comes out even your office may not be immune."

Of course the prefect did not dare hush it up, but wrote a report to his superior, who passed it on to his ministry.

12. A censor who lived from 1516 to 1555.

When the ministry communicated it to court and Quan was summoned to the palace, the case was finally brought to a close.

As he entered the Forbidden City, Quan noticed that all the creams and soaps in use by the palace women, like the ornaments they wore at their waists, bore the imprint "House of Gathered Refinements," and he said as much to the women: "All these things come from our shop. It must be fate; first the goods come here, and now the shopkeeper comes to join them."

"So you're the owner of Gathered Refinements! A good-looking lad like you—why didn't you marry and have children instead of getting yourself castrated?"

"There is a reason, but I can't go into it just yet. If it got out of the Forbidden City and came to the ears of that gang of traitors, I would never be able to avenge the wrong they did me. I prefer to explain everything to the Imperial Father when I see him."

The women went at once and tattled to Emperor Shizong: "That eunuch who has just arrived used to be in business but fell foul of the tyrant and has been forced into his present situation. He's suffered some wrong that he wants to protest, but he won't tell anyone about it except Your Majesty."

The emperor had his aides bring Quan into his presence and questioned him again and again. Quan gave a detailed account of the castration, adding nothing and omitting nothing. The emperor was enraged. "They told me that he used his power to oppress the people and did nothing fair or just, but I didn't believe them. In the light of this, he really is a tyrant; there can be no doubt about that. But while living in his household all that time you must have learned about other actions he took. Apart from this case, are there other crimes that might harm the court or nation?"

Kowtowing endlessly, Quan cried out "Long Live Your Majesty!" over and over again. "The fact that Your Majesty condescends to ask about such matters is due to the nation's glorious destiny as well as the spiritual power of ancestors and gods. This man's villainies are too numerous to count. Out of concern for the court, your humble servant set to work to spy on him. I wasn't able to record all the things he did, but I do know a good portion of them. I have a little notebook here in which I jotted down only those incidents that I had heard or seen myself. If it contained a single incorrect word, I wouldn't dare inflict it on Your Majesty and commit the unpardonable crime of deceiving my sovereign."

The emperor took the notebook and read it. Then a thunderous roar escaped him, and the sun broke through the clouds. Rapping on the imperial desk, he exclaimed: "What a fine man Yang Jisheng was! A second Bi Gan or Ji Zi![13] Every word of his memorial was right. In wrongfully killing a loyal officer, we have made ourselves an object of scorn to all eternity and brought ruin upon our nation! Our original intention was to let the thunder roar and then follow it up with gentle rain, waiting until people's feelings had cooled before reappointing the Yans. But in the light of your evidence, dismissal and exile are too good for them. We must certainly bring them back and execute them in the marketplace—to avenge the fury of a

13. Bi Gan protested against the tyrannical actions of the last Shang ruler and was disemboweled for his trouble. Ji Zi protested against the same actions and was thrown into jail. Although rescued by the Zhou, he continued to regard them as usurpers.

loyal officer and bring joy to the innocent hearts of the people. Every day they live, even in some malaria-ridden place, will be spent stirring up trouble for us. How do we know they aren't calling on the barbarians to rise in rebellion at this very moment?"

As the emperor was pondering his course of action, fate decreed that Yan should die a cruel death, for others now arrived to pour oil on the flames. Several loyal officials came in with a sealed report: "The Japanese are invading, sent by Yan Shifan, who has been bribing them for some time. The officials at court and in the provinces knew all about it but didn't dare say anything because of his enormous power. Since his exile, however, numerous people have come forward. We beseech Your Majesty to enforce the law with all due haste and eliminate this threat!"

This report confirmed the Emperor's own revised opinion, so he handed down a secret order dispatching a commander to bring Yan back to the capital as quickly as possible and execute him under the law.

Quan waited until Yan Shifan had been brought back and was about to be executed, then went to the execution ground and, jabbing his finger at him, denounced him bitterly. He also wrote a fine poem and presented it to Yan to vent his own outrage and warn all who heard it that the wages of sin are quickly paid, in the hope that no one in power would ever try to emulate him. After the execution he made Yan's skull into a chamber pot. Yan had drooled with desire before doing this evil thing, and then, in taking his pleasure, had used a great deal of spit. Quan now settled accounts with urine.

The poem, in old-style verse of irregular line length, contained a powerful moral message. It ran:

You took my manhood;
Your head I'll claim.
A high for a low—
Surfeit of shame!
You played with my rump;
In your mouth I'll piss.
A clean for an unclean—
The stench will not cease.
And now I urge all mortal men:
Let not your hearts be cruel and cold.
For when you come to pay the price,
Your schemes will be assessed twofold.

*C*RITIQUE

Since catamites take the woman's role in sex, their genitals
are superfluous, and it is really a convenience to have them
removed. However the decision must be that of the youth
himself, as it was in the case of You Ruilang in the *First
Collection*.[14] Yan Shifan failed to obtain this young man's
consent and took action on his own account that was
distinctly brutal. Small wonder Quan ached for revenge! I
also mock Yan for the lack of discrimination he showed in
using castration in the wrong case—the result of having a
successful intriguer's power but not his talents or skills. Had
he been a real master of intrigue, he would have done to
Jin and Liu what he did to Quan and deprived those who

14. The homosexual lover of a story in Li Yu's *Silent Operas* collection. See "A Male Mencius's Mother . . ." in Patrick Hanan, ed., *Silent
Operas* (Chinese University of Hong Kong Press, 1990).

possessed the catamite of *their* underpinnings. Not only would it have brought joy to his own heart, it would have been greeted with paeans of praise from the entire capital; people would have said that Yan Shifan had actually been responsible for *one* heartwarming action in the course of his life. Alas, he was not perceptive enough to see this. He lost his chance for goodness, both in name and reality, and the episode became just another instance of his wickedness.

THE CLOUD-SCRAPER

CHAPTER 1

*A beautiful girl is even more beautiful with her
    makeup removed;*
*An ugly wife seems even uglier when flaunting her
    looks.*

Poem:
> Who first contrives a young girl's ruin?
> A treacherous maid will arouse her feeling.
> With flashing glance she'll hold the stranger
> And send, like the oriole, news of spring.
> From the boudoir steals a whiff of blossom
> That quickens the beat of a butterfly's wing.
> Without Hongniang there to unravel the clues,
> Would Zhang have ever been found by Ying?[1]

1. Zhang and Yingying are the hero and heroine of *The West Chamber*, Hongniang is the maid.

This poem, like the story that follows, emphasizes the willfulness and treachery of serving-girls and maidservants. The story's aim is to alert heads of households to the danger and induce them to take precautions and check on their maids' activities, lest their womenfolk suffer dishonor through inadequate segregation. It is a work of moral education, not a tract to promote immorality and decadence.

The word *meixiang* (plum-blossom fragrance) has been in use since ancient times as a general term for maidservants. People who take it for granted assume that it is meant to be flattering, not realizing that the ancients had a profound purpose in coining it: *mei* (plum-blossom) stands for *mei* (matchmaker) and *xiang* (fragrance) stands for *xiang* (hither and thither).[2] The plum sends the message of spring and its fragrance drives the bees wild. But when the message of spring is inside the house and the bees are outside, how are the twain going to meet—unless she goes hither and thither and brings them together? The ancients gave maidservants this name to remind people of the danger and put them on their guard. A single slip, and trouble will ensue, trouble that will ruin the mistress's reputation but leave the maid's intact.

Suppose for a moment that that was not the ancients' intention. The names available for maids are legion—at one time or another every flower, every vessel you can think of has been drawn upon—so why is the term *meixiang* the only one to have been handed down unchanged from ancient times?

In the Ming dynasty there lived a chaste widow who preserved her chastity from the age of fifteen—when she lost her husband—into her forties, despite pressure from

2. Pairs of homonyms. The characters are quite distinct.

her husband's relatives and even her own parents. Unyielding as iron or stone, she did many things that showed great fortitude, until suddenly one night she was defiled in her sleep by an adulterer. Still only half awake, she felt a man's weight on top of her and, thinking she was back in the days when her husband was alive, clasped the adulterer in her arms and indulged her passions to the full. Only when it was over did she awaken with a start and realize that the man in her bed was an adulterer and that she was a widow.

She asked him who it was that had let him into the house and allowed him to make so sudden an appearance. Now that he had defiled her, the adulterer felt confident there was no ulterior motive behind her question and told her the truth. It turned out that her maid had been carrying on with him for some time and had more than once brought him in to spend the night. Fearing that her mistress would find out and punish her, the maid had told her lover that he might as well help himself to both women and secure his pleasures over the long term.

"The mistress is a very sound sleeper," she told him. "She won't wake up unless you shout. Choose a time when she's fast asleep to sneak into her bed and have sex. To succeed, all you need do is get inside her. Even if she does wake up, she'll be far too embarrassed to call the constables and have you arrested." Emboldened by this advice, the adulterer had crept into the widow's bed and done this evil deed.

Although bitterly resentful, the widow valued her reputation too highly to risk a scene. But once the adulterer had left the house, it struck her that her chastity, maintained at such terrible cost for over twenty years, had been sacrificed in an instant by the machinations of a maidservant, and she could not live with the thought. Unable either to endure what had happened to her or to reveal it, she summoned the maidservant and denounced her bitterly, then heaved a few deep sighs and hanged herself.

Eventually her family found out the truth and filed suit. The adulterer was sentenced to summary execution and the maidservant to a lingering death. The judge's summation included the lines,

> The wrong was righted after her death,
> When her name was ruined beyond repair.
> How hard to stay pure and avoid a slip!
> Let those with lax regimes beware.

And then there was another maidservant, responsible for all kinds of remarkable achievements, who succeeded in arranging a marriage between a brilliant young man and a beautiful young woman that had hitherto defied the most strenuous efforts. She belongs in quite a different category from those maids who devote themselves to lechery and adultery, and when you learn her story, gentle readers, you will undoubtedly see it as an amusing anecdote and protest that she should not be spoken of in the same breath as that first maid. But what you may not realize is that this author is well versed in the principles of the *Spring and Autumn Annals* and knows that everybody in the world may serve as a matchmaker *except* a maidservant.[3] For a maidservant who plays the matchmaker in her mistress's marriage is obeying the same principle as the traitor who betrays his country and his lord. Thus my story is presented to you as a negative, not as a positive, example.

3. A terse chronicle allegedly compiled by Confucius. Some of its commentaries specialize in finding moral judgments in the chronicle's terminology—a view that was generally believed in Li Yu's time.

In the Yuanyou period[4] of the Song dynasty there lived a young licentiate named Pei Yuan, styled Zidao, who, as the seventh boy in his generation, was known as Septimus. He lived in the city of Hangzhou and was noted for his refined good looks. He was talented and learned as well, and had set his heart on succeeding in the examinations. In his early youth he married a Miss Feng, the daughter of a local magnate, a girl whose dowry was as handsome as her looks were ugly, and whose opinion of herself was as high as her behavior was low. Septimus was deeply ashamed of her. Before his engagement to Miss Feng, his father had betrothed him to a Miss Wei. He was just a boy at the time and quite unknown, but when he came of age the whole town was buzzing with talk of his talent, and all of the wealthier fathers wanted him as a son-in-law. Miss Feng's father sent a matchmaker along with a proposal, and when Mr. Pei heard that the dowry would be over ten times that of the Weis', he could not bring himself—under the influence of the current mores, as he was—to pass up the opportunity. He broke off the engagement to Miss Wei in favor of one to Miss Feng.

After the wedding Septimus noticed how peculiar his wife looked. She, however, far from being aware of her own ugliness, made a point of sporting the most vivid makeup and the gaudiest dresses and of flaunting herself in public under the impression that she was the ranking beauty in all Hangzhou. Every month she would insist on making several jaunts to the West Lake in the company of her women friends. Indulged from her childhood on, she was accustomed to such gallivanting and would tolerate no restraint.

4. 1086–1093.

Septimus was a young gallant who had boasted to his friends before marrying Miss Feng that he would either find a dazzling beauty or else remain single, and in his present situation, with a gorgon for a wife, he was terrified that people would find out and laugh at him. He let his wife take her jaunts but never went with her and would not even allow her to be escorted by any pages whom his friends might recognize. Her escorts were all drawn from among their women servants, so that when his friends saw her they would not know whose wife she was. If they gave a catcall or two as she passed, or made critical comments, he would be not be personally affected.

During the Dragon Boat Festival the whole population turned out to watch the races on the West Lake. Septimus went, too, and watched with a group of young men. In the midst of the excitement, a hurricane struck the lake, the waves began pounding on shore like thunder, and the West Lake in the fifth month was suddenly transformed into the Qiantang River in the middle of the eighth.[5] Waves five feet or more in height came crashing in and drenched the boatloads of women sightseers to the skin. Unable to control their boats, the boatmen shouted at their passengers to go ashore at once—a moment's delay, and they'd be thrown into the water—and the women scrambled for safety. The passengers from several hundred boats rushed ashore at the same time, crowding every inch of the Su Embankment and almost collapsing its six bridges beneath their weight.

Among the male onlookers, a couple of frivolous youths floated an idea: "From the look of it, this storm is

5. The Qiantang River is noted for the thunderous tidal waves that occur at the equinox.

certainly not going to let up. It's most unlikely that these women will be able to get back on board again, so they'll have to walk home. Let's stand at the intersection and check them out as they go past, to see how many classic beauties there are in this city of ours. According to the old gibe, Hangzhou is all beauty aids and no beauties. Today's downpour is obviously a gift from the Lord of Heaven, who wants us to examine them for genuine talent. He's sent down this rain to wash off their makeup and reveal their true looks, so that we literary men can rank them properly. We can't disobey the Will of Heaven now, can we? Come on, everybody, let's go!"

It was the perfect idea, they all agreed. Even Septimus, who had failed to make good on his boast, claimed to have an eye for such things and duly appointed himself the chief examiner. The young men rushed off to take up positions on Xiling Bridge, where they found paving stones to stand on that would give them a better view. Hardly had they done so than the first women came swarming in their direction. Some held umbrellas over their heads, and some held fans in front of their faces. Others covered their heads with lotus leaves that they had picked. They looked like hibiscus flowers blown down and floating in the stream. And there were still others who had neither umbrellas nor fans nor lotus leaves and looked like pear blossoms stripped from the trees by the storm and exposed to the common gaze. Carefully the observers scrutinized the women but judged them of middling quality at best; no superlative beauty was to be found. Even after several hundred groups had gone by, the same opinion held, which made the observers sigh and quote the *Four Books:* "Talent is hard to find—how true that is!"

Just as they were lamenting this fact, another friend

dashed up from the rear. "There's a real stunner on her way up here! Take a look!" They looked and saw a woman approaching who was escorted by a bevy of maids, a woman of truly extraordinary appearance. Not only could she herself have toppled a nation or a city with a smile, those who saw her felt like laughing fit to topple a city or a nation themselves. As a lyric to the tune "Moon Over West River" bears witness,

> Her face was dark, lackluster paint;
> Her skin like crackleware grew.
> Curious blotches marked her cheeks—
> The stains on mottled bamboo.
>
> Her teeth were silver, tarnished black,
> Her fingers porphyry.
> A glance from her eye would melt the soul—
> And make the suitor flee!

Who do you suppose she was? None other than the daughter of Master Feng and the wife of Septimus Pei, that wife whom he didn't dare accompany lest his friends learn her identity but whom his friends could run down behind her back as long as he himself wasn't there to see it. He had never dreamt that she would make a spectacle of herself right in front of him, but by now it was too late to flee. The friend who first spotted her, noting how ugly she was, had rushed up and told everybody to watch out for an angel, hoping they would get a good laugh when they found an ogre instead. As she came abreast, they put their hands over their mouths and bent their heads. "It's bad luck to see a ghost in the daytime," they muttered, covering their eyes as she passed.

Septimus flushed crimson with embarrassment and wished there were some place to hide. Thanks to the advance warning he had recognized her while a long way off and had had time to duck behind the others and take several inches off his height, in the hope that she wouldn't recognize him and call out, exposing his secret. When she came up to where he was standing, he wished she could have been swept by on some cloud, for the longer she took, the more ugly remarks he was bound to hear. But alas, those tiny feet of hers sported a hump in the middle from forcible arching, and whenever she needed to hurry her shoes would restrict her feet and prevent them from straightening out, making it impossible for her to go fast.

But even if she had sauntered by, she would still have taken only a minute or two. Instead she chose to flaunt her bewitching beauty and, wherever onlookers were gathered, to slow down and proceed with mincing steps, laying on the charm to win their admiration. Not even the heaviest downpour could have induced her to hurry. Alas, the mud underfoot and the paving-stones on the bridge proved to be her nemesis; instead of cooperating to enhance her beauty, they plunged her into disgrace. As she minced and postured her way along, one of the paving-stones caught her toe, the mud held her high heels fast, and down she went, spread-eagle on the ground and far too flustered to think of posturing anymore. Of course she cried out to high heaven and called on people for help, displaying in the process every odious trait known to man and sending the hundred or more young men present into paroxysms of laughter.

Septimus had shrunk in height before her accident, but only by a few inches. Now, to hide the sight from view, he rolled himself up in a ball like Yuan Rang squatting down and ignoring the world.[6]

At the height of the uproar another group of women came up and, seeing that Miss Feng had fallen, helped her to her feet. Their looks varied greatly, but there were two genuine beauties among them, both about fifteen, with a rare, delicate beauty that dazzled the eye. Their sopping wet silks clung to their bodies and revealed in all clarity the rich fullness and soft bonelessness of their figures. Even their tender flesh and jade-fair breasts were half exposed.

The observers were unanimous in their praise. "Now we have our Prima and Secunda," they said. "What a pity we don't have a Tertia to round out the top group![7] We'll just have to leave the third place open until next year's festival and choose someone we've overlooked."

At these words Septimus cautiously poked his head out. Still afraid that his wife might see him and involve him in her shame, he pulled out a fan to shield his face. A pair of covetous eyes were all that appeared above the fan as they carefully surveyed the two young women and concluded that they truly were peerless beauties.

By this time Miss Feng had been helped to her feet. Her servants found that her clothes were too badly soiled for her to walk home in, so they took her to a temple to wait while they called a sedan chair.

The frivolous young men, now that they had found some outstanding beauties, were like hungry hawks at the sight of a hare or starving dogs at the smell of meat; they couldn't bear to be separated from the girls, but followed

6. See *The Analects*, p. 131.

7. The translator has feminized the Latin equivalents of the first three graduates in the national examinations.

in a pack close behind. Septimus, still afraid that he might give himself away, was forced to abandon his wife and join them.

The two young women, with a single umbrella between them, walked quickly for a little while, then slowly for a little while longer. When they went slowly, they looked lovely, and even when they tried to go fast, the sight touched a chord of sympathy in every observer. Even in their most harried moments they were never less than charming, which goes to show that theirs was a genuine beauty and not the result of artifice. But for the downpour, their beauty would never have been discovered.

After crossing Partition Bridge, they sought shelter in a private house while waiting for sedan chairs to come out from the city. The young men, unable to follow them into the house, tore themselves away and headed home.

The two young beauties may have been chosen Prima and Secunda, but we still do not know their names or whether they are engaged and, if so, who their fiancés are. I must apologize, gentle readers, for keeping you in the dark about these questions until the next chapter, where the answers will be revealed.

CHAPTER 2

Renewing an old bond, he once more proposes;
Losing his new love, he is thrice humiliated.

When Septimus saw his wife exposing her numerous failings in public at the Dragon Boat Festival and leaving him with no place to hide, he was mortally ashamed.

Among his friends, however, the consensus was as follows: "A woman as ugly as that ought to stay home. Why incur all this ridicule by visiting the lake? It's really her husband's fault for not helping her hide her shortcomings. What a pity we don't know his name! If we knew it, we'd have the makings of a play here. She'd be the clown and he the villain, of course; the two painted-face roles are all set. In addition we'd have the two beauties for the heroine roles, and since you need someone monstrously ugly to highlight a great beauty, we'd use this tower of strength to round the thing out."

"Now that we have our heroines, all we need are the heroes," said someone. "Let's try our best to find out their fiancés' names as well as their own. If we show an interest in writing the script, the fiancés will undoubtedly pay us for our work. Such fascinating material—it's practically asking to be written up!"

"If you're going to find out their names," put in another, "you ought to find out who the painted faces are, too, so that you can give discredit—as well as credit—where it's due."

At this point Septimus felt more than ashamed, he felt afraid, afraid of those two streaks of white paint that would be daubed on his villain's face,[8] and he tried by every means he knew to conceal his connection. He not only hid his own embarrassment, he even joined the others in condemning the woman's husband. Dissatisfied with their ridicule, he in effect ridiculed himself.

Reflecting on the incident after his return, he was consumed with loathing. Although he could not express

---

8. The role-types on the Chinese stage are distinguished by facial makeup as well as by costume.

the feeling to his wife, he began to feel estranged from her and prayed constantly for her early demise.

But any woman who has attained the ultimate degree of ugliness has already infringed the Creator's taboo. There is no need for her husband to lay a curse on her, for the demons and hobgoblins will already have marked her out as a companion and issued their own invitations. After being caught in the storm Miss Feng came down with a fever. To make matters worse, she had always loved to dress up prettily and play the coquette in the belief that the men who saw her would praise her beauty to the skies and spread her fame abroad. It was only when she fell and overheard those malicious comments that it dawned on her that her looks might be less than perfect.

In my panic I showed what I really look like, she thought, and in the heat of the moment they said what they really felt. All that effort I put into mincing and posturing has been *wasted*! She sank into a depression that became more and more acute, then took to her bed and died within a few days.

> She who had lived for others' praise
> Now chanced to die from their contempt.

To Septimus the loss of his ugly wife was like having a mote plucked from his eye, so ecstatic did he feel. Needless to say, he at once reverted to his boastful ways. When I remarry, he thought, I'll have to find a real stunner who meets with universal admiration if I'm to wipe out the shame of that last marriage. The only women I know who would qualify are those two we saw the other day. I don't suppose I can get both, but either one would impress people. I'd not only be carrying out my current boast, I'd also be vindicating the previous one. And I wouldn't be given the villain's role in the play either. I'd get the hero's part instead!

He joined his friends in their efforts to identify the women. Days of searching brought no result, until he happened to hire the same bearer who had taken the women home. They proved to be none other than the girl to whom Septimus had once been betrothed, Miss Wei, and her maid Nenghong, neither of whom was engaged.

Storyteller, your previous narrative was plausible enough, but not this last point. If the women were maid and mistress, the people at the lake that day would surely have been able to discern the fact. Why did they leap to the conclusion that the girls were sisters on an outing and not discover their mistake until now?[9]

Gentle reader, there is a point here that you have failed to grasp. When the storm first struck the lake, panic reigned, and all thought of social status was cast aside as the two women raced along together. Moreover they were holding the same umbrella and their bodies touched; they were a double lotus blossom and you couldn't tell flower from leaf. That was why people assumed they were sisters.

When the young men pressed him for information, their informant did not content himself with a vague response but went on to describe the girls' social positions and background, all of which deeply impressed his audience. "For a single family to produce two such gems—and a mistress and maid at that—why, it's unheard of!"

The maid, who was actually two years older than her mistress—seventeen to the latter's fifteen—was originally called Peach Blossom. She had studied alongside her mistress, and since she was extremely bright as well as beauti-

9. A passage of simulated address to the narrator.

ful, her tutor felt confident that she would one day make a good marriage herself. Lest the name Peach Blossom cause people to think of her as a maid, he got the master's permission to change it and call her Nenghong, a name that retained a suggestion of Peach Blossom from the line "The peach blossom excels at red, the plum at white."[10]

On learning this, Septimus went out of his mind with excitement. If I manage to pull this off, he thought, I'll have a beautiful concubine as well as a charming wife. What a bargain—two for the price of one! And my proposal won't be coming out of the blue either; it was agreed on before, and I shouldn't have any trouble renewing it.

He told his parents of his wishes and asked them to renew the engagement. Now that he planned to remarry, his father, who had hurt his son deeply by insisting on that first, unfortunate marriage, accepted the decision without a murmur and called in the same matchmaker who had negotiated the original agreement.

But Mr. Wei no sooner heard the name Pei than he exploded: "He repudiated the engagement before for the sake of money. What a double-crossing scoundrel! Why, I'd rather cut off his head, rip out his heart and liver, and make a meal of them, than give him my daughter in marriage! He's got a rich father-in-law and a beautiful bride, what does he need an impoverished father-in-law and a humble helpmate for, that he should come and seek us out again? I'll have no trouble finding a match for a daughter like mine. But even if she were crippled, blind and deaf, and no one wanted her, I'd rather support her the rest of her life than sink so low as to marry her to someone I detest! Don't even mention the subject!"

10. *Nenghong* combines the words for *excel* and *red*.

Faced with Mr. Wei's battery of objections, there was nothing the matchmaker could say. She apologized and returned to Pei's house to report.

Mr. Pei knew the situation was hopeless and urged his son to choose another wife. "If I fail to marry Miss Wei," said Septimus, "I intend to give up my life, and not after living out my days either, but within a year at most. If the Weis are adamant about this and don't come around, I'll just have to die an unnatural death to atone for the wrong I did her."

At first his parents were struck dumb by the outburst. Then they knelt down in front of the matchmaker and pleaded with her to do what she could. She had no choice but return to the Weis' and repeat her proposal.

This time Mr. Wei sent his wife out to receive her. Now, a woman expresses herself differently from a man, and Mrs. Wei gave the matchmaker a piece of her mind: "It's always the girl's family that spurns the poor husband for a rich one. Is there a single play or novel in existence in which it's the boy's family that breaks its word? He's got it all upside down—as if he thinks his son's something out of this world and my daughter's trash! His son's been married for years, and if he managed to get his parents appointed to the Royal Family, I've yet to hear of it, while this worthless daughter of mine has received countless proposals from provincial and national graduates alike. The only reason we haven't accepted any of them is that none of the horoscopes has matched. But as for *his* chances, tell him to snap out of it and stop daydreaming!" She then launched into a highly personal diatribe that was even livelier than Old Mother Wang cursing her chickens. The embarrassed matchmaker took her leave and gave the Weis a terse report advising them to drop the whole foolish idea.

At this news Septimus sank into an even deeper depression, turning the following thoughts over and over in his mind: How can I ever forget the girl I met or the engagement we agreed on? From what the matchmaker says, her parents are adamantly opposed, but I still don't know how *she* feels about it. Perhaps her parents aren't very well educated and are letting petty grudges stand in the way of fundamental issues, and that's why they've broken off relations. But she's a well-educated person and knows it's a woman's duty to remain loyal unto death to a single husband. During our engagement, we were united by the marriage bond, she and I, and perhaps she has vowed not to marry anyone else except her former fiancé. Let me make some discreet inquiries and see if I can find some woman with access to their house. If I find one, I'll court her with lavish presents and beg her to find out how matters stand with the daughter. So long as she isn't met with outright rejection, she should work on the girl with the precepts of fidelity and loyalty in marriage. So long as *she*'s prepared to accept me, her parents will surely fall into line. It's not inconceivable that those cold ashes of hers can still be fanned into flame!

Intent on his new plan, Septimus set about making inquiries. He learned that there was a needlework teacher named Mother Yu who used to give embroidery lessons to Miss Wei and Nenghong and who lived close by and visited frequently. Her husband was an assistant proctor at the county school, and it so happened that when Septimus was first admitted there, he had been entrusted to the husband's care and had come to know him well. Septimus now thought he had a chance of success and, after preparing some lavish presents, he got the husband to introduce him to Mother Yu. He begged her to accept his presents, expressed his anguish over the broken engagement and his sincere desire for marriage, and then asked her to convey that message to the daughter without informing her parents.

"Miss Wei is a highly principled young lady," said Mother Yu, "and she won't hear of anything that isn't absolutely proper. I wouldn't dare pass any other suggestion along to her, but she does like to hear about fidelity and loyalty. Let me give her your message."

Septimus was so delighted that he couldn't bring himself to return home but stayed nearby to await the news.

At the Wei house Mother Yu chatted with Miss Wei before steering the conversation around to the subject of her visit. She relayed Septimus's own words, merely giving them a persuasive, rather than a tactical, cast.

"You're wrong, Mother," replied Miss Wei. "Fidelity and loyalty are inseparable. Only when you have a faithful husband can you have a loyal wife. There's no rule that says a girl should remain loyal when the fiancé has been unfaithful. If he was determined to marry me, he should not have been so eager for money as to break off the engagement. By doing so he showed himself an ungrateful, faithless wretch! What bond do I share with him any more? That was a most specious argument of his, without rhyme or reason to it. Mother, an upright person like you oughtn't to be delivering messages for him."

"His parents forced him to break the engagement, it wasn't his doing. You ought to make some allowances."

"His parents could never have forced him into it if he hadn't been willing. The same moral laws apply to both of us, so why should I disobey *my* parents while he obeys his? The Four Virtues and Three Obediences were instituted for women,[11] not men, but in this case it's the man who is apparently supposed to obey his father before marriage. Am I as a woman expected to obey my *husband* before I marry! That's even more ridiculous!"

"We mustn't be too conservative about marriage," said Mother Yu, "but adapt ourselves to our own destinies. At first he did want to marry you but was deceived by a matchmaker's arguments into changing to Miss Feng. Now after a short marriage he's single again, while you're still waiting for the right man. Obviously the Feng girl did not share a predestined bond with him, but you evidently do. Moreover this gentleman is both extraordinarily handsome and also the outstanding talent in the whole of Hangzhou. My husband is assistant proctor at the school, and if anyone knows the licentiates, he does! I'm giving you this advice out of my concern for your future, not in hopes of any reward!"

"Whether or not a predestined bond exists between us is tied to our emotional reactions. I feel utterly opposed to him, which means we have no such bond. How can one be *forced* into existence? Man's estate in this life is foreordained; it cannot be forced. We simply accept what fate has in store for us and carry out our parents' decisions."

When she saw how adamant Miss Wei was, Mother Yu changed her tune and praised the girl's response before taking her leave. At the entrance to her own house she met Septimus, who had come to hear the news. She invited him in and told him what Miss Wei had said.

11. The virtues were in respect of conduct, speech, demeanor, and accomplishment. The obediences were to one's father at home, to one's husband in marriage, and to one's son in widowhood.

"Your proposal has come to a dead end," she added. "Try another girl at once. Don't delay such an important matter as marriage."

For a while Septimus sat bemused. "If that's the case," he said at last, "I have another suit I'd like your help with. If the daughter isn't willing, I won't press her again. But I understand that the Weis have a maid named Nenghong whose beauty and intelligence are the equal of Miss Wei's. Since there's no bond between the mistress and me, I'll have to turn my attention to the maid. I'm asking you to persuade Mr. Wei to consider Nenghong his daughter and marry her to me as my second wife. In the first place, the marriage would fulfill our previous agreement. Secondly, it would put an end to my obsession with Miss Wei. And thirdly, it would show the world that Mr. Wei is such a proud man that he disdains to marry his daughter to someone he has quarreled with and fobs the fellow off with a maidservant. It will look as if he's humiliated me, which ought to please him. If he remains inflexible and won't budge, I beg you to go behind his back and inform Nenghong. Tell her that I lost my heart to her when I saw her at the lake and that I never expected to find such a heavenly flower growing on the earth below. Ask her to take into account my heartfelt love for her and find some way for us to marry. Wouldn't that be the ideal solution?"

He followed up his request by offering Mother Yu another generous present, but this time it was neither money nor silk. As the poem explains:

> In sending off a go-between,
> Don't hand her a feeble brew;
> You need to find another gift
> To show your heart is true.

His treasury was far from bare;
Much silver did it hold.
But he chose to kneel upon the ground—
A gift of the purest gold.

As he spoke, Septimus began slowly to shrink that six-foot height of his to a dwarf's stature. By the time he had finished speaking he was on his knees, where he spent a considerable amount of time as a dwarf before she reached out and helped him up again.

Mother Yu's heart melted at the sight of his solicitous demeanor and pathetic pleading. "In the daughter's case I wouldn't dare promise a thing. In fact I couldn't even raise the matter with her father. And since he won't agree in *her* case, he'll never agree in the maid's! It would only fuel his anger to mention the subject. But this girl Nenghong is wonderfully clever—resourceful as well as persuasive. In fact she considers herself superior to the rest of the family, with the sole exception of the young mistress, to whom she still defers—up to a point. Should she take a fancy to you, she may well come up with some marvelous scheme for manipulating the master into accepting you. You'd better go off now and let me try to persuade her in my own good time. The moment I have any news, I'll send someone over with it."

Septimus felt his hopes rekindling and, beaming broadly, thanked her again and again. After losing the daughter he had set his heart on the maid, still fearful that he might not succeed. But now, before gaining one prize, he was dreaming of a second; he cherished the hope that, by enlisting Nenghong's aid, he might get the other girl as well. But he could scarcely voice this thought, lest Mother Yu think him too ambitious and refuse to serve, so he confined himself to elaborate bows and repeated expressions of gratitude before taking his leave.

What will happen next, I wonder. Let me suspend my discussion for a moment before taking up the whisk again.[12]

CHAPTER 3

With a word or two a persuasive talker brings off a double marriage;
By kneeling once a sentimental suitor wins a pair of beauties.

Mother Yu kept Septimus's suit constantly in mind. One day on a visit to the Weis' she was about to broach the matter to Nenghong behind Miss Wei's back when the girl anticipated her, as if she knew what was coming.

"Tell me, Teacher," she said, "am I right in assuming that you've come here to play the advocate? If so, I'm afraid you'll find me even harder to convince than the mistress. I won't listen to any improper suggestion or help with anything underhand, so you might as well not start. He knelt down in front of you, and of course you want to repay him with interest. I find it highly amusing, this loss you're going to suffer."

Mother Yu shivered with apprehension. Even if Nenghong were an immortal, she reasoned, she wouldn't have *this* sort of power! How does she know every little thing

12. An elaborate fly whisk made from the tail of a brown deer was a conversational aid for wits and raconteurs.

that goes on at my place? I couldn't even keep his kneeling secret. Surely she hasn't got superhuman eyes and ears! But since she's seen through our little scheme, I can't very well deny it.

"You're perfectly right," she said. "I've come to play the advocate, to talk you, a beautiful young woman, into marrying a brilliant young man. And he *did* kneel down in front of me, that's perfectly true. But what puzzles me is how you came to know all about it while sitting here at home."

"Haven't you heard the sayings, The whispering of men on Earth echoes in Heaven like a roll of thunder, and A shameful deed in a darkened room flashes before the gods like a bolt of lightning? I'm an immortal incarnate, that's what I am, and I know *everything* that you and he talked about; I gave you only the gist of it just now. There's only one thing that's not clear to me. The scheme he entrusted you with was aimed at the mistress, so why not try to persuade *her* instead of coming to me? I suppose you want to go through me to get at her, is that it?"

"You've described our discussion exactly—except for the last point, where you guessed wrong. It was for *your* sake, not hers, that he went down on his knees. He never even mentioned the words *young mistress*, so why slander the man?"

Nenghong hung her head in thought.

"If that's the case," she said at last, "if he even went down on his knees for someone like me, I wonder what kind of pathetic appeal he made for the mistress. He must have kowtowed until he got a bloody forehead or knelt until his knees ached!"

"That just shows what a phony immortal *you* are! What you said was a lucky guess, nothing more. When he asked me to propose to the young mistress, he didn't kneel down, he didn't even bow. After he was rejected, he gave up all hope of her and turned his thoughts to you. In asking me to act for him, he was so afraid I'd beg off on the grounds of difficulty that he actually went down on his knees. Such a heartfelt appeal it was—you can't *fail* to respond!''

Nenghong now confessed. The Weis' house faced the Yus' with only a wall in between. In the back garden was a tower named the Cloud-Scraper, which had a balcony for airing clothes that was encircled by a trellis. From inside it one could see out, but from outside nobody could see in. The day Mother Yu returned from delivering the proposal Nenghong had calculated that "that fellow Pei" would be waiting in front of her house, so she climbed up to the balcony to see what reception the messenger got. On arriving home, Mother Yu did bring a man inside, and Nenghong was able to get a full view of Septimus. When she saw him suddenly sink to his knees, she assumed he was doing it for the young mistress, to persuade Mother Yu to arrange not merely a marriage but an illicit rendezvous, and she was continually on her guard. This time, when Mother Yu wished to talk to her behind her mistress's back, Nenghong thought: the old bitch, she's been commissioned to get me to serve as a Hongniang. *Some hope!* That was why she had exposed the scheme before the other woman could open her mouth. But her stern expression had also concealed a good deal of envy, and now, on learning that Septimus had bent the knee for *her*, the envy turned to sweetness and the vinegar to honey, and she was eager to get on good terms with Mother Yu and discuss what steps to take next.

After her confession Nenghong continued: "He really is a handsome gentleman. If he's prepared to lower himself, how can I, a mere maid, not do my best to aspire? But there's one thing that troubles me. I'm afraid 'the Old Tippler's mind may not be on the wine,' and he may want to marry the maid first and summon the mistress to court later. If he's successful, he's sure to forget the fish-trap after catching the fish, and it will never be my turn for so-called love. On the other hand, if he's unsuccessful in getting her, he'll regard me as even more useless and not only treat me coldly but actually resent me, which I couldn't bear. Now, tell me the truth, was it really for me that he knelt down, or was it a way of getting at the mistress?"

"As Heaven is my witness," exclaimed Mother Yu, "you're doing him a terrible injustice; he really and truly did kneel down for you. If you're willing to accept him, of course he'll hire a matchmaker, arrange a proper marriage, and hire four sedan chairs to bring the bridal party to his house. It's absurd to think he would marry a maid as his principal wife and then take her mistress as his concubine!"

Nenghong burst out laughing. "You've banished all my suspicions! From what you say, he must be a real romantic, no doubt about that. Well-known scholars and writers have no trouble finding wives. Why, rich young ladies are ready for the taking, let alone mere maids! And he was actually willing to go down on his *knees*! Tell him that if he'd been trying only for the mistress, he wouldn't even have been able to get me into his house, but since he wants to marry me, he shouldn't give up hope of getting the mistress as well. We're on the same plane, she and I; there's never any difference between us. His family and ours are sworn enemies, and with a matchmaker working from outside, he'd never get anywhere. Fortunately the whole family knows I have a little commonsense. They don't come and meekly ask for my advice, mind you, but they always sound me out, usually without realizing it. If

I say go ahead, they go ahead. If I say better not, even if it's something they've already decided on, they find they can't do it after all. This suit is a case in point; unfortunately I got so furious on the mistress's account that I said some very nasty things about him. The whole family took their cue from me and now hate him with a vengeance, which is why his matchmaker didn't even get a hearing. If he'd told *me* before kneeling down, I'd have been a willing collaborator from inside the household and I expect the marriage would have taken place by now. But it would be rather embarrassing for me to change my tune at this point and start supporting the match, and it would be even harder to jettison the mistress and argue the case for myself. Not even an immortal could pull *that* off! I'll just have to play it by ear and try to come up with something. I'll need to give the impression that I'm planning things for the mistress's sake, but if the public interest can be served, perhaps my private interest can be served also. Two birds with one stone!"

A delighted Mother Yu asked Nenghong what plan she proposed to use.

"Oh, one can't think up that kind of thing in a matter of minutes," said Nenghong. "Just tell him to be patient. As soon as I see an opportunity, I'll send for you and get you to tell him, so that we can decide how to proceed. Far be it from me to boast, but the only thing to worry about would be my disapproval. Once I've approved of him, no ordinary mortal would stand a chance with the mistress and me. Why, even if the emperor himself were choosing new concubines, and the authorities had recommended us and taken us off to the yamen, this quick little tongue of mine would still get us out of it—to say nothing of other predicaments."

"I certainly hope so. Everything depends on your skill."

On returning, she invited Septimus in and gave him a full account of what Nenghong had said. Delirious with joy, Septimus realized that the good news resulted entirely from his kneeling. Thinking he might as well carry humility to the extreme, he faced the Cloud-Scraper and gave four deep ceremonial bows.

At the sight Nenghong felt an even greater fondness and sympathy. If only she could have received his proposal now, accepted it in one hour, and married him in two! She looked upon marriage as an official excursion, with the runners going on ahead and the magistrate bringing up the rear, and her private hope was that she, as junior wife, would lead the way. But the difficulties she faced were too serious for any hope of quick success, and so she took care to spend all her time in her master's and mistress's company to see what transpired. If you want to patch up failed negotiations, she reflected, you can't simply propose it. To have any hope of success, you need to get someone else to stir things up first—then seize the chance to jump in yourself.

But where Septimus was concerned, the family's lips were sealed. To make matters worse, matchmakers now began arriving in an endless stream, bringing at least three or four proposals a day, and the suitors they represented were all superior to Septimus in social terms. In addition a number of the local gentry were prepared to pay a large price for Nenghong as a concubine. None of them would accept the slightest delay. After presenting their proposals, they would take a quick turn elsewhere and then come back and demand an answer, as if by waiting a few minutes longer they might miss their chance and see the prize snatched away from them.

How was it that this mistress and her maid, who had come of age without receiving a single proposal of marriage—except that from Septimus—now found themselves in such demand at the same time? You should understand that Mr. and Mrs. Wei were a straitlaced couple who had refused to let anyone see their beautiful daughter or charming maid. The girls were like brilliant pieces of jade buried in a rock or glistening pearls locked in an oyster. How was any outsider to know what they looked like? Even when they visited the lake at the Dragon Boat Festival, they were in a group of elaborately dressed and made-up women with powdered cheeks and carmined lips. The most avid of girl-watchers could scarcely have gotten within ten yards of them, at which distance even a superlative beauty would have gone unnoticed. It was solely due to that freak storm, which served the girls like some monstrous matchmaker, that all the talented young men in the land had started thinking marriage. They knew of Septimus's misfortune in letting the perfect match slip away and felt, as the saying goes, "When the state of Qin has lost its deer, only the most talented and fleet of foot can catch it."[13] They rushed to propose, fearful lest they miss their chance.

Nenghong was not in the least put out by this development; on the contrary she felt it might well produce an opportunity for Septimus. Knowing that the whole family believed implicitly in astrology, she "forged an imperial decree" and proclaimed it in Mr. and Mrs. Wei's presence:

13. As the Qin empire collapsed, numerous contenders arose. This statement is adapted from one made by Kuai Tong to the successful contender, the first emperor of the Han. See Kuai's biography in *Shi ji* 92.

"The young mistress has a secret desire that she is too embarrassed to tell you about but that she has confided to me. She thinks marriage too important a matter to be entered into lightly and insists that the suitors' dates and times of birth be obtained and some capable astrologer invited to cast their horoscopes. The better horoscopes will then be matched with hers, and if one matches perfectly, that suitor will be accepted. Anyone whose horoscope is even slightly at odds should be rejected. We must not make the same mistake as we did with the Peis, when we failed to have the horoscopes checked and accepted his proposal on the spot, not realizing it was unsuitable. It was sheer luck that he backed out before the wedding. If he'd married her and the two of them had not gotten along, he'd have wanted to make a change later, and what a hopeless mess that would have been!"

"Of course horoscopes must be checked in the case of marriage!" exclaimed Mr. and Mrs. Wei. "But if we send them out for checking, how is she going to be sure of the results?"

"She also told me," continued Nenghong, "that it's *her* marriage that's in question, and that if someone outside the household approves a match, she won't be convinced unless she actually hears him say so. From now on we shall have to invite the astrologers into the house to do the checking. Even if she is too shy to listen to them herself, she would be happy to have me stand in for her as a witness. She also told me that we shouldn't invite astrologers from here, there and everywhere, but settle on one and accept his decision as final. That way we'll eliminate all those conflicting interpretations that only raise doubts in our minds."

"That's no problem," said the Weis. "We have a great

deal of faith in a Jiangxi astrologer named Iron-mouth Zhang. If there's any checking needed, let's call him in."

Having secured their approval, Nenghong promptly told Mother Yu to send word to Septimus. "Tell him to go and see Iron-mouth Zhang, bribe him handsomely, and say that he must do such-and-such before settling on Septimus.[14] With me working on the inside, Septimus can count on their sending a matchmaker over. He shouldn't accept the proposal at once, but do such-and-such before agreeing."

For Septimus these instructions were more than an imperial decree, they were the word of God, and he obeyed them to the letter.

Nenghong also raised the subject with Miss Wei. "Your parents are afraid we'll make the same mistake as before, so from now on they are going to be guided by destiny. When your suitors' horoscopes are being cast and matched, they want you there as a witness, lest you complain later on about their choice."

Miss Wei was more than pleased and never suspected she was being duped. But let us wait for the horoscopes to be cast and matched in order to see how Iron-mouth Zhang will begin his spiel and what kind of transition he will use to bring the choice around to Septimus. Although this episode is connected to what follows, I shall have to interrupt it here, so that the tale may gain in interest. For a story is like a riddle—if you simply tell it without a pause, not giving your listeners time to guess the answer, it falls awfully flat.

14. The narrator is hiding the plan from the reader.

CHAPTER 4

*Consulting her own interests, she hatches a plot to
    deceive her master;*
*Fabricating consensus, she plans a mission to see her
    fiancé.*

The Weis assumed that what Nenghong told them
really had come from their daughter, and from then on
they asked every suitor to supply them with his date and
time of birth. After accumulating a few dozen dates, they
invited Iron-mouth Zhang in to cast the horoscopes and
match them with their daughter's. Iron-mouth would say
they were all inauspicious and that none of them matched.
He made five or six visits, casting dozens of horoscopes
each time, but found not one of which he approved.

"But this is absurd!" exclaimed Mr. Wei. "Do you
mean to tell me that out of all these horoscopes there's not
one that's worth considering? In that case my daughter will
never be able to marry! Go over them carefully, I beg you.
So long as there's one that shows part of the Husband Star,
so long as it has no destructive effect and doesn't block the
Wife palace, we'll accept him!"

"It's not that there are *no* horoscopes worth considering," replied the astrologer. "But because the men's de-
structiveness is rather weak and they've never lost a wife,
I'm afraid they might do harm to your daughter, which is
why I wouldn't dare accept them lightly. If I were just
looking for a good horoscope without regard to such matters, any one of these would do."

"But it's a *good* thing if the destructive effect is weak!
Why do you insist on their losing a wife?"

"Please don't take offense at what I'm about to say.

Your daughter's horoscope shows only half of the Husband Star, which means she is not destined to be a first wife. Her horoscope would match only that of a man whose first wife had died and who was seeking to remarry. If this were his first marriage and he had never lost a wife, even if he became engaged to your daughter, he would still want to back out. If he went through with the marriage, within a few days disaster would occur, and it's far from certain that she would live to a reasonable age. But although the best solution would be marriage as a second wife, she would still find it too onerous to handle all the domestic duties herself, and if she is to have a long marriage, she ought definitely to find a concubine to share them with. If she occupies the empress's palace alone, her horoscope won't match even half of the Husband Star, and she'll suffer crisis after crisis and won't live beyond the age of twenty at the outside. This is my honest opinion. No one but Iron-mouth Zhang would have the courage to tell you."

So appalled was Mr. Wei at the news that his eyebrows shot straight up and for a moment he lost the power of speech. After showing the astrologer to the gate, he returned and discussed the matter with his wife.

"From what he says, she's fated to be a second wife," said Mr. Wei. "Someone looking for a second wife certainly won't be young, and a daughter like ours will never consent to marry a middle-aged man, let alone one who's been married before!"

"But that's the way it is! You heard him say that a man who is marrying for the first time, someone who has never lost a wife, will want to back out of the engagement. That was right on the mark! The Peis' proposal, now—wouldn't that have been a first marriage? But after the engagement

148

they suddenly changed their minds! We blamed *them* for it, not realizing it was the work of fate!"

"He recently lost his wife, so he qualifies perfectly. He's not too old either; in fact he's ideal for our daughter. Had we known all this before, we wouldn't have rejected his proposal."

"The only question is whether *we* are willing. If we're sure in our own minds, we'll let the word out, and he's bound to come back asking for her hand."

"You're right," said Mr. Wei. "Let me drop a hint to the matchmaker and see if he comes back."

At just this moment Nenghong came in. Mr. Wei gave his wife a meaningful look and left the room to allow her to consult the maid.

Mrs. Wei told Nenghong of their discussion. "Now, you're a sensible girl, Nenghong. Do me a favor and give this a little thought, would you? Ought we to accept him or not?"

Nenghong put on a pained expression. "You may be worried about finding a fiancé for your daughter, but do you have to marry her to your *enemy*? And in my opinion marriage to a man in his thirties or forties would be just too humiliating! You mustn't breathe a word of this to her. She'd be terribly upset. You ought to choose a fiancé from among the young men, preferably someone younger than he is, but if there's no one qualified, you'll just have to get *his* date and time of birth and have Iron-mouth Zhang cast his horoscope and match it with hers. If it's a perfect match, pocket your pride and marry her to the man. But if he's going to stay a licentiate forever, you'd be far better off with someone else."

"Very true," said Mrs. Wei. She promptly consulted

her husband and told him to give the matchmakers the following instructions: "Any suitor who is looking for a second wife and is under twenty should send us his date and time of birth without falsifying them. If anyone makes himself out to be younger than he really is, even if his horoscope is a good match, he'll be found out and rejected, and his efforts will be in vain." She added: "While you're about it, let the Peis know, so that they can send in their son's date."

Mr. Wei did so, and within a few days the matchmakers brought along a number of cards with the relevant details. "Actually we have no one *under* twenty," they reported, "only people *in* their twenties. It was their idea to send their dates in, and it's up to you whether you want to match them."

Mr. Wei glanced at the cards, over twenty in all, but found none from Septimus. He asked the Peis' matchmaker about it. "When you rejected him, he lost all hope and now has no further interest in the match," she replied. "That's why he didn't send in his card. Moreover there are far too many suitors already. He wants to make a careful choice, not a snap decision, and is no longer so set on his ex-fiancée. I told him he wouldn't be losing anything by letting you have the information, and he said he wrote it out for you a few years ago. He's three years older than your daughter, born on the same date but at a different hour. One was born at one o'clock, the other at three. Think it over by all means."

Mr. Wei took the message back to his wife. "That's right!" she exclaimed. "He *is* three years older, born just two hours before her. Go and invite Iron-mouth Zhang to come and cast his horoscope."

Mr. Wei was afraid that if he simply told Iron-mouth

Zhang the date and time, the astrologer would think him biased in Septimus's favor, so before inviting him over, he copied out the date and mixed it with the others.

As he had done on earlier occasions, Iron-mouth disparaged every card he looked at—until he came to Septimus's, when he burst out in astonishment: "Now, here's a date I know only too well! I've matched this man's horoscope several times already for different people. But he *has* someone! What's his card doing here?"

"Which families have asked you to check his horoscope?" asked Mr. Wei. "And which one has he accepted? Would you say he is likely to have any success on the basis of his horoscope? Please give us the details."

"A number of families, all of them distinguished, have obtained his details and asked me to cast his horoscope. I told them that I have rarely in the course of my career come across a horoscope like his. There'll simply be no stopping the man after the age of twenty; he's destined for a meteoric rise to the very highest levels of government. Some of the girls' horoscopes happened to match his, others' didn't. Of course the former, once they took a look at his horoscope, didn't want to let him get away. But even the latter said they wouldn't mind if the horoscopes were slightly at odds, so long as his destiny was good enough. I assumed the fellow would have been snapped up ages ago. I can't *believe* he's failed to settle with anyone and has sent his card along to you!"

"You're quite right. I understand a number of gentry families have made offers, but I imagine he's too ambitious to settle for second best and that that's why he's delayed his decision until now. To be quite frank with you, this fellow used to be my daughter's fiancé, but he broke off the engagement and married another girl for the sake of a bigger dowry. Within a couple of years his wife died, and he later renewed his suit, but I blamed him for backing out of the engagement and firmly refused him. However when you told us that our daughter was fated to be a second wife, this man came into our minds. He didn't supply the card, we did."

"That explains it," said Iron-mouth. "I wouldn't expect a man who is being fought over by so many others to bother about sending in his card!"

"You say his horoscope is exceptional, but I wonder how it matches my daughter's? Would she really gain from marrying him?"

"Her horoscope's a *perfect* match! There's no end to the riches and honors she'd receive! The only problem, as I see it, is that too many people are after him, and you may not get the chance. Let me take another look at your daughter's horoscope to see how her luck stands now. Then we'll know whether to approach him or not."

He took her card out again, placed it in front of him and scrutinized it, then burst out laughing. "Congratulations! It's as good as settled, but you can't afford any delay. There's a benign star in her destiny that's shining on the Love Star, which means you'll succeed at your first attempt. But if you wait more than three days, the star will have left the palace, and your chances will be doubtful at best." After offering this advice, he left.

Mr. and Mrs. Wei were atwitter with excitement. Putting aside the animus they felt for Septimus, they sent a matchmaker to him with a proposal. Even Miss Wei was concerned. She felt sure that he would put on airs and that it would take more than a word or two from a matchmaker to persuade him. If only she could stop that benign star in its tracks for a few more days!

Of the whole household only Nenghong remained at her ease, urging Miss Wei not to fret. "If it's in your destiny, no one can take it away from you," she said. "But even if the horoscopes do match, in my opinion it's just as important that a couple's looks should match too. By rights the man ought to arrange a time and place where she can look him over, and only if he's really good-looking should her family accept him. It may even be worth their while to eat a little humble pie. But if his looks are grotesque, how could anyone bear to force a delicate flower of a girl into the arms of a jackass?"

"He's putting on such grand airs that it's by no means certain he'll even accept our proposal. He'd *never* agree to a viewing!"

"Never mind, I've thought up the most marvelous idea. Mother Yu's husband is an assistant proctor at the school and knows all the licentiates. Let's get him to play the decoy and invite Septimus to his place for a talk. Before he arrives, you and I will go over there and hide. That way we'll get a good look at him."

"It would be a lot easier to get him to come here than for us to go there. You're a maid, so you're at least allowed to visit the neighbors, but how can an unmarried daughter like me even get beyond the gate? The only solution is for you to go in my place."

"If you don't want to go, I'll have to. But there's one problem. What if *I* think he looks fine, but you don't and later on you take a dislike to him?"

"You have a good eye for quality, as good as mine, I daresay. You go."

Gentle reader, why do you suppose Nenghong, who already knew exactly what Septimus looked like, volunteered for this trivial task at a time when the marriage was practically arranged and she should have been pressing ahead to victory? You must understand that this venture was strictly in her own interests. The question of her becoming his junior wife had been discussed, but although Septimus had given a verbal assurance, he had never put it in writing. How could she be sure that after the event he might not be carried away with his own importance? A brand new head of household is scarcely going to get down on his knees and propose marriage to his wife's maid! What if he were to deny the promise she had received only at second hand and to go on treating her as a maid? *That* was why she had arranged this turn of events, knowing perfectly well that her mistress would not be able to attend the viewing herself but would ask her to go instead. To prevent any backsliding on Septimus's part, she had devised this plan to get out of the house and obtain a commitment signed in her presence. This shows just how devious Neng-hong could be. Although it was her own private interests that were at stake, she acted as if for the general good. Mr. and Mrs. Wei had to explain to her how necessary it was for her to go before she would even ask Mother Yu to arrange a meeting.

Their meeting is bound to produce a fine comedy. Not only will she secure her own position, she may even, who knows, win first place ahead of Miss Wei. Keep your honorable eyes peeled as you watch the next scene of this silent opera.[15]

15. Li Yu's first collection of stories was entitled *Silent Operas*.

CHAPTER 5

Before agreeing to marry, she lays down the law;
Fearing a total loss, he signs the contract.

Although Mother Yu had given her approval to Neng-hong's plan for the meeting, she was still on edge. Dry tinder must not be allowed near a naked flame, she reminded herself. Verbal flirting plus a bit of ogling, or a little hand-holding and footsie as they amuse themselves on the sly—that I could accept. But with the stake I have in this marriage, I can't allow them to get carried away, forget all sense of propriety, and set to in earnest. For that reason she kept a close eye on them when they met, lest they try to deceive her and sleep together.

Little did she realize that this most peculiar girl had something very different on her mind. With Nenghong, when you expected one thing, she would always do another. On this occasion there was no trace of lust in her heart, not even a smile on her face, as she threw herself into the role of a puritan.

When Septimus came in, he was about to kneel in gratitude when she stopped him, a stern expression on her face.

"A man can kneel twice if he has to, but not a third time. It cheapens the sentiment. Well, the marriage is now as good as arranged—and thanks to whom, I wonder. Do you happen to remember those instructions I gave you?"

"I regard madam's instructions as imperial edicts and repeat them to myself every morning and evening. I've not forgotten a *word*!"

"In that case, you must now repeat them to me. Get one word wrong, and it will prove that you were simply trying to ingratiate yourself and have no real affection for me. Both marriages will then be off, and I would sincerely advise you to give up your foolish hopes forever."

Septimus grew alarmed again, assuming that she had changed her mind and was looking for some way to put him off. He mentally rehearsed what Mother Yu had told him and then recited it perfectly, with not a word too many nor a word too few. He even got the grammatical particles right.

"That shows that the front hemisphere of your heart loves me, but I'm afraid the back part may not be quite so reliable and may change after you marry. I have three conditions that I want you to agree to in my presence—my basic law,[16] so to speak. You may as well tell me outright whether you mean to obey them, so as to prevent any backsliding in the future."

Septimus asked what the conditions were.

"First, from the moment I join your household, I am no longer to be called Nenghong; I must be referred to by everyone as Second Lady. For the first offense you will slap your own face. If the offender is someone on the staff, the blame will still rest with the head of the household, and you will be called to account in the same manner.

"Secondly, I have observed that your behavior is most licentious. You're a frivolous young man, and I don't doubt that you're an old hand at love affairs. From the moment I join your household, you must put a stop to all adultery and whoring. If I find any evidence, you'll never hear the end of it. Having knelt down for my sake, you are *never* to kneel down for anyone else. Of course, should you

16. A set of legal guidelines announced by the first Han emperor.

become an official, you'll be permitted to kowtow at court and pay your respects to your superiors, but for every unauthorized kneeling you will strike yourself on your feet. The mistress is the sole exception to this rule.

"Thirdly, you must reconcile yourself for the rest of your life to marriage with just the two of us. After me there will be no further embellishments. Even if you succeed in the higher examinations and become minister or premier, you'll still not need a third wife. Should you develop any evil hankerings and so much as mention the word *concubine*, you will have to beat your head on the ground until it bleeds. If by some chance we are both unable to bear sons, endangering the ancestral shrine, you will have to wait until the age of forty before receiving a special dispensation, and even then you will be permitted to take only a personal maid, not a concubine."

Hearing all these harsh strictures in the course of his first meeting, Septimus felt more than a little nervous. But then he noted that her looks and bearing were far superior to those of other women and qualified her for the title of supreme beauty. He also recalled her miraculous talents and superhuman abilities. One such woman would give him pleasure enough to last a lifetime, but in addition to her there was also *another* girl, the most beautiful in the world. He accepted Nenghong's conditions without a murmur.

"He's committed himself," said Mother Yu, "and I doubt that he'll change his mind. I hope that you'll now wind this up as quickly as possible."

"He's broken his word once already," said Nenghong. "If he was capable of breaking off his own engagement, why not other obligations? A verbal promise can't be relied on. If I'm to wind this up, he will have to prepare and sign a contract which I shall trouble you and your husband to witness. Then, if he should stray, I'll have some evidence when I take him to task."

"Excellent idea!" said the Yus. They set writing materials and a sheet of parchment in front of Septimus and asked him to draw up a deposition. Far from objecting, Septimus picked up the brush and wrote:

The person drawing up this contract, Pei Yuan, acted in bad faith and allowed himself to be deceived by an unscrupulous matchmaker into abandoning his fiancée, thereby incurring widespread condemnation. Fortunately the one who succeeded to the throne died early, before the other was betrothed.

Respectful overtures to restore the relationship, although conveyed repeatedly by a matchmaker, met regularly with angry rebuffs from her parents because of his earlier breach of trust. Due to a certain lady who graces the women's quarters—a lady capable of turning the heavens around and making the sun rise in the West—a remarkable plan was devised that shrank the gulf and repaired the breach between the two families. Wherefore, to attest his sincerity, the undersigned has devised the following plan in recognition of the lady's services. Not only will he divide the kingdom, he will agree to her sharing the empress's palace. How can one who is soon to declare herself a ruler be classed as a common servant? Sage Emperor Shun held no other love in his heart; a third consort could not have joined his two.[17] Since there's gold at a man's knee,[18] how can I kneel again? It may seem unreasonable of her to lay down a basic law and also the penalties for its infringement, but in truth it is a selfless endeavor to uphold the feminine virtues and nip evil in the bud. The undersigned will scrupulously obey the law and not dare transgress. Should he ever break it, he will allow her to wield the rod!

Nenghong read and admired it except for one point: The opening phrase was too vague for her liking, not consistent with the standards of denotation used in *The Spring and Autumn Annals*, so she told him to change the phrase, the *person* drawing up this contract, to the *husband* drawing up this contract. After getting the Yus to sign the document, she accepted it.

Septimus had another question. "I wouldn't dare disobey a word of madam's instructions, but there is one point that bothers me. I shall control my servants and see that they don't call you by your name. But the young mistress will be new on the scene, and I shan't be able to bring *her* into line all at once. What if I call you Second Lady, but she doesn't follow suit and insists on using your name? That would be a case of a family member breaking the rules, but you wouldn't hold me accountable as head of the household, would you?"

17. The legendary emperor Yao gave his two daughters in marriage to Shun, his chosen successor.
18. I.e., a man's kneeling is a precious gift that is not to be casually bestowed.

"You leave that to me, it's no concern of yours. I suspect the mistress will want me to be Second Lady but that I shall decline, and that she will have to plead with me again and again before I accept."

She took leave of Septimus and went off without a single backward glance.

In reporting to the family, she praised Septimus's talents and looks to the skies. "Sons-in-law like that are few and far between! No *wonder* everybody's after him! Send off a proposal as soon as you can. It might even pay to eat a little humble pie."

Mr. Wei was thrilled and went off to see that the proposal was delivered.

Meanwhile Mrs. Wei had a question for Nenghong. "There's one thing I've been meaning to ask you for the longest time, Nenghong, and I can't put it off anymore. Ever so many gentry families have asked for you as a concubine. Every day someone comes with a proposal. But I've always preferred to keep you here as a companion for my daughter until her own marriage plans are settled. But now that we've sent off a proposal, it's only a matter of time before she's married, and after that, of course, it will be your turn. What I need to know is whether you would be willing to be someone's concubine."

"Don't even mention the word! I may occupy a menial position, but I do have some pride, and I wouldn't even consent to being a poor man's wife, let alone someone's concubine! I'd much sooner wait for an acceptable husband to come along. I don't wish to boast, but my modest talents and not so modest abilities are bound to earn me a wife's position. If you find that hard to believe, ma'am, you just watch me."

"In that case are you thinking of going with the young mistress when she marries?"

"That's up to her. If she's worried about having no one to advise her in her new home and would like to have me at her side, I daresay I'd be of some help if I stayed awhile, to see how things work out. But if she thinks of her husband as her confidant and doesn't need anyone else, I shall be perfectly happy to remain here. However I do have one nagging concern about her marriage, something that ought to be settled before she leaves home."

Miss Wei was present at the time, and her curiosity was piqued. She and her mother asked Nenghong what she meant.

"Don't either of you remember what Iron-mouth Zhang said? He told us that the young mistress's horoscope contained only half of the Husband Star and that she would need to find a helpmate in her marriage or disaster might strike within a few days of the wedding; unless she persuaded her husband to take a concubine, her life would be in danger. But if she succeeds in getting him a concubine, she will have another kind of problem on her hands. How many concubines devote themselves wholeheartedly to the wife's interests? Either you are jealous of them, or they of you. When quarrels break out, you inevitably want to retaliate. But our poor young mistress is simply *too* good-natured. I've spent half my life with her, and she's never said a cross word to anyone. Here, where she has no occasion to be upset, she has me to cheer her up. But soon she'll have occasion enough and no one at hand to calm her down. With a delicate constitution like hers, how can she help but fall ill?"

At this point Nenghong looked so wretched, as if she

were on the brink of tears, that Mrs. Wei and her daughter broke down and cried. After raising the subject this once, however, Nenghong never mentioned it again.

Let me tell how Mr. Wei sent the matchmaker off with the proposal and how Septimus prevaricated and then declined. Only after she had argued her case several times did he finally make good on his original promise and choose an auspicious day for the wedding.

Meanwhile the Weis, alarmed by Nenghong's warning, were preoccupied with worries about half of the Husband Star. They were convinced, too, that Nenghong was extremely close to their daughter and should on no account be separated from her. Even if she could not give long-term support, she should at least go with the daughter for the present. In a few days' time, when they had seen whether Iron-mouth Zhang's predictions came true, they would reconsider. And so it was decided that the maid should accompany her mistress.

Nenghong had a further suggestion. "While I'm in this house, of course, my duties should be those of a maid. But after I accompany the young mistress to the other house, although I'll still be a maid where she's concerned, I shan't be subordinate to anyone else, and no one will be allowed to call me Nenghong. And even with the mistress I'm not prepared to be truly subservient in matters of etiquette. One day I intend to make a good marriage myself, and I would ask her to show me a degree of respect. Although the sedan chair taking me there will not be the same as the mistress's, it should not be a maid's either. I'm not being given in marriage along with the bride, and the proper form would be to allow me two additional bearers as if I were her escort. Otherwise I shan't go!"

Mrs. Wei and her daughter assented, noting how reasonable her demands were and how hard it would be to leave her behind.

When the day came, the two sedan chairs traveled together. Although Nenghong let her mistress take the lead in all the wedding formalities, when it came to the reality of lovemaking, it was she, fittingly enough, who took first place. How did that happen? Because in Septimus's mind Nenghong had been his bride all along, and before her arrival he had prepared a separate bridal chamber for her with its own marriage bed. He felt he could scarcely expect her to spend the wedding night on her own, so he told her he would ask his mother to join her while he slept elsewhere. In fact he planned to sleep with the mistress during the first half of the night and then make an excuse to leave and join his second lady for a second celebration.

But the mistress refused to change with the times and clung to the old wedding decorum, throwing herself into the role of the traditional bride. No matter how Septimus pleaded with her and tugged at her, she refused to get into bed. Little did she realize that her bridegroom, accustomed to feeling repelled by an ugly wife, had never been with a beautiful woman before. Finding himself suddenly in the company of a superlative beauty, he was like a ravenous eagle at sight of a nesting chicken or a starving cat in front of a tasty morsel. How could he stand the strain? Without any other recourse, he would have had to curb his impatience and wait there beside her. But in addition to the plump chicken there was also a goodly duck, and in addition to the tasty morsel there was also a delicious treat. Why not enjoy the easy pickings first and tackle the difficult ones later, rather than vice versa? So he made the excuse that he had to see his parents to bed—and brought forward to the evening hours what he had planned for after midnight.

Nenghong realized, when he arrived so early, that the mistress had allowed her concern for decorum to spoil the occasion, and she refused to follow the outmoded convention and subject him to a similar experience. Instead she received him with special warmth while dispensing high-sounding advice that he go back to the mistress. She even quoted a couple of lines from the *Poetry Classic*:

The rain falls first on my lord's fields,
And then on my private plot.[19]

But she immediately began to worry that he really would go back, so she tried to save the situation by quoting from the *Four Books*: "Having persuaded him to come, give him comfort." In his overwrought state, Septimus was afraid to delay a moment longer. Without a word he pulled her to the bed—a case of being "in too great a hurry to spell out the message." Entrusting herself to experienced hands, Nenghong made no resistance as he undid her sash, took off her gown, and brought her to bed, where she was the first to celebrate the wedding. To her way of thinking, however, she had sacrificed none of her respect for her mistress by so doing; she saw her mistress as the magistrate and herself as the runner preparing the way for his superior. But I am not sure that she sacrificed very much by this respect of hers. All those who ignore real disadvantages in their concern for a hollow reputation should take heed of Miss Wei's example.

19. See Arthur Waley, trans., *The Book of Songs* (New York: Grove Press, 1987), p. 171.

CHAPTER 6

*Fictional dreams become fact, as anxieties are
    cunningly raised;
An imperfect woman perfects herself, as treachery yields
    to loyalty.*

After consummating one marriage, Septimus returned
to his bride's chamber, treating her this time in a composed
and respectful manner. Miss Wei wanted to play the old-
fashioned bride and he the old-fashioned bridegroom—as
he ignored the modern fashion while waiting for his strength
to come back. He sat with her until midnight, when they
both grew tired of being old-fashioned and quickly modern-
ized themselves. Climbing happily into bed together, they
performed a certain act several times over, becoming steadily
more decadent. Finally they fell asleep in each other's arms.

They slept until dawn, when Septimus, still only half
awake, suddenly began a hysterical sobbing. The harder he
sobbed, the more tightly he clung to his bride, who had to
call him a dozen times before he awoke and cried out: "So
it was all a bad dream!" But when she asked about the
dream, he refused to explain. Instead, noticing it was dawn,
he got up and went out.

Once her husband had left the house, Miss Wei called
Nenghong in to brush her hair. As they chatted, a young
maid came into the room.

"I wonder what lucky dream you had last night,
ma'am," said the maid. "I wonder what it was. *Do* tell!"

"I didn't sleep a wink the whole night," said Miss Wei.
"What lucky dream would I have?"

"Then why did the master send for the dream interpreter the first thing this morning?"

"That's it!" said Miss Wei. "He had a bad dream and woke up sobbing from a sound sleep. He wouldn't say a word when I asked him, but went straight off and called the dream interpreter. That *must* be the reason. But when is the interpreter due?"

"They went for him some time ago. I expect he'll be here at any moment."

"Well, you come and tell me the moment he arrives, then take me somewhere near to where he's giving his interpretation. I want to hear what got my husband so upset that he jumped out of bed and sent for him."

Before long the maid came rushing back. "The interpreter's here! The master doesn't want anyone to overhear, so he's taken him into a side-room and shut the door. They're still just chatting and haven't gotten on to dreams yet, but if you want to listen, ma'am, now's your chance!"

Miss Wei was so anxious to hear about the bad dream that she ignored the time-honored rule that a bride should remain in her chamber until the third day. Pulling Nenghong along with her, she headed for a place from which they could eavesdrop.

As it turned out, the dream was extremely unlucky. Septimus had been asleep with his bride in his arms, he said, when a band of malignant ghosts burst into the room, bound his wife with steel wires and would have dragged her off had he not clung to her desperately.

"We've just become husband and wife! What possible reason could you have for seizing her?" he demanded.

"It was in her destiny to have only half a husband," replied the ghosts. "What is she doing with a whole one in her arms? Moreover your first wife is waiting for her in Hell and has begged us to come and seize her." Once more they tried to tear her away.

A heartbroken Septimus pleaded with them again and again. "Take me instead! Let her go!"

In response the ghosts drew their swords and split Septimus in two from head to foot. He was awakened from the excruciating pain only by the sound of his wife's voice. Wouldn't you expect a dream like that to bring shock and horror in its wake? The fact that it occurred on their wedding night only made it worse. It must surely mean something, which was why Septimus had called in the dream interpreter.

"Of course the evil omens predominate," said Septimus, after recounting the dream. "What I don't know is when they will take effect."

"Evil it certainly is," said the interpreter, "but fortunately we have the word *half* there to provide us with the explanation. Your lady is destined to have a helpmate rather than to occupy the women's quarters alone, which is why you were given this omen. First the ghosts said she was destined to have only half a husband, and then they split your honorable body in two, to correspond to the word *half*. They're telling you to divide yourself and give half to someone else, in which case they won't take your wife away. Such a transparent dream—it's child's play to interpret!"

"With such a fine wife, how can I bear to make her share my love with another woman? *Anything* would be preferable to that!"

"She'll lose her life if you don't, and it will be your love that caused her death. You'd be far better off taking a second wife! If you're still not convinced, why not call in another astrologer? Get him to look at her horoscope, calculate her life-span, and see whether she is destined to have a helpmate. Then compare his reading to mine."

"Good idea," said Septimus. He produced a packet of silver for the interpreter and saw him out.

After eavesdropping on this conversation, Miss Wei and Nenghong stole back to her room. She spoke to no one else about it, only Nenghong.

"The dream's message is absolutely right," she said. "It corresponds exactly to what Iron-mouth Zhang told us. What's the point of bringing in another astrologer to give us yet another reading? From what this man says, the prophecy about half a husband is absolutely right. It would be best if I were the one to suggest the concubine. So long as he takes one, I'll be safeguarding my own life and also doing him a favor. He won't need to bring the subject up himself and will be terribly grateful."

"That's all very well," said Nenghong, "but you should consider it very carefully first. I'm afraid this concubine may not defer to your wishes in everything and that you might do better to put up with things as they are."

Miss Wei did indeed put up with things—for one night, during which she said not a single word.

Just then, by a coincidence arranged by the Lord of Heaven, another urgent invitation arrived. As the proverb says, Speak not of yin and yang, they have no ears to hear. It is always a mistake to talk of gods and spirits or of good and bad fortune. Once you do, you don't need to search for ghosts and spirits by night or for good and bad fortune by day. They spring up from your own mind. Every little thing you do will take on an eerie significance.

Even before her marriage, Miss Wei had been affected by the astrologer's prophecy, and her incipient doubts were now further aroused by the dreadful things she had heard. No matter how brave a girl was, she would inevitably start to fear the supernatural. Another proverb applies here: Our worries by day are the stuff of our dreams at night. Septimus had been coached in how to recount his dream by Nenghong after he slept with her on his wedding night. His summoning of the dream interpreter and his commissioning of the maid to get Miss Wei to come and eavesdrop—these were both parts of a preconceived plan that sprang from her ingenuity rather than from his dreams.[20]

Once Septimus's story reached Miss Wei's ears, she converted dream into reality and fantasy into fact and began to have terrifying, ill-omened dreams herself about malignant ghosts seeking her out as a substitute or telling her that Septimus's first wife was waiting for her company. Inevitably, after dreaming of ghosts, she came down with a ghostly illness and barely clung to life, her only desire being to die.

One day she called Nenghong to her bedside and asked her advice. "Look, I can't go on like this. There's something very important that I want to discuss with you, something on which I also need your help, although I'm not sure you'll give it to me."

"We may be from different positions in society, but there's never been any difference between us as friends. Of course I will—as long as it's within my powers."

"I'm looking for a concubine, and you're looking for a husband. Why don't we combine our searches, so that I don't need to look for a concubine nor you for a husband? Instead you'd stay on here as our second lady. Wouldn't that be the perfect solution?"

Nenghong gave a calculated reply. "Absolutely impossible! I've served you half my life in hopes of getting ahead.

20. The text plays on a common expression for *nonsense*: "a foolish man talking of dreams."

If I were willing to be a concubine, I'd have left ages ago! Why would I wait until now? He has enough money to find a woman anywhere. Why does he have to make *my* life miserable? Let him get someone else!"

"You and I have spent half our lives together and share the same temperament. It would mean adding another wife, true, but she'd be a kindred spirit, and even though I'd have to share his love with her, it wouldn't be like sharing it with an outsider. If you have a son, he'll be treated exactly like a son of mine. How happy we would be! If I send my husband outside for a concubine, it will be just as you predicted: I'll be jealous of her or she of me, and what's the good of getting so upset? Let me appeal to you on the grounds of our sixteen years of friendship. Don't deny me this! Grant me my heart's desire!"

Unable to hold out against her pleas, Nenghong consented. Of course, being Nenghong, she came up with another set of conditions that Miss Wei had to meet before she would consent to marry Septimus. Intent on saving her life, Miss Wei did not hesitate to accept. At that point Septimus was told of the arrangement.

On Nenghong's instructions, he first displayed all the false humility of a Wang Mang or a Cao Cao and made many unctuous remarks, refusing to mount the throne until the imperial robes had been thrust upon him.[21] A servant was then sent to inform Miss Wei's parents, who were elated. They provided a dowry for Nenghong and chose a day for her wedding, which she celebrated for the second time.

Nenghong had not dissembled during the first celebra-

21. Like Julius Caesar, Wang Mang and Cao Cao refused the throne until they were "forced" to accept it.

tion, but this time she played the role of the new bride from the start, surprising Septimus by fighting off his advances and refusing to undress. Why? Only after the first watch would she give the reason: She wanted him to go to the mistress's chamber, as he had done before, and ask if he could stay the night, then return only after repeated urgings from Miss Wei. Ostensibly Nenghong was showing her gratitude, but in fact she was repaying a debt. This was typical of the things she did.

The marriage relieved Miss Wei of her anxieties, and of course no disaster ever befell her. Her eating returned to normal, and her nightmares ceased. She and Nenghong began to swell up at the same time and both were delivered of sons before a year had passed. Relations among the husband and his two wives were exceptionally loving. Later Septimus won first place in both examinations and rose from county magistrate to governor of Beijing. However, bound by his contract with Nenghong, he never did dare to take a concubine.

Nenghong had behaved deceitfully toward Miss Wei before her marriage, but afterwards she was loyalty itself, "fearing her as a father, loving her as a mother," and never daring to deceive her in the slightest. She gave Miss Wei a lifetime of devoted service, bearing all her burdens and vexations and seeing that they didn't tax her. Yes indeed, there *are* people who possess the talents of Cao Cao and Wang Mang but who behave like Yi Yin or the Duke of Zhou![22] Just look at the latter part of Nenghong's career!

22. Wang Mang and Cao Cao were arch-rebels; Yi Yin and the Duke of Zhou were loyal ministers who helped others establish their dynasties.

first professional writer of China
   wrote with intention to make one laugh

☐ = chapter grabbing audience's attention
   story-telling atmosphere

delightful and instructive
   entertaing ~~moral~~
philosophical?
Chinese readers = young scholar + beautiful lady
Ming dynasty - rare breeding, experience dinner
   they always get separated

Li Yu wants to play w/ this formula in a
subversive way
                              Stoic attitude to love

1. Duan   Jade
2. Yu   Pearl

romance - passion blw boy + girl (Qing)
         intimacy
"if you're too passionate, you blow it"

reversability, irony, paradox
   ambitious people lose everything

HOMING CRANE LODGE

Passion for intimacy becomes destiny (handwritten)

Duan Yuchu = cut off desire
yu = desire (handwritten)

Yu Zichang = desire naturally emerges (handwritten)

CHAPTER 1

Happy in his quiet existence, he receives the highest rank;
Averse to romantic love, he gets a beautiful wife.

Poem:
How bright the Milky Way that parts them!
She, fair maid, in the East, and he in the West.
Tilling clouds and weaving mists, they gaze;
Tonight a year of love must be expressed.[1]

1. The reference is to the oldest Chinese romantic myth, that of Herd Boy and Weaving Girl, who represent the stars Aquila and Vega, situated on opposite sides of the Milky Way. The granddaughter of the Emperor of Heaven, Weaving Girl is allowed to meet her lover only one night a year, on the seventh of the seventh month, when she is drawn by a dragon-chariot over a bridge formed of magpies.

The dragons pulling the car, the magpie bridge,
The sudden wind in the tree, its leaves aswirl—
Flinging aside the loom, she adorns herself,
For soon they'll meet, Golden Lad and Jade Girl.[2]

Blissful as ever is the love they feel,
Till Chanticleer, they fear, will end the night.
Beside the screen heartbroken words are said.
"Linger awhile. The East is not yet bright."

"You hesitate to cross to the farther shore.
But parting in life is all that you abhor,
And you'll meet and love again this time next year.
Have you never seen two lovers part in death?
Their rosy youth once gone, they come no more."

This old-style poem by a Yuan dynasty poet describes
the poignant love of Weaving Girl and Herd Boy as they
meet for one night each year. But numerous good poems
have been written on that topic; why choose this one in
particular? Because all the others stress the pain of parting,
while this one tells of its pleasures. The theme is contentment, like that of the following story, which is why I have
chosen it as my opening.

Now, parting from one's own flesh and blood is the
most heartrending experience in life. What could possibly
justify my associating it with the word *pleasure*? You must
understand that parting will not of itself bring pleasure, but
if we look beneath the surface and think of those torments

2. Another legend, of two attendants of the Queen Mother of the
West who fell in love and were sent down to Earth to become husband
and wife before finally being recalled to Heaven.

from which there is absolutely no escape, we will actually prefer to be off in some remote corner of the world than in the bosom of our own families, convinced that a lonely pillow will bring us the blessings of a quiet life. The condemned sinner in the Eighteenth Hell who envies the sinners in the Seventeenth is observing the same principle as the living buddhas in the Thirty-second Heaven who long for the Thirty-third.[3]

There was a case recently of a rich man on a journey who put up at an inn. The night was oppressively hot, and the drone of mosquitoes reverberated throughout the room. Draping a silk net over his bed, he lay down safe from the mosquitoes, although their noise continued to bother him. As his mind dwelt on the pleasures of his life at home—the maids gently fanning him, the servants driving off the mosquitoes so that he no longer even heard their noise—he grew bitter.

Sharing the room was a poor man who lacked not only a mosquito net but even a sheet, and who by midnight was so badly bitten that he had to get up and move about. Back and forth he went past the mosquito net like a hunted fugitive, trying to keep his body in motion and prevent the mosquitoes from settling.

The rich man felt sorry for him, but the poor man, far from complaining, congratulated himself on his good fortune and stressed again and again how "happy" he was. Astonished, the rich man asked him what pleasure he found in such hard labor.

"I complained at first, too," said the other, "but then I suddenly thought of a different situation and cheered up."

The rich man asked what he meant.

3. The eighteenth was the worst hell, the thirty-third the best heaven.

"I thought of a convict suffering in prison, where he's chained to the rack and can't move. Even if the mosquitoes are biting him to death, he can only lie there like Lady Bare Sinews,[4] not stretch and move about freely the way I do. That's why, although it's a physical strain, this doesn't upset me in the least. In fact I can't help feeling rather pleased with myself."

At this point the rich man broke out into a sweat. He realized how wrong he had been in feeling homesick while ensconced in his mosquito net.

If only the wretched of the earth would utilize this method, they would come to see their hells as heavens and their inns as pleasure domes and enjoy playing the lute beneath the gold thread[5] or living in a slum. Their faces wouldn't wither nor their hair turn prematurely white, and their troubles would shrink as their blessings grew.

The poem I quoted claimed that parting in life in Heaven was preferable to parting by death on Earth. But this romance of mine will claim that parting by death on Earth is preferable to parting in life in Heaven. It is fully consistent with the passage in the *Four Books* that urges people "in a position of sorrow and difficulty to do what is proper to such a position."

In the Zhenghe period[6] of the Song dynasty there lived in the city of Bianjing a scion of an old-established family

4. A Tang dynasty martyr. Caught outside the city in the dark, she allowed herself to be bitten to death by mosquitoes rather than seek shelter, which would have been unseemly.

5. Gold thread is a plant that is known, like wormwood, for its bitterness. The expression is an example of verbal play; the plant stands for bitterness and the music for joy. (*Music* and *joy* are written with the same character.)

6. 1111–1117. Bianjing, the modern Kaifeng, was the capital.

whose name was Duan Pu and whose style was Yuchu. He showed his intelligence early in life and earned a reputation as a prodigy, but spent the ten years from eight through eighteen as a licentiate without taking the provincial examination. When people asked him why, he answered: "It's unlucky to succeed when you're very young. If I were to pass now, I'd be utterly ignorant of the world and all its hardships, and if I trusted to my own foolish instincts and behaved recklessly, I'd not only be letting down court and society, my very life might be endangered—I could well die an untimely death. It is far better to spend a few more years as a licentiate, postponing the examination and acquiring a little learning—like capital that steadily accumulates interest. That's why I'm quite content to go on with my studies and not try to leap ahead."

He took this attitude not only toward the examinations, but also to marriage, fearing that the sooner he married the sooner he would have a son. "I'm still a child myself! How can I be a father to someone else?" An additional reason was that he had lost his own parents in infancy and had never learned how to behave as a son; he now felt uneasy about receiving someone else's filial attentions too early in life. For these reasons he refused to become engaged, even though he was approaching twenty. He was a man of placid temperament, always prudent about good fortune and constantly worrying that things might turn out for the worse, so he lived one day at a time and never entertained any hopes for the future.

He had a friend and classmate named Yu Tingyan, styled Zichang, another student of high talent and wide learning whose temperament was exactly like his—with one striking exception. Yu was, if anything, *more* indifferent to riches, rank, and examination success; even his friend's steady accumulation of interest failed to attract him. He would rather spend a single day as a licentiate than a whole year as an official, and when he compared the delights of leisurely conversation with his friends to the chores of the official's life, he thought it best not to pass. But in one respect he did differ from Duan—marriage, which he considered the ultimate reality, worthy of man's highest concern. "In the course of his life on Earth," he used to say, "a man may forget every other attachment save his delight in his womenfolk, his sexual bliss, which is the area of Confucian doctrine set aside for our enjoyment. It differs from all other pleasures and must not be neglected under any circumstances. Inhibited as we are by the bonds of morality, we inevitably become bored and apathetic, which is why the Sages who opened the heavens and laid down our moral standards created this path for us and set it among the ethical relationships, enabling us to cast aside our prudish restraints. Moreover, if there were no hus-band-and-wife relationship among the Three Bonds, where would all the rulers and subjects, fathers and sons come from? And if the Five Obligations lacked such a relationship, how would we practice the virtues of filial piety, friendship, loyalty, and goodness? Obviously mar-riage is the most important of the Five Obligations, and we must not only marry young, we must marry well. Beautiful concubines may be easy to obtain, but beautiful wives are not, and in the last resort it is only with the latter that we find the highest pleasure that Confucianism has to offer. To marry a wife who is not beautiful and then feel a compel-ling urge to take a concubine—that's the result of ennui. Subject though we are to Confucian doctrine, our desires will have already transgressed."

With such an attitude, Yu naturally felt an urgent desire

to get engaged, his only problem being that the two parts of the prescription, *marry young* and *marry well*, were impossible to reconcile. Marrying young meant he couldn't marry well, and vice versa. From his childhood on he tried to arrange a marriage, but by the time he came of age he was still, like Duan, unattached. The young man who had hoped to marry young and marry a beauty found himself in exactly the same position as the friend who wanted to do neither. If anything it was the friend, content with his lot, who came off better, enjoying six or seven years of peace and quiet on a lonely pillow—unlike Yu, who had to endure much stress and strain, scrambling up and down complaining about the Lord of Heaven, and rushing hither and thither begging matchmakers for their help.

One day Emperor Huizong issued a decree aimed at recruiting men of talent for the civil service. All licentiates in school, without exception, were to take the examinations; absentees would be charged with opportunism. What lay behind this decree? The fortunes of the Song dynasty were steadily declining, while the power of the Jin was as steadily rising.[7] What's more, China was at loggerheads with both the Liao and the Xi Xia and so had enemies on three sides, a situation that produced several crises a year. Many of the officials stationed near the frontier had lost their lives, and replacements were urgently needed. The emperor feared that licentiates in school would consider the civil service too dangerous and be reluctant to risk their lives, so he issued this directive to drive them from their sanctuaries.

7. The Liao kingdom lay to the northeast, the Xi Xia to the northwest. The Jurched, also in the northeast, conquered the Liao and established the Jin empire.

Much against their will Duan and Yu were forced to sit. In writing their essays, however, lest they pass and so break their private resolutions, they wrote carelessly, doing just enough to prevent the examiner from reporting them absent. But literary ability is like a gift for chess or a capacity for wine—those born with only a little of it cannot increase it, while those born with a great deal cannot reduce it. Both men finished high on the list in the provincial and metropolitan examinations, with Duan ahead of Yu.

Let me point out that good things in life seldom come singly; one invariably leads to another. Before Yu succeeded in the examinations, he had looked everywhere for the ideal beauty he had set his heart on but never found her. It was as if no more great beauties had been born after Xishi and Wang Zhaojun,[8] and he used to wish he'd had the luck to live thousands of years before his time. After he succeeded, however, Wang Zhaojuns and Xishis sprang up everywhere, and he felt lucky to be alive. Otherwise he might have missed out on all these marvelous opportunities.

There was an official named Guan, the Director of Seals, in whose household were two girls, Embraced Pearl and Enfolded Jade. Pearl was his daughter and Jade his niece, one year younger. As an orphan with no immediate family, Jade depended on her uncle to arrange her marriage. Both girls would qualify as classic beauties, but if forced to choose *la crème de la crème*, one would have to put Jade above Pearl. A jingle circulated in the capital:

Pearl's a gem in the hand,
Jade's a jewel among men.

8. Classic beauties of the Zhou and Han dynasties, respectively.

If even a king cannot have both,
He'll take the jewel instead of the gem.

How did a great man's daughters come to be seen by the person who made up this jingle and spread it around town? The reason lay in Emperor Huizong's ordering a new selection of concubines for the imperial palace. No commoner's daughter had been chosen, just these two girls. "They are the only truly outstanding beauties among the millions of girls considered," the eunuch in charge of the selection had reported. "The rest are all mediocre."

"But which of the two is Number One?" asked the emperor. The eunuch recommended Jade over Pearl, which led the emperor to focus his attention on her. That was how the people in the capital came to hear of the girls and make up the jingle.

Jade was just about to enter the palace when suddenly the Liao army descended. For two months the capital held out, until troops could be summoned from all over China and the siege lifted. An outspoken censor then submitted a memorial recommending that in a time of national crisis like the present the emperor ought to make personal sacrifices to regain the lost territories. He ought to free his present concubines and so gain a reputation for putting wise counsel ahead of sensual gratification. How could he delegate power to malicious eunuchs and charge them with selecting even more concubines? By taking such actions how could he hope to keep the aggressor at bay?

The embarrassed emperor reluctantly agreed. He issued a decree accepting personal responsibility for the disaster and ordering the girls married off. In this way both beauties were spared.

Director Guan heard there were two unattached young

men on the first list who were known for their exceptional talents and extraordinary good looks. He promptly dispatched their examiners to propose marriage with his daughter and niece.

Yu was beside himself with delight, his only concern being that he didn't know which girl he would be allotted. Before, if someone had proposed a match with Pearl, he would have been thrilled, but now that both girls were available, he inevitably wanted to "take the jewel instead of the gem." Only his friendship with Duan stood in the way; he had no desire to profit at his friend's expense. But as it happened, Heaven granted his wish. Guan had ranked the young men according to their positions on the list and the girls according to their ages, and since Yu stood a couple of places below Duan and Jade was a year younger than Pearl, he had matched Duan with his daughter and Yu with his niece. In reality this was just a doting father's attempt to secure the higher candidate for his daughter and bring her more prestige; the talk of ranking was only a pretext. Yu understood this, but said nothing. Indeed he blessed the fact that his writing was less than perfect and had brought him a slightly lower place; good luck had sprung from bad and given him the outstanding beauty. If his name had stood a few places higher, his secret wish could not have been fulfilled.

Duan's reaction was precisely the opposite. He feared that his ambitions were too extravagant and had already infringed the Creator's taboo. When he heard that Pearl was to be his wife, he was appalled that the second most beautiful girl in the world should become the wife of a poor student and feared that he had exhausted his good luck and ruined his career. But because it was his examiner who was proposing the match, he had to accept. After all, what wilder ambition could he cherish?

After arranging the betrothals, Guan still would not permit the couples to marry. He wanted to wait for the palace review, when the men would receive their appointments, so that the girls could begin their marriages as titled ladies.

As it turned out, the palace review reversed the order: Yu now found himself at the bottom of Honor Group Two and Duan at the top of Honor Group Three. Slight as the difference was, it meant that Yu would receive an appointment in the capital and Duan one in the provinces. Furthermore a provincial post was no longer what it had been; most vacancies were in the dangerous border regions. In all probability there would be not a single good post to be had. Snobbish as ever, Guan evolved a devious scheme to switch the couples. Without revealing his intentions, he waited until the wedding day and then called in the matchmakers and gave them fresh instructions. Neither couple suspected a thing; both assumed they would marry the partners they were engaged to. Little did they realize that their examination rankings were to be the blueprint for their weddings, which would follow those rankings precisely. The groom who was content with his lot obtained the most beautiful bride in the world, while the one with extravagant ambitions failed to attain them, even if he avoided an outright loss. It is clear that fate lies behind everything that happens to us and that there is no point in our striving against it. But we do not yet know how the couples will get along after their marriages and what the outcome will be. Let me give my gentle readers a chance to rest their eyes before I narrate the next chapter.

CHAPTER 2

An emperor is jealous of his officials;
Love's pleasures draw to a close.

By getting Pearl as his wife after he had counted on Jade, Yu could not help feeling mortified. As time went by, however, he became reconciled to his situation, and he and his wife forgot their differences. Pearl was really extraordinarily beautiful; it was only in comparison with Jade that she suffered at all. If, as now, she were parted from Jade, she became the most beautiful girl in the world, while in terms of grace and charm, at least in Yu's eyes, she had always been superior to Jade. (As the proverb so aptly puts it, your essays don't need to impress the whole world, just the examiner.) Yu had always had a romantic temperament—only a Zhao Feiyan or a Yang Guifei would have satisfied him—and since Pearl was the perfect match, he felt grateful to the father-in-law whose highly questionable behavior had produced such a satisfying result.

He and Pearl were an exceptionally loving couple. He swore that he would never take a concubine, whether or not Pearl had a son, and that he would never leave her behind no matter where he was posted. They would play lovebirds forever and waste not one moment out of their lifetime of wedded bliss.

Let me turn now to Duan, who was delighted to note that his wife was of the old school and refused to let her physical beauty overshadow her moral nature. Like Yu he accepted the fait accompli, but unlike Yu he was constantly on tenterhooks about possessing so much beauty. The most beautiful girl in the world is like a priceless jewel, he told himself. Why am *I* so lucky as to possess her? My friend

184

hadn't the right destiny and lost her after first winning her. Even a romantically minded emperor wasn't fortunate enough to enjoy her but sent her back after choosing her as his consort. Who am I, with my brief spell of luck, to outdo an emperor? "The commoner's only crime was to be caught with a piece of jade on him."[9] This could lead to my *whole family* being liquidated!

He felt anxiety in the midst of joy and sorrow in the midst of laughter and did not dare abandon himself to pleasure. Even when he was making love to Jade, these thoughts would flash through his mind, and he would start having qualms—as if the beautiful girl in his arms was not his own wife, and as if what he was doing with her was somehow disreputable.

Jade misunderstood his feelings. Because he had passed only in Honor Group Three and would not get a post in the capital but be sent to some provincial danger spot instead, she assumed that he was plagued with worries like the man of Qi.[10] She often consoled him with the maxim: "Rest secure in the knowledge of a just fate, for Heaven comes to the aid of the good man."

"Life and death are governed by fate; riches and rank are in Heaven's gift," countered Duan. "If I'm posted to the frontier and sacrifice my life there, I'll have merely done my duty as an official. My death will have been decreed by fate, so how could I complain? No, the thought that plagues me is that I'm a luckless wretch of a student

9. Proverb quoted in the early chronicle *Zuo zhuan*, tenth year of Duke Huan. The citizen's sole crime was possession of a gem.
10. The Chinese Chicken Little. From a story in the *Lie Zi*.

who has enjoyed three different kinds of excess. The Creator abhors excess and topples all those who enjoy it. One way or another, openly or in secret, I'll meet with disaster. That's what worries me."

Jade asked what excesses he was talking about.

"Firstly, I was a bright child who acquired a reputation as a prodigy. Secondly, I succeeded in the examinations at an early age and received undue distinction. Thirdly, I've taken over the Land of Love, the Isle of Bliss, snatching away a prize that my ruler and friend had both hoped to win. Any one of these excesses would have been enough to jeopardize my good fortune. Think how certain my ruin is, now that I have all three! How would *you* go about saving me, if disaster were to strike?"

"It will never come to *that*! Just don't covet any more blessings, and try to find some way to ward off disaster. But since you feel such concern, you must already have a solution in mind. Do tell me."

"As I see it, the only possible remedy is the maxim, Be prudent with blessings, content with hardship. But even that is just hoping against hope. There's really no escaping the consequences." *fatalistic*

"What do you mean 'prudent with blessings, content with hardship'?"

"To be rich and famous without license—that's what 'prudent with blessings' means. And to be cast down but not bitter—that's what 'content with hardship' means. In the last analysis the former concept was designed to promote the latter; it means that anxiety over the future toughens your mind and body so that you can withstand the trials to come. Your clothes shouldn't be too splendid, your food too lavish, or your house too grand. In each case you ought to leave a little leeway for building up your fortunes in the nether world, not enjoy yourself too grossly or pamper yourself so that you can't withstand privation. That principle is easy enough to grasp. But even the love between husband and wife, the passion of the bedchamber, ought not to be too exuberant. You should enjoy yourself only up to seventy percent of capacity, reserving the other thirty percent for the period of separation. Now, *that* is a most subtle principle that no one has yet grasped, but married couples must grasp it, particularly in wartime. As the twin proverbs say, A loving marriage doesn't last into old age, and There's no joy greater than meeting, no sorrow greater than parting. A husband and wife can spend their whole lives together, but the time will come when they have to part. Loving couples part sooner than unloving ones, and for every extra measure of joy while together they have to suffer an extra measure of sadness while apart. In trying to be prudent about our blessings, we must take the following as our starting point: our passions shouldn't be too ardent, lest our happiness be short-lived and sorrow develop at the peak of joy; and we oughtn't to repeat those words that touch us most deeply, lest they stab us to the heart when we recall them later. If you and I continue like this and enjoy a long and happy marriage without ever having to part, perhaps our prudent attitude toward our blessings may be the cause, allowing us a few extra years of love."

Jade now understood what her husband meant. She asked when the appointments would be made; perhaps by the grace of Heaven they might get some quiet post in which to live out their lives.

"A luckless student with my excesses would surely be

struck down by some unforeseen disaster even in peace-time. You don't imagine I'll be lucky enough to escape in time of war?"

Jade burst into tears.

"There's no need to be sad, my dear. My maxim, be prudent with blessings, was designed for just such a situation as this. Before disaster strikes, we must act prudently, and when it strikes, we must resolve to be content with hardship. If I'm given a post, good or bad, of course I'll take you with me, and your safety will depend on my luck. Even if we spent a lifetime together, we would still have to part in the end. People just don't *understand*! They imagine that parting in life is better than parting by death, whereas in my opinion it's a hundred times worse. If by the grace of Heaven we are able to die together in some danger spot and so avoid the pain of parting, that would be the best thing that could happen to us in the course of the longest life. But I'm afraid that the Creator in his jealousy will begrudge us the chance."

"Parting in life may be painful, but at least it's tempo-rary as compared with parting by death. What makes you say death is preferable? Kindly explain."

"Let's say a husband is stationed at the opposite end of the world from his wife, and although she longs for his return, they never meet—that's parting in life. If either the husband or the wife dies and Heaven and Earth prevent any chance of a reunion—that's parting by death. As the prov-erb says, It's easier to be a real widow than a grass one. A married couple who part in life live for a single hope and inflict endless torments on themselves. By day they long so desperately to meet that the finest food tastes like chaff in their mouths and the brightest clothes feel like shackles on their flesh. By night they yearn so badly to be reunited that their embroidered quilts and pillows bristle with thorns and needles. And because their days drag by like years, they age before their time. Some husbands go so far as to set a date for their return before leaving home, but then one partner will die and bring them to a final parting. This is common with parting in life, and it is really better that one of them die, because then the other has no one left to pine for. The widow or widower simply accepts the situation, just as the priest who is approaching death doesn't hanker after the layman's life but gets as much pleasure from the prayer mat as he ever got before joining the order. Doesn't this show that parting by death is more enjoyable than parting in life?

"There is another kind of couple who enter into a pact to die together before they are born. At exactly the same time they complete their natural span with no need of deathbed farewells, funeral tears, or mournful faces. It is even better than parting in life, in fact it is the same as translating one's whole family to Heaven, an exceptional destiny available only to those who have perfected themselves through many lives. You and I will go together to the frontier. If we meet with disaster, we'll need only a pair of sashes tied in lovers' knots in order to go to our reward. The proverb may say, If you die beneath the peony blossoms, you'll turn into a romantic ghost, but that refers only to sexual passion, not to the Three Bonds and Five Obligations. If we are able to do as I have suggested, one of us will die a loyal official, the other a chaste wife, and together we'll have been a couple in life and in death. Wouldn't that be the most joyous outcome of all?"

These words transformed Jade from a creature of exquisite sensitivity into a gallant, stouthearted woman who longed for a heroine's death. She was no longer afraid to hear talk of the dangerous frontier, but even felt a touch of envy, as she spent her days waiting anxiously for news of a favorable posting.

News did come, but only after several months of waiting. There was such a shortage of officials in the capital that the few dozen names in Group Two were not sufficient to fill all the vacancies, and so the top names in Group Three were also given ministry posts. Yu was chosen for the Ministry of Revenue and Duan for the Ministry of Works. Soon each would be installed in the perfect job, and Jade was thrilled.

"When the old man on the border caught a horse, it wasn't necessarily a blessing,"[11] cautioned her husband. "Don't be too quick to celebrate. This is what I had in mind when I told you the Creator was too jealous to let us part by death."

This time Jade decided that he was being unduly pessimistic and paid no heed. But as bad luck would have it, he was sent on a mission that really did spell disaster.

Emperor Huizong had heeded the censor and halted the selection of concubines, but he couldn't help regretting his decision. Another jingle circulated in the capital:

When the city gates are closed,
The way to criticism is open.
When the city gates are open,
The way to criticism is closed.

The benefits from the emperor's responsiveness to criticism had not been yielded up of his own free will. His was a temporary maneuver to protect himself at a time when the

11. From an anecdote in *Huai Nan Zi* 26 about the illusory nature of good and bad fortune.

gates were open again but the public was still restive, and as soon as the war subsided he planned to resume his old ways. Not only was he loath to give up the most beautiful candidate, he even wanted to keep as an alternate the girl who had been recommended with her. He never anticipated that that high official, evidently lacking the good fortune to become an imperial relative, would take the decree so seriously as to marry his girls off. When the emperor heard that his beauties had fallen to two new graduates, he was full of regret, and when his mind dwelt on the pleasures those graduates would be enjoying, he was overcome with jealousy and gave orders to his Grand Secretary: "Those half-starved paupers have no right to such beauties! You mustn't let them get away with it. Find a couple of distant posts to pack them off to and don't allow them back for three or four years. Make them pay for their *lèse majesté* in marrying imperial consorts by doing a term as Herd Boys separated from their Weaving Girls. I'd also like to see the relative gravity of their crimes indicated by a difference in penalties. Let the one who married Jade serve a few years longer than the other."

"We're about to send emissaries to the Jin to deliver the annual tribute. It's the joint responsibility of Revenue and Works. May I suggest that we send these two?"

"But the tribute is easy to deliver, and the Jin court is no great distance. I hardly think *that* would atone for their crimes."

"The tribute used to consist of large quantities of silk and silver, but the Jin deliberately made trouble and fined our emissaries, so that it's now extremely difficult for them to complete their missions. Those who deliver the silver have to stay there between two and three years, while none of those who have delivered silk over the last ten years has yet come back. It's the most grueling mission of all, more than enough to atone for their sins."

Highly gratified, Huizong ordered Yu to deliver the silver and Duan the silk. Each was to be responsible for his own sphere rather than to merge operations. After assembling the tribute, they would travel north together to deliver it.

Once the imperial directive has been handed down, it will surely change these lovebirds into shrikes and swallows.[12] But if you are wondering how their missions came to be so grueling, please turn to the next chapter.

CHAPTER 3

Parting by death is better than parting in life, so he bids a casual adieu.
Returning from afar is like a honeymoon, but joy turns to ashes.

The delivery of tribute began in Shenzong's reign.[13] Tormented beyond endurance by the Jin, the emperor began the insidious practice of paying a quantity of silver each year to defray the costs of their armies and stop their harassment. As the years went by, the amount was regularly negotiated upward until by Emperor Huizong's time it had reached a million. At first it was known as annual tribute,

12. Cliché drawn from a song in *New Songs of the Jade Terrace* 9. The birds fly off in different directions.
13. The Xiaoxianju edition leaves a blank before the word *reign*, whereas later editions give Shenzong, who reigned from 1068 to 1085. Li Yu's account of these tribute relations is largely fictional.

although the payment was entirely in silver, but then some Chinese nationals taught the Jin how to make more money by pointing out to them that silk came from the southeast where it was cheap and of high quality and suggesting that half of the amount be paid in silk. The Jin then sold off the silk and doubled their profit, so that one million from the Song became a million and a half in their hands. At first, while the payment was all in silver, a single emissary sufficed, but when silk was added, a whole wagon train became necessary. The job was now too much for one man and had to be split between two, with one in charge of the silver and the other of the silk. Lest the silver prove of poor quality or the silk underweight, which would have allowed the Jin to build the dispute up into a pretext for a border raid, the emissaries were ordered to collect or purchase the tribute themselves. The same man acquired it as delivered it, to prevent the shifting of responsibility that would occur if the goods changed hands.

When the silk was first delivered, the Jin were unable to judge its quality and accepted what they were given, which made it easy to cover up any deficiencies. The silk emissaries showed a certain finesse by starching the cloth and powdering the silk and then setting top prices for both, all without the court's knowledge. They simply delivered it to its destination and reported back; it was the perfect job—and very hard to obtain. After a few deliveries of this sort, however, some Chinese nationals taught the Jin how to test the material: before accepting the tribute, they should insist on rinsing out any starch and powder and then weigh each bale separately. If a bale was found to be short by even a fraction of an ounce, the emissary would have to make up the loss. Eventually this practice became the rule and the emissary had to pay the fees whether the goods were acceptable or not. But even after the fees had been paid, the Jin would still accuse the emissary of deceiving his own court and cheating a neighboring country and, seizing the evidence of malfeasance, make further outrageous demands. The emissary would be unable to meet them and would have to remain behind as a hostage, prevented from returning home and stalled in his career for years at a time. Such were the trials of the silk emissary.

His colleague's trials arose from the fact that the Jin scales weighed light and a supplementary payment was always needed. Moreover, however large the payment, there was always another one on top of it. The reason is that the Jin were crafty, and when they found one additional payment forthcoming, they assumed the emissary was wealthy enough to pay more and concocted another pretext. This was why the silver emissaries, rich or poor, had to remain with the Jin for several years before their cases could be cleared. No more than two or three in every ten returned in the same year as they set out.

Taking up their arduous tasks, Duan and Yu went their separate ways, one to purchase silk, the other to collect silver. Once they had gathered the tribute, they returned home together to take leave of their families before setting off on their mission.

Yu was infinitely loving toward Pearl and, we need hardly say, took the tenderest of farewells beneath the quilt, paying in advance the debts that would accumulate between his departure and return with one of those nights of which every moment is precious. He also reminded Pearl that, despite the arduous task he had been given, he had her father's backing. Even if he had to pay something, he didn't suppose her father would begrudge a mere pittance in order to rescue him. "We'll be together again in six months, perhaps in as little as three—unlike our brother-in-law, who has a lonely fate in store for him and will have to spend at least ten years away from his wife."

When Jade realized that her husband was setting off on a long journey, she packed his bags for him, taking care to include a ten years' supply of clothes and shoes that she provided herself. When he returned from purchasing the silk, she set them in front of him. "I doubt that this journey will be over in a few years, and I can't deliver your winter clothes myself, my feet being too small to travel that distance, so

> I've emulated the love of Meng Jiangnu,
> And tried to follow Su Huiniang's intent,[14]

wearing out the midnight loom in preparing a ten years' supply for you. Please take them with you, so that whenever you look at one, you'll feel you are looking at me. In the seams there are specks of blood where the needle has pricked my finger. Miss me, miss me terribly—and the love I've shown you will not have been in vain." At this point she wept as if her heart was about to break.

"Your intentions were perfectly sincere, but unfortunately you wasted your valuable efforts in a futile cause," said Duan. "The journey I'm going on is still a parting by death. Don't think of it as parting in life. What's a penniless

14. Meng Jiangnu's husband had been conscripted to help build the Great Wall. She traveled there with winter clothing but found that he was dead, then wept so piteously before the wall that it tumbled down and revealed his bones. Su Hui in the fourth century embroidered a palindrome, destined to become the most famous in Chinese history, and sent it to her husband on the frontier. Chinese palindromes, of which the units are characters, can run to great length.

scholar to do when assigned the most arduous task of all
and required to repay an unlimited amount of money?
Since I've abandoned all hope of returning alive, why eke
out my existence? The day I deliver the silk will be the day
I die. I doubt that I'll live long enough to wear out a single
pair of shoes or a suit of clothes, so why do I need to take
all these things with me? Even if my time is not up and I
fail in my attempt at suicide, at most I'll have only a few
more years of misery left in which to pay off my debts of
hunger and cold. How can someone who has lost his
sovereign's favor expect good treatment when a prisoner in
a foreign land? The clothes that Meng Jiangnu delivered,
the embroidery Su Huiniang wove, went only to the frontier, not into enemy territory. Even if I took these with me,
they'd be seized by the Jin, and I'd never get a chance to
wear them! It makes far better sense to store them at home,
where someday they may come in handy."

"But since you don't intend to return alive, they'll be
useless! What's the point of keeping them?"

Duan was about to say something but thought better of
it and gave a sardonic sigh. Jade's suspicions were aroused
and she continued to question him until he explained.

"Have you never read those heartrending lines in the
Classic of Poetry?" he asked. " 'When you are dead, someone else will enter into your house.'[15] When I'm dead,
some other man is bound to move in, and once he's here,
the clothes are sure to be worn. Every garment you keep
will spare you so much trouble when you come to serve
my successor. Think of all the needles and thread you'll be
saving! What a *boon*!"

Jade had assumed that he was speaking from a genuine

15. See Arthur Waley, trans., *The Book of Songs*, p. 200.

love for her, but when she heard this, she felt as if "in the act of worship, her fervent heart had been dipped in icy water." Exploding in anger, she retorted in scathing terms. "Oh, a man like you, you have a heart of *stone*! I spent my heart's blood on you and get not so much as a kind word in return! Instead you slander me! What makes you think you'll be a loyal official but I won't be a chaste wife? If that's your opinion, you can take these clothes away and burn them, lest they add to your suspicions!"

Suiting her actions to the word, she made a pile of the clothes and shoes and poked some kindling underneath, as if she were burning paper garments at a funeral. In a matter of minutes the brocade and silk were reduced to ashes.

Duan tried to dissuade her but was reluctant to pull her away. It was almost as if he wanted her to burn the clothes rather than leave them behind for someone else to wear.

Jade sobbed as she burned the clothes: "How devoted *other* husbands and wives are to each other! *They're* about to part for a year at the most, yet he comforts her in every possible way to keep her from feeling sad. In our case it's not parting in life but parting by death that we face, and yet you haven't a single loving word for me but come out with these outrageous slurs! What's the point of being *that* kind of husband and wife?"

"Other women perfected their conduct in their last existence and obtained good husbands in this one, husbands who bring them both love and good fortune and from whom they never part, in life or death. Why did you have to misbehave and earn such bad karma as to get a coldhearted, luckless wretch like me? Disaster by death, no pleasure in life—that is your fate. If you hadn't broken your engagement but gone through with the marriage, you'd be in a loving relationship now and wouldn't have to listen to these harsh remarks. It's the fault of whoever broke off that engagement; it has nothing to do with me. Who knows, after I die he may carry out his original desire and unite Ehuang with Nüying again?[16] The selection may have been halted, but the city gates are open now, and you can be sure that the way to criticism will soon be closed. If His Majesty chances to think of someone out of the past, he might well choose you again. Highly unusual, true, but as one who is about to leave for a foreign country, I can't help being concerned about it. Now, don't take this to heart. Two maxims sum it all up: Life and death are governed by fate, riches and rank are in Heaven's gift; and Our every little move is foreordained. If it's your fate to lose your chastity and remarry, I couldn't prevent the knot from being tied, no matter how kind and considerate I tried to be. On the other hand, if it's your fate to leave a good name behind as a chaste wife, there's no need to take offense just because I've been a little rude. Perhaps *because* I've revealed all this in advance—mankind isn't permitted to learn the secrets of Heaven—who knows, it may never happen."

He prepared to travel light, packing only a few well-worn garments instead of those Jade had made for him (such as remained after the fire). He also attached a name to the upper rooms in which they lived—Homing Crane Lodge, an allusion to Ding Lingwei's flying home in the form of a crane—to indicate that he would not be returning alive.[17]

As the men were leaving, the two couples said good-

16. Daughters of the legendary emperor Yao, whom he gave in marriage to his chosen successor Shun.

17. A Han figure who studied Taoism, became an immortal, and returned home in the form of a crane.

bye. Yu gazed at Pearl again and again, and even as he rode away still turned and looked back at her several times. If only he could have painted a miniature portrait of her to keep on his person and worship like an image of the bodhi-sattva Guanyin! Duan, on the other hand, bowed once and then set off on his long journey without a trace of sadness in his expression, despite his wife's weeping and wailing.

After enduring the rigors of the journey, the two men delivered their goods to the Jin who, needless to say, applied their tests and as usual claimed that the goods were either fake or underweight and insisted that the emissaries make up the difference.

"I'm a new graduate," protested Duan, "and have nothing to call my own. I've never received a salary from the court or collected any taxes from the people. I couldn't produce a single tael if I tried, let alone tens of thousands. And there's no starch or powder in the material I've brought; by all means rinse it out and see for yourselves. If you continue to make demands and try to force me into coming up with that unwarranted payment, all I can offer you is my life, which your honorable country is free to dispose of as it wishes."

Needless to say, the Jin humiliated him in public, then demanded payment again, and finally tried to strike a deal, hoping in each case to force him into writing home and asking his family to sell up their property and ransom him. But Duan had resolved to take "content with hardship" as a novel remedy, to which he added the comparative method, as a tonic. Whenever he reached fifty percent on the misery scale, he would compare that with seventy percent, and when he reached seventy percent, he would compare it with one hundred percent. He felt that the torments of this world were easier to bear than those of the next. No matter how intolerable the beatings and tortures became, death was always there as an escape hatch. The other world was a place of retreat, for when you reached the point of desperation, you could take your own life. After death you felt no pain; the knife, the saw, the cauldron could do you no harm. But the torments of Hell were a different matter, for having died once, you couldn't die again. Whether you strangled yourself or cut your throat, there was no other world to flee to; no matter how severe the torture, the demons were inescapable. One heard of living people who couldn't bear their punishment and who escaped to the other world but never of dead people fleeing back to this world in desperation. Having arrived at this conclusion, Duan looked on torture merely as a boil or abscess; he was fated to suffer and would have to put up with a spell of misfortune, but once the boil burst, the pain would be gone. With the aid of this secret formula he was able to find contentment in any situation and to feel no misery in his bondage.

Yu's father-in-law had reassured him: "If there's a shortfall, just send a letter home and I'll make it up." Buoyed by this promise, Yu decided to play the big spender, bribing officials at all levels and avoiding any public humiliation. Noting how free he was with his money, the Jin treated him to the best of food and wine. Even his brother-in-law, with no one to turn to, came in for some of his largesse. In less than five months Yu paid off his debts, took leave of Duan, and returned to report on his mission.

The rule under the Song was that any official returning from a mission abroad had to report to the emperor before going home. It was midmorning when Yu arrived in the capital, and the emperor was in court, but Yu assumed there would still be time after delivering his report to get home that day. As the proverb so aptly puts it: Not even a honeymoon is as sweet as a homecoming. Yu's craving for pleasure was even keener than at his wedding, and he could hardly wait to give the briefest of reports and then rejoin his wife. However, the court was locked in debate over whether to join forces with the Jin for an attack on the Liao. Numerous opinions were offered, and the issue could not be resolved. The emperor began the session early in the morning and did not make his decision until evening. He then immediately withdrew, and his ministers, knowing how tired he felt, would have hesitated to disturb him with the most urgent military dispatch, let alone with something that could easily be deferred, like the report of a tribute mission. For six months Yu had been on tenterhooks, but because the unlucky star had not left his horoscope, he had to endure an extra half night at court, not daring to return home. But that half night was harder to endure than half a year, as the Tang poem points out:

It seemed as if all the waters of all the seas
Had filled the water clock, so long was the night.[18]

When Pearl heard that her husband had arrived at Court and would soon be home, she felt as if the moon had tumbled out of the sky, she was so excited. She hurried off to perfume the embroidered quilt and iron the silk coverlet in readiness for a night in which they would confide all that had happened to them in the period of separation.

But although she watched from sunrise until the moon went down, she saw no sign of him. Up and down the

18. Adapted from a poem by Li Yi (748–827).

deserted steps she tripped, wearing out her tiny slippers. Then next morning when she climbed the stairs to their rooms and looked out, she saw an official with a large escort of mounted men waving flags and shouting slogans. She assumed it was some officer passing by—until the cavalcade suddenly halted before her gate. She stared. It was her husband! Flying downstairs, she welcomed him with the most radiant of smiles. Such sweetness after so long a drought would surpass even the pleasures of the wedding night, she thought, expecting to find him aglow with anticipation. But after they had greeted each other, her husband began to weep tears of frustration, and when she asked him why, was so racked with sobs that he couldn't explain.

After reporting on his mission, he had been given another task: to oversee military supplies. He was to set off at once, without a moment's delay, lest the army be held up. Even to make this call at his own house he had had to deceive the court and see that no one knew. How had this situation come about? Before he returned, the Jin had sent an official message asking the Song to join them in an attack on the Liao, but the court had been unable to reach a decision and had delayed its answer. Receiving no reply, the Jin had then sent a demand, threatening, "If your honorable country refuses to commit itself, that fact will constitute a breach of our alliance. This court will make no further demands, but will turn against the Song the troops that are now poised for an attack on the Liao. It will then be too late for you to honor our treaty."

The emperor was paralyzed with fear, which was why the debate had dragged on for days and he had been unable to dismiss the court. Had Yu come one day later, someone else would have been sent. But fortune was against him. At first the court could not reach a decision, and then, just as Yu arrived, they set a time for the army to march. The generals had been appointed the evening before, except for the quartermaster-general, who was to be chosen next day. Yu had broken the taboo by his temerity in marrying a royal consort, and the emperor, seeing him back so soon and about to make love to his wife once more as if he had never been away, turned Yu's achievements against him. He declared that since Yu had done so well on his tribute mission, completing it so quickly, he would be able to give excellent service to the army with his rapid delivery of supplies. That was why, after barely finishing one task, Yu was immediately assigned another, one that would keep him away from a reunion with his wife.

Pearl's red-hot passions were plunged in icy water, and two columns of tears poured endlessly down her cheeks like the streams of the Yangzi Gorges. She tugged at her husband's sleeve and was about to tell him she loved him, when his fellow officers began to protest: "It's a serious matter, moving an army! You can't worry about your private feelings! We *all* have wives! If *we* hung about like this, each of us would delay the operation a bit longer, and the army would need *weeks* to get off. If the court gets wind of this, there'll be trouble!"

Yu had hoped to delay another few minutes and, pulling his wife inside, was about to give her an idea of why he had returned, when he heard these ugly threats and suddenly lost his ardor. All he could do was cry bitterly and act out an unhappy reunion, which was how they parted. Before leaving, he gave Pearl a letter from his brother-in-law and asked her to pass it on to Jade.

Jade's mood brightened when she received the letter. She assumed that her husband regretted his mistake in not saying he loved her as he set off, and that the letter would express his repentance and his resolve to do better. On opening it, however, she found it to be something quite different—a four-line poem that ran:

Your weaving showed a wife's affection;
But away with love—it's only wise!
All our passions end in parting;
Alone, I'll see suspicion rise.

She realized then that he had not altered his callous attitude but was still the most coldhearted man in history. In any case there was no prospect of a meeting, so even if he *had* shown a loving attitude, it would have made no difference. Her best course was to resign herself to the role of chaste widow and cast aside all thought of sexual pleasure. She would make a living with her spinning-wheel and not try to save her earnings but enjoy herself to the full.

After a year or more of this life she was much plumper than when Duan was at home—unlike the cousin who was so pleased with her husband. *She* spent her days moping, sighing, and cursing Heaven and Earth, and grew thinner and thinner until her bones stood out like matchsticks—the very antithesis of voluptuous womanhood.

Let me turn now to Yu, as he trailed after the army supervising its supplies. Day after day he kept up with the cavalry, braving high winds and freezing cold and enduring every conceivable hardship. As the proverb says, A young man grows old on the road. If a traveling merchant tends to age on the road, how can a young fellow in an expeditionary force be expected to keep his youth? If it were merely the hard labor and combat, there would still have been opportunities for rest and recreation, and even if a man did tend to age rapidly, the fact would show in his face only when he actually grew old. But this young man had never cared for success, only pleasure; he regarded his beautiful wife as the be-all and end-all of his existence and could not put her out of his mind. Besides, she had been incredibly solicitous in his marriage and anticipated his every desire. The endearments they exchanged on the pillow, their passion beneath the quilt—he had only to think of such things to feel his soul melt and almost expire. And so in less than three years he came to resemble a grizzled old man, with the hair of his mustache and beard turning white as soon as it appeared above the skin. Even if he had been allowed home, he could not have returned as the dashing young husband who had set forth. In any event his horoscope still showed the Posthorse Star, and he had no prospect of returning. The campaign lasted into a second year, during which the army was never at rest. Back and forth they marched, laying waste to dozens of towns, before they were lucky enough to gain the victory and annihilate the enemy.

The army's withdrawal happened to coincide with the date of the annual tribute mission. An official attuned to the emperor's feelings realized that if Yu returned he would only arouse the imperial wrath and be sent off again, so he made a most disingenuous recommendation: "Yu Tingyan carried out his tribute mission efficiently and expeditiously and has conspicuous achievements to his credit. Furthermore he has had many years of experience with the Jin and knows their temperament. It would be advisable to promote him and put him in charge of the whole tribute operation, including the administration of the officials who deliver the silver and silk. Not only would this move save much expense, it could also prevent an outbreak of hostilities on the frontier, which would be a great boon to both ruler and people."

The memorial conformed exactly to the emperor's jealous predisposition, and that same day he issued a directive to the Ministry of Personnel that Yu be promoted to vice-president and given charge of the tribute operation. He need not return to court on receiving the promotion, but should take up his duties on the frontier at once. After the operation he would be promoted and rewarded.

When he read the news in the *Imperial Gazette*, Yu was shocked almost to death. Without waiting for the ministry's decree to arrive, he tried to commit a certain foolish act, but in the nick of time met a messenger bearing a letter that saved his life. But who sent the letter? What did it say? And why did it arrive at such an opportune moment? For the answers to these questions please turn to the next chapter.

CHAPTER 4

Two cousins differ vastly in their circumstances,
And a husband and wife become a newly married
couple.

Who sent the letter, do you suppose? And what did it say? It came from a certain close relative, a fellow graduate of Yu's class who was in the identical predicament and wanted to express his sympathy. Afraid that Yu might be misguided enough to fall into the same trap and repent only when it was too late, Duan sent him some salutary advice. When the news of the Liao defeat reached the Jin court, he knew that Yu, concerned about his wife, would rush home at once and sow the seeds of further disaster. Not only would he have to part from her again, he might even die. Duan advised him that the only safe course was to petition the emperor for leave on the pretext that he had fallen ill along the way, then wait for a year or more before reviewing the situation and deciding what to do.

The letter arrived on the same day as the *Imperial Gazette*. Reading the letter, Yu realized that his brother-in-law was an immortal incarnate whose every word was wonderfully prescient. His readiness to endure hardship and his lack of interest in returning home were evidence of a profound purpose. Even his losses had worked out to his advantage. What a pity that he, Yu, had not emulated Duan instead of enduring so much pointless hardship! He sent in his petition at once, as the letter advised, but unfortunately it arrived after the decree had been issued by the ministry, and Yu was told he could not excuse himself from service but must apply himself to his new duties.

He had no choice but to wait for the tribute emissaries at the border and accompany them to the Jin court. When the Jin realized that he was in charge, they were delighted, assuming that he could bribe them as he had done before. In the past he had been in charge only of the silver, but now that he was in charge of both items, they reasoned, he would need to instruct only one source to pay and both accounts would be cleared up. The officials in charge of the tribute held banquets in his honor at which they offered him gifts and addressed him as *my Lord* and *Mr. Vice-President*. Little did they realize that the situation was now radically different. Previously Yu had exerted himself on his own account and had had a father-in-law to back him up. Moreover he was responsible only for the silver; when a supplement was demanded, it was for a limited amount only, and he cheerfully paid it. But this time he was managing the operation for others, and although he tried his best, he could not come up with the money. When his family at home realized they would be unable to ransom him, they declined to waste any more of their limited resources. Moreover there were now such large deficits in both accounts that Yu could not have made them up even if he had been blessed with the golden touch. His only course was to put on a bold face, stiffen his backbone, and emulate Duan in letting the Jin do with him as they pleased. The punishments they inflicted on him were even harsher than those inflicted on Duan and included every conceivable cruelty.

Meanwhile Duan had settled down. The Jin, noting his capacity for withstanding hardship and realizing they could not squeeze anything out of him, gave up hope of extortion and treated him as a visitor. They escorted him to scenic places, subjected him to no further hardships, and allowed him freedom of movement. Had he wanted to return home, they would have made a special provision and let him go. But this particular emissary preferred to regard the desert as his Peach Blossom Spring and adopt it as a temporary refuge.

When Yu could bear the torture no longer, he had to ask Duan to intercede, and his worst ordeals were somewhat lightened. After two years of this treatment, when still no one came to his aid, the Jin realized that Yu was not a wealthy man and gradually relaxed their grip.

Yu and Duan had been relatives at home, and now, in a foreign country, they naturally drew closer together and shared each other's fortunes. "Everything you've ever done, brother," remarked Yu on one occasion, "shows the evidence of deep thought. But I must say the way you treated my sister-in-law when we were leaving did strike me as a bit excessive. A husband's love for his wife oughtn't to be quite so shallow!"

Duan laughed. "That was precisely when I showed how loving I am. No husband has ever had such a love for his wife! Why not check your facts, brother, before you go accusing me of being shallow?"

"You forced her to burn the clothes because you suspected she would remarry, and you never smiled while you were with her or showed any sadness when you left. That's cold-hearted enough for me! How can you call it love!"

"You must surely be the most *naive* person in the world! No wonder you kept pining for your wife and suffered all that extra hardship! What young women fear most in life is loneliness, and what they love best is excitement—except when the husband dies and the wife, with no one to long for, resigns herself to widowhood. If I had wantonly left her pining for me, she'd inevitably have suffered for a few years and then died of grief. Ours was a very loving marriage, but we were forced to part. If I'd shown her something of what I felt and caused her to miss me so badly that she dreamt about our lovemaking, my departure would have been a draft of poison consigning her to an early grave. If I managed to return and wanted to resume our marriage, I couldn't do so. Far better to pick a quarrel, pretend I didn't care for her, and leave in a huff. Naturally her desires will cool, she won't hanker after the pleasures we enjoyed, and she'll find her loneliness easier to bear. As the ancients said, 'Condemn them to death and they'll survive.' The misery I inflicted on her was designed precisely to save her life. As an educated man, you must surely understand the principle involved?"

"So *that*'s why you did it! All very well, but women are changeable creatures, unpredictable. You treated her as immoral while she was still a chaste wife. What if she so resents your insinuations that she puts them into practice and does something she wouldn't otherwise have done?"

"My method has to be tailored to the individual. I knew that I could trust her. I knew that she believed in the Three Bonds and Five Obligations and would never do anything to transgress them, and that's why I treated her this way. In another case I'd have used a different treatment, one with less risk to it."

"Then you ought at least to have given her a little consolation as you set off, shown her some tact, left her with some hope for the future—even if you couldn't get back alive. You should never have put that ill-omened name on your house. Have you *really* made up your mind to follow Ding Lingwei's example and not return?"

"My motive in choosing that name was the same as when I quarreled with her. I picked a quarrel because I wanted her to forget the pleasures we enjoyed together, so that time would pass more easily for her. I chose a name denoting a final farewell because I wanted her to give up her fantasies and not count the days until my return; my sole purpose in both cases was to ward off disaster and prolong her life. This technique of mine is essential not only for husbands in desperate situations, but also for men in general, whether they be merchants setting off on their travels or students leaving for the examinations. If they know they'll be gone one year, there's no harm in saying they'll be away for two. If they've decided to leave for a month, they shouldn't specify four weeks. Travelers are at the mercy of the roads anyway; there's no such thing as a definite date of return. It's far better to surprise your wife before she expects you than miss the date and cause her to worry. If all men who loved their wives were able to do this, they would assure themselves of long and happy marriages and avoid the *pretty face, sorry fate* outcome. If you doubt my word, brother, just compare our wives' figures when you get home, and you'll see what I mean."

Yu was only half convinced. Admittedly Duan's advice showed a great deal of shrewdness, but in the end it was simply too heartless; if I were in his shoes, he thought, even if I were capable of thinking up such a plan, I still wouldn't be able to put it into practice.

Years went by, and their exile continued. When the throne passed to Emperor Qinzong and they had been away eight years and had seen the start of two reigns, the Jin launched a sudden invasion, and the Song suffered a major defeat. The Jin took the capital, captured Emperors Huizong and Qinzong, and brought them back to their own court.

Duan and Yu met the emperors and, needless to say, wept bitterly and kowtowed to them as to reigning sovereigns. On learning who they were, Emperor Huizong felt a twinge of remorse. His jealousy had been pointless, he now realized, for even if he hadn't halted the selection eight years ago and the cousins had joined him in his palace, he would now be as far removed from them as Herd Boy from Weaving Girl. Giving them up had been the best course after all.

Let me explain that before capturing the two emperors, the Jin had valued nothing but jade, silk, and women. They had never thought in terms of conquest, which was why they had put such emphasis on silver. Although they knew that no more money could be extracted from Duan and Yu, they held onto them like leftover chicken ribs—no meat on them, but hard to part with nonetheless. But after their great victory they knew that there was no one left at the Song court and that the glorious Central Plain was theirs for the taking. They wanted to install a benevolent regime and to show their magnanimity issued a directive releasing all Song tribute emissaries over the past ten years who were unable to pay the supplements. The emperors urged Duan and Yu to return, but they protested: "When Your Majesties were forced to leave your court, it was a subject's duty to give his life to avenge your shame. If we were in our own court now, it would be our duty to rush up here and risk our lives for you. How can we even think of evading our duty when we're already here?"

Again and again the emperors urged them to depart, consoling them with the thought that they could do no good by staying, merely shame their rulers further, and at length the two officials made their kowtows and took their leave.

Although Yu was still under thirty, his hair and beard were completely white. As he drew near his home, it occurred to him that he could scarcely meet his wife looking the way he did and that he should find some way to dye his hair. Lest he disappoint her, he bought a miraculous darkening substance and touched himself up with it to look like a new bridegroom.

To his surprise, although his sister-in-law came out to meet Duan when they entered the gate, *his* wife did not appear. He assumed that, not having seen him for so long, she felt shy and preferred that her husband go in and see her. Yu greeted his father-in-law and was about to enter the bridal chamber when he noticed an ominous shape looming in the hall. Stuck on the front was a column of small characters that read: COFFIN OF OUR DECEASED

DAUGHTER OF THE SONG, MISS GUAN OF THE YU HOUSE.

So great was Yu's shock at the sight that he broke out into a cold sweat. Clutching at Guan, he pressed him for the cause of her death.

"You had hardly left," explained Guan, sobbing as he spoke, "when she began counting the days until your return. Her eyes would fill with tears, and she would sob all the time. After several days like that she fell ill. I called in doctors from all around, but they said she was suffering an emotional trauma brought on by frustration and would recover only when reunited with you. At first she still hoped you might come back, and although she had stopped taking solid food, would force herself to drink a little broth to keep herself alive and see you one last time. But after the victory when she heard that you had been given another assignment, she knew she could never wait long enough. She cried her heart out, stopped taking any food or drink at all, and died. That was three years ago. She gave me instructions on her deathbed not to bury her but to allow her to meet you once more through the boards of a coffin, in a kind of family reunion. That's why she's still unburied."

In his despair Yu was going to dash his head against the coffin and join her in the grave, when Guan dissuaded him. "There's no need to be so distraught," he went on. "Even if my daughter were alive today, she would not be the Pearl you knew. She had grown so thin that her bones stood out like matchsticks, and her face had become sallow and her body dark. She had turned into a skeleton, a mere wraith, enough to make you cover your eyes and flee in terror. It's far better that she find refuge in here where she can hide the way she looks."

Yu remembered Duan's suggestion that he compare

their wives' figures, and he knew that Duan had been right. Not only was one wife plump, the other had wasted away. I was the cause of her death, he thought, declaring his repentance again and again before her coffin. Men should model themselves on Duan, not on me. Loneliness *is* excitement after all, and true love is not to be found in sentimental passion. "Condemn them to death and they'll survive"—those are the words of a romantic genius, not of a puritan.

Let me turn now to Duan, who found his wife fuller in the face, as if she had exchanged the svelteness of Zhao Feiyan for the voluptuousness of Yang Guifei, and felt elated at the success of his novel technique.

With a broad smile on his face, he asked his wife how much peace and quiet she had enjoyed over the past eight years and whether in idle moments she had missed her husband. Jade's face fell, and she said nothing, no matter how he questioned her.

"In that case I suppose you're still resentful and want an apology before you'll say anything, is that it? I don't want to boast, but there's not another husband in the world as loving as I am. I might expect *you* to bow down and thank me, but instead you expect *me* to apologize!"

"Why should I bow down? And why do I need to thank you? Explain yourself."

"We've been apart for eight years, and you're not the least bit thinner, in fact you've gotten quite plump. That's the first reason you ought to bow down and thank me. You're eight years older but your complexion hasn't changed at all; in fact it looks younger and softer than ever. That's the second reason. And of two cousins in identical situations, the other one is dead and you're alive, and thanks to whom, may I ask? That's the third reason. Her husband aged rapidly while away from home, but I still look the same; I haven't changed a bit and so I don't disappoint you. That's the fourth reason. That other couple parted in life, while you and I have already parted in death. Who would have guessed that after all this time they would be parted by death and you and I only parted in life? Thanks to the karma from your last life you had the good luck to marry a husband like me with the power to bring people back from the dead and turn the heavens around; otherwise we could never have arrived at this stage. That's the fifth reason. Also you didn't feel lonely even though you slept alone; you found the cold pillow better than the warm one. The clocks kept the same time for everybody, but *they* complained it was too long while you complained it was too short. You and she saw the same spring flowers, but you enjoyed them, while she was heartbroken. I can't begin to describe all the hidden benefits, all the blessings of secret love you've enjoyed, merely give you a general idea of them."

Jade understood not a word of all this. She still believed that he was trying to transform his sins into virtues, and that his talk was totally insincere, calculated merely to cover up his misdeeds.

"In case you don't believe me," said Duan, "eight years ago I sent you a magic charm. Get it out and try it, and you'll see what I mean."

"I never saw any magic charm!"

"When our brother-in-law came back, I gave him a letter for you. That was a magic charm. Don't say you never saw it?"

"That was no charm, it was a letter of separation. You tried to end our love and deny me any further hope. Why are you turning everything upside down and trying to make out that the letter was well-intentioned?"

Duan laughed. "Don't accuse me of being fickle! When we parted, you made up a couple of lines: 'I've emulated the love of Meng Jiangnu, And tried to follow Su Huiniang's intent.' As I see it, you may qualify as a Meng Jiangnu, but certainly not as a Su Huiniang, because you know nothing about that palindrome she wove. The poem I sent you was a palindrome that can be read forwards or backwards. Read forwards, it's a letter of separation. Read backwards, it's obviously a magic charm. If you still have it, get it out and read it, and you'll see what I mean."

Jade was now even more suspicious. She brought out the poem and read it forwards, then backwards, and finally realized that it was well-intentioned, not callous as she had first thought. It ran:

Suspicion and doubt I caused to rise
But our love I'll renew once I'm home.
Cold-hearted, I spurned your affection,
But with love I now weave a palindrome.

For some time she sat silent, pondering the poem's meaning. Then her sadness turned to joy and her cherry-blossom lips parted in a smile. "In that case were *all* of your actions meant to cool my desires and stop them from becoming too passionate? If so, why didn't you make it clear to me when you wrote the poem? Why be so devious and give me eight years of vexation? What was the point?"

"If I'd stated my meaning clearly, I might just as well have done nothing. It's only because I *was* so devious that I managed to keep you alive. Otherwise, as in your cousin's case, we could only have met through the boards of a coffin, not held each other in a passionate embrace and acted out a true reunion. The first palindrome in history was sent by a woman to her husband, but I've turned the tables; this time it's a husband weaving a palindrome for his wife. How's that for a novelty?"

Nearly out of her mind with joy, Jade not only cast all her old grievances to the winds, she felt convinced that Duan had done her a great kindness and was about to bow down and thank him in earnest.

"One of us wants to show her gratitude and the other to apologize," put in Duan, "but these ceremonies should be exciting; we mustn't let this most precious of occasions pass in too dull a fashion. On our wedding night I was such a bundle of nerves that I got no pleasure from it at all, but now that I've escaped a great disaster, I'm free of worry. Even if the emperors return to court, I doubt that they'll remember old scores and retaliate. You and I parted in death, but I've returned alive, which is something I never expected. It's as if I'd been reborn. We're newly matched, you and I. Let's not think of ourselves as an old married couple."

He ordered his servants to make preparations for a new wedding and called in two bands to play together. The couple made their bows again in the ceremonial hall and retired once more within the brocade curtain, where their joys that night were beyond description. His skill was a hundred times greater than it had been, and she displayed a reckless abandon. They realized that to attain bliss in lovemaking we cannot afford any sorrow in our hearts or tears in our eyes. The finest sex tonic in the world is composed of just two words—*don't worry*—beside which all the nostrums peddled on the streets are nothing but a swindle.

In later years Duan rose to the rank of chamberlain. He

lived into his seventies, and he and Jade enjoyed a long and happy marriage. All five of their sons followed in the family tradition of scholarship.

Yu married another great beauty after his wife's death, but within a few years she, too, was dead, of consumption, the reason being that his passion for women was all-consuming and the Creator insists on toppling heroes and preventing people from achieving their hearts' desires. Eventually Yu was promoted to grand councilor, an exceptional honor, although he had no great interest in a career and no desire for that particular honor—which is why, paradoxically, he received it. It appears from these examples that we have no choice in our lives but to follow our destiny; our own decisions are of no consequence. The foregoing events are taken from *A History of the Duan Clan*,[19] which contains a section "On Homing Crane Lodge" that I have developed into this story. It is not imaginary. *So you will take the story to heart!*

playful aspect of Chinese fiction

— ‖ CRITIQUE ‖ —

The purpose behind this work is exceedingly profound and its course extremely convoluted, for it is a variant on the age-old romance. Men who cherish tender feelings toward women may not undergo the experiences related in this story, but they must adopt its attitude. Romantic young fellows will inevitably condemn that attitude as too cold, but I maintain that without such coldness the torrid excitements of passion would be impossible to disperse. If you

19. An imaginary work.

What is the true goal? → *greater pleasure*

"second" honeymoon

↪YOUR OWN HAPPINESS↩

read this story after "Combined Reflections"[20] and "Cloud-Scraper," you will feel as if, when you are sweltering in the midsummer heat and running with sweat, someone has handed you a chilled melon. You slice open the melon, you bite into it—and your mouth gushes with its cold juice!

Hardly a superficial pleasure!

20. The first story of *Twelve Lou*, the collection from which these translations are made.

中文

wife dies . . . always, tortured by true love

boy meets girl.
boy leaves girl.
girl stops eating.
girl dies.

= Chinese story!

also! 2 categories of beauty:
fat + slim

Duan gets it all!
and Yu continues
to kill girls by
loving them ☺

no depression

NATIVITY ROOM

CHAPTER 1

Against his rule he builds a house to conceive a son;
With a strange device he tries to sell himself as a
father.

Lyric:

Holocaust of the ages—
During my life it came.
Nation and family gone, myself dishonored,
All things brought to a nothingness—
It's the Lord of Heaven that I blame!

Mine was a momentary slip;
It's pointless to regret the shame!
So many martyrs there are! So hard to find him!
But Yellow Springs is a narrow track
Where I'll have to meet him, cheeks aflame.
(To the tune "Gazing Toward the South")

This lyric was discovered during the Dashing Bandit's advance south.[1] Someone found a small quantity of Zhangzhou tobacco at the side of the road and noticed this lyric on a piece of paper that the bandits had wrapped the tobacco in. The man who picked it up didn't know what it meant and thought it merely scrap paper. But afterwards it came into the hands of a literary man who realized it was a poem by some gifted woman whom the bandits had captured. Full of remorse over her lost honor, she had wanted to kill herself but been ashamed to face someone in the netherworld. In her cruel dilemma she had written this poem with its haunting grief and rage. In light of the words *nation and family gone* in line three, she cannot have been any commoner's wife or official's concubine; the man she is to meet on the narrow track in Yellow Springs must have been a ruler with family and nation in his care. I imagine that before the capital fell she was either a favorite of the late emperor, the consort of a feudatory prince, or the wife of some member of the royal house. If indeed she held such an exalted position, certain other facts can be concluded about her, and since she was so skillful a poet and had such literary knowledge, yet other facts can be inferred.

In the light of this example our judgment of people in war-torn ages ought to differ from our judgment in ordinary times; we should examine their motives rather than their actions. If there is the slightest thing to be said in their favor, no one with any concern for moral education will feel able to reject them outright. As the saying goes, The laws must be harsh, but their execution lenient. Since the

1. Li Zicheng, the rebel who captured Beijing in 1644, was known to his admirers as the Dashing Prince. (*Dashing* refers to his mobility, not his looks.) Li Yu is using a satirical version of the name.

ancients believed in examining the motive rather than the crime, people today ought to obey the same rule. When a man acts like a faithful officer but thinks like an unctuous rogue, he is condemned in *The Spring and Autumn Annals*. By the same token if some woman is taken off to a foreign land but stays true to her lord in her heart, she ought to receive the praise of those of us living at the end of an era. Motive was the one factor above all others that the ancients stressed.

After this woman was dishonored, her natural reaction must have been to behave like an ingrate and put the dead man out of her mind. But since she proved capable of uttering such a moving lament and then of writing it down, she deserves to come under the heading of *tout comprendre, c'est tout pardonner*. She ought not to be mentioned in the same breath as those women who lost their honor under ordinary circumstances.

This discussion has little to do with the story I am about to tell, so why do I choose it as my lead-in? Because the neighboring stories are about abduction, and I want the reader to suppress his feelings a little and not apply his most critical standards. Changes of dynasty have always brought with them periods of separation followed by periods of reunion. Now, separation is a tragic experience, but it may occasionally lead to good fortune, either by our meeting someone we have never met or by finding someone we have been looking for. The Creator's ingenuity in arranging our destinies often manifests itself in such ways.

Let me tell how in the last years of the Song dynasty there lived in Zhushan county of Yunyang prefecture in Huguang province a rich farmer named Yin Hou. For generations his family had worked the land and honored the simple life, acquiring vast wealth from their hard labor and frugal habits. Yin's wife, Miss Pang, was a farmer's daughter herself and wore raw silk and plain cloth and even hulled the rice with her own hands. Actually this hardworking, thrifty couple lived rather well, much better than other families, although they set no store by luxury and took no pleasure in display. To give just one example, their house had an impressive air of its own. A passage in the *Four Books* says, "Riches adorn a house and virtue adorns the person,"[2] but scholars have never known how to interpret that word "adorns." It is not necessary to build a brand-new house for it to be "adorned"; even a thatched hut in an overgrown garden, provided a rich man lives there, will possess an aura of prosperity that is projected automatically by the situation. If the "adornment" of the house were to result from a new building, we would have to change our looks and create a whole new body to lay claim to the "adornment of the person." How dreadful, if all our efforts to "rectify the mind and make our thoughts sincere" were thought to be based on an unsound interpretation of the classics![3]

Yin had spent a lifetime as a rich man without doing any building—until his wife proved unable to bear a son and he concluded that his house was the inhibiting factor and built himself a chalet next door to the ancestral home. The locals chaffed him about it: "For all his millions the rich man never builds a stately home, but after saving his money all these years, he finally puts up a chalet. We ought to call you Chalet Yin."

Yin was delighted with the nickname and adopted it as his sobriquet.

2. From *The Great Learning*. See James Legge, *The Confucian Classics* (Oxford University Press, 1891), vol. 1, p. 367.
3. Loc. cit.

Once the chalet was finished, he and his wife moved in and slept there, and Mrs. Yin soon became pregnant. At the end of her tenth month, she gave birth to a boy, whom they called Lousheng (Born in the Chalet). He was a big child and grew rapidly, his only handicap being that he was born with a single testicle. Yin had heard that a man with one testicle could not father a child, but he decided to take care of this generation and not worry about the next until the time came.

However when the boy was only two or three years old, he went out to play with some other children, and when they returned that evening, one was missing—the rich man's son! There was a tiger scare at the time, and both people and livestock were being lost. A search was mounted that lasted several days but produced no results, and they concluded that the boy had been devoured by a tiger.

Yin and his wife scarcely wished to go on living. They had once been concerned about the next generation but, such was their misfortune, had not even been able to protect this one. Friends offered encouragement: "The only thing a young woman needs to fear is infertility. Once she has carried one baby to term, her body will have adjusted, and she'll always be able to have a second."

"Quite right," said the Yins.

From that day forth they devoted even more attention to their lovemaking, reserving all their energies for conceiving a child. Unfortunately, from the age of thirty to well past fifty, although Mrs. Yin had over three hundred periods and Mr. Yin sowed his seed at least three thousand times, all of it fell on stony ground. There was no crop to harvest.

Yin took a prudent attitude toward the blessings of life,

and whenever anyone urged him to take a concubine, would loudly intone the Buddha's name, adding: "The very mention of such a thing will reduce our blessings in the other world! If we actually take one, it cannot help but lower our moral credit!" And so at the age of fifty he and his wife were still childless.

Yin's friends and relations urged him to name an heir, but he demurred: "Naming an heir is no small matter, you know. You need to be able to entrust everything to him, and I don't see any child around who's *that* lucky. What's more, before I bestow a fortune on someone out of the blue, he'll have to have shown me affection over time and I'll need to have become extremely fond of him. That way the legacy will seem like an act of appreciation on my part, and I shan't regret it from Yellow Springs. But if I ignore the question of love and trust and take the first boy I see as my heir, he'll be eager enough for my property while I'm alive to fawn on us and call us Mother and Father, but after we're dead he'll deny the relationship altogether. There've been cases where a man names an heir and then, once the heir gets control, he starts calling the tune and even trying to force his adoptive parents to his will, exploiting the fact that they have no children of their own. When he can't budge them, he tries to drive them to their deaths, because the sooner they die the sooner he'll be master. This is quite common with adopted heirs. We earned our property with our blood and sweat and I'm certainly not going to turn it over to someone else for *nothing*. I far prefer to wait for a son who will give me some real affection. Before I name him my heir, I expect him to set my mind at rest by showing me gratitude, after which I'll do the same for him. Other people expect to earn interest on their capital, but I want someone to *exchange* his interest for my capital and strike a fair bargain with me. But what do you think of my idea?" His listeners were merely puzzled and dismissed what he said as sophistry.

One day he discussed the problem with his wife. "Everyone in this area knows how much we're worth and would like to be named my heir. Once they hear about this idea of mine, there are bound to be some who'll lay a trap for me by faking their affection. I'd be far better off traveling about the country testing people's feelings in chance encounters. If I met someone born under a lucky star who gave his heart to me of his own free will, I'd bring him home and name him my heir. Wouldn't that be a good idea?"

"An excellent idea!" she agreed, packing up her husband's things and sending him off on his quest.

On leaving home Yin dressed quite differently, in ragged clothes, well-worn cap, hempen socks, and straw sandals, so that people took him for the inmate of some poorhouse or hospice. All that was needed to complete the picture was a walking stick, which he planned to acquire.

All well and good. But in addition to this outfit, he also had a wisp of straw tucked into the brim of his cap to indicate that he was offering himself for sale.

"A man your age," people would expostulate, "with one foot in the grave—what earthly use are *you* to anybody, that you should try to sell yourself? From the looks of you, you're not from the lower classes either. If someone does buy you, what are you going to do for him, be a servant or a tutor?"

"You're right, I'm old and not of the slightest use. But I *am* accustomed to a certain status in life. It wouldn't suit me to work as a servant and I don't have the ability to teach. I'm looking for some rich orphan who'll purchase me as his adopted father. I'd do my best to help him manage his property and arrange a secure old age and a decent funeral for myself at the same time. That's all I ask."

The bystanders assumed he was joking and paid no attention. When he found that nobody believed him, he bought a sheet of parchment, mounted it on several layers of cardboard, and wrote a few columns of characters on it in a bold hand—a placard advertising himself for sale. It ran:

OLD MAN WITH NO SON WILLING TO SELL HIMSELF
AS FATHER. ASKING PRICE ONLY TEN TAELS.
SAME-DAY CLOSING. LIFELONG COMMITMENT.

Whenever he came to a new place, he would parade up and down the streets with the placard held in front of him. Sometimes, when he grew tired, he would sit cross-legged on the ground with the placard dangling from his neck, like a priest begging for alms. When people saw him like that, they would laugh and jeer fit to burst, assuming he had gone out of his mind. Yin let them laugh and jeer but never changed his ways. He spent his time traveling from town to town, crossing rivers and mountains, determined to find himself a buyer.

If you wish to know how long he had to search, turn to the next chapter.

CHAPTER 2

Ten taels are paid to a father in a limited investment;
Ten thousand are repaid to the son at an enormous
profit.

With his placard Yin visited countless towns and brought smirks to tens of thousands of faces before he encountered a remarkable man who, amidst the laughter and jeers of the crowd, accepted his offer! A popular jingle sums it up:

A drawn bow will vegetables chop
And a chamber pot fit the oil jug's top.
Few things need be discarded, we're told;
Sour wine can as vinegar be sold.

One day when he arrived in Huating county of Songjiang prefecture and sat down at a street corner, a number of ignorant young punks came up and began badgering him, telling him the old people's home needed a beggar chief and the Tortoise Bordello a head musician. Some rapped him on the pate, others kicked him in the shins, and he was utterly bewildered.

In the midst of his ordeal someone pushed his way through the crowd, a good-looking young man, tall and pale complexioned. He stopped the taunts by telling the bystanders to cut out their nonsense: "Widows, orphans, and the like are the most vulnerable of the poor. The emperor wishes to show them mercy and the officials want to help them. We younger people ought to be respectful, not take it upon ourselves to insult them!"

"Since you're so sympathetic, why don't *you* put up the

ten taels he's asking for and buy him as *your* father?" the crowd asked.

"There's nothing so strange about that! You can tell from his face that he's a man of quality. My only worry is that some relative of his might turn up and claim him and he wouldn't want to stay with me the rest of his life. If he does want to, well, I'm an orphan myself and I'd be willing to pay his price and adopt him. Why, it would be *wonderful* to leave a name behind as someone who had succored the weak!"

"I'm all alone in the world," said Yin, "and the placard specifically mentions lifelong commitment. If you're really willing, hurry up and pay me my price, and I'll go home with you."

"Since you're selling yourself, it's up to him to provide for you," said the bystanders. "What do you need money for?"

"To be frank, I have an insatiable appetite and need snacks in addition to my regular meals. I've always loved to eat and can't start scrimping now. You wouldn't expect me to go to him for every little thing I want, would you? I need to have money enough to last me the first month or two, and then, once we've established a good relationship, I'll pressure him for more. That's how a father ought to behave."

The bystanders began to fear for the buyer and assumed that he would pull out on hearing these remarks. But instead he praised the seller, claiming that one could tell from the older man's considerateness *before* the adoption that he would show an unconditional love after it. He invited Yin into a wineshop where he ordered an array of hors d'oeuvres and a jug of the best wine and closed the deal as they chatted.

The youths followed them into the wineshop, ostensibly to buy a drink but actually to see what happened. They saw the seller take the place of honor while the buyer poured out the wine with all the respect due to a father. After they had drunk it, the buyer fetched several packages of silver from his money belt and counted them out, sixteen taels in all, then offered them with both hands to his guest. "Here are another six taels in addition to the purchase price. I'd like you to keep the money for me, Father. From now on you'll be in charge of my purse, which I shan't check on. Whatever you need, go ahead and buy it. So long as I can continue to make money, you shall live well all your life."

Yin took the money without a trace of embarrassment, then detached the placard and gave it to the younger man. "Let this serve as our bill of sale. Put it away with your things as proof of the deal."

The young man took the placard, bowed deeply, and tucked it away. As head of the family, Yin opened the purse and counted out enough to pay the bill. Then they left the wineshop together.

Watching from a nearby table, the youths were goggle-eyed with astonishment. "What a pair of freaks. They must be immortals or demons! No honest-to-goodness human beings would do anything half so weird!"

Let me explain that Yin, although he had been bought, still did not know the buyer's name or family situation—or even whether he was married. To find out he would have to wait until he reached the young man's house.

Entering the house, the young man pulled up an easy chair, placed it at the head of the reception room, and invited Yin to sit down, after which he kowtowed reverently four times and asked Yin's name and where he was from. Yin feared that if he revealed his secret he would no longer be able to test the young man's affection, so he gave a false name. He was equally reluctant to say where he was from and picked a neighboring county at random. Then he asked the young man *his* name and whether he was married.

"My name is Yao Ji," said the latter, "and I come from Hankou township of Hanyang prefecture in Huguang. As a child I lost both my parents and had no one to turn to. When I was fifteen, I went with a local merchant, Cao Yuyu, to Songjiang selling yard goods and earned a few taels a year to live on while I learned the trade. Later, when I was familiar with the dealers and had saved up a few taels in capital, I left my employer and did a little business on my own in the same line. The Caos are cotton brokers, and when I come to buy cloth every year, I stay with them. I'm twenty-one but still unmarried. Father, it seems that we come from the same province, if not from the same town. As the proverb says, We may be neither kith nor kin, but we share a native heath. Our meeting today is surely the result of karma. When I look at other fellows my age, I see that they all have parents, and I feel lonely. I'm tempted to join another family as an adopted son, but I'm also afraid that people won't understand and will take me for a sponger with designs on their property. They don't realize that so long as I keep my health I can make money anywhere—I lost my parents at the age of six or seven and have survived well enough so far—and I'd never dream of using adoption as a way to get at someone else's money! But you happened to be homeless as well as penniless, and I knew that if I adopted you, no one could make that charge against me, and that's why my heart went out to you and I did this good deed. Since losing my parents as a child I've had no one to guide me; I hope you'll give me daily instructions and help me grow into a good man. That would give it all meaning—my establishing this bond with you so late in life. But now that we're related, I shall have to change my name; it would never do for a father and son to go by different names. I beg you to let me take your honorable surname. And please choose a personal name for me."

Yin knew that this was a son capable of supporting a family, and he was completely satisfied. But he still feared that the situation might change and his son tire of him, so he wished to try one more test. He could hardly pass on the false name he had taken, so he improvised: "If *I* had paid for *you*, you'd have been obliged to take my name. But you paid for me. How can I trouble the buyer to change his name? No, since your name is Yao, let me use that and call myself Chalet Yao."

Yao Ji had found a father, but he could not bring himself to repudiate his origins. To justify keeping his name, he quoted the old saw: Obedience before politeness.

Father and son loved each other dearly. Yao Ji would buy his father his favorite delicacies, and Yin would play hard to please, complaining that the choicest titbits weren't tasty enough, and Yao Ji would have to go back and exchange them several times before Yin would consent to eat. The son indulged his father's contrariness without the slightest irritation. After a few weeks of living together Yin decided to fake an illness in order to see how Yao would look after him. If he passed the test with flying colors, Yin would reveal his secret.

Instead disaster struck. Suddenly news came that Mongol troops had broken through the Shanhai Pass and, sweeping all before them, were expected in Nanjing at any moment. Other reports came in that Huguang province swarmed with bandits and no place was safe from looting.

Frightened out of his wits, Yin gave up all thought of faking an illness. He called Yao Ji in and asked how much capital he had with him and whether it was too late to collect the goods for which money had already been advanced.

"The total comes to over two hundred taels," said Yao Ji. "The goods I've collected amount to less than half that. The rest of my money is with the farm managers, and in the face of this news we'll never be able to collect the goods. The only thing we can do is pack up what we have in hand and take it home. Once we've gotten through this turmoil and peace has been restored, we can come and collect the rest. The trouble is that we're short of most of the travel money and have no way of raising it. What are we going to do?"

"We have the money, don't worry about that. But in this chaos, you'd be afraid of running into rebel troops if you had *nothing* with you. How can you hope to take any goods with you? Why not deposit what you've collected with an agent and get a receipt? Then when peace has been restored, you can come back and get it. In the meantime we'll flee home, traveling as light as we can. That's the only safe course."

"Father, you don't *have* any money—you sold yourself! Even if you do have some, it can't amount to very much. I was on my own before I met you and, money or no money, I always got by. But now that I have you, we're a family, and if we go back empty-handed, what are we going to live on? *I* might go hungry, but how can I allow *you* to do the same?"

When Yin heard this, tears streamed down his cheeks.

He reached out and patted the young man on the shoulder.

"My loving son! I wonder what karmic bond we share from a previous existence that you show me such love? To be honest with you, I'm not really a poor man, nor did I actually sell myself. I'm an old man without a son, and I wanted to name an heir with some affection for me, so I thought up this hoax as a way to test people's feelings. By a providential chance I did meet a good man, and now I willingly and unreservedly entrust all my worldly goods to him. Far be it from me to boast, but my property is more than enough to meet all your needs. When you bought me, you paid a mere ten taels. I'm paying you back a thousand-fold. *You're now a ten-thousand tael man*! Even if you lost your entire capital, it would be just a drop in the bucket. Hurry up and get ready to return with me and live the life of a rich man."

Yao Ji's cheeks streamed with tears. That evening he made an inventory of his goods and deposited them with an agent, and the next morning he and his father chartered a large boat sailing upriver.

Gentle readers, I daresay you are expecting father and son to travel home and bring this story to a close. In fact, this world of surprises is just the beginning. Along the way these two will experience tragedy and joy, separation and reunion—at far greater length than can be told at a single stretch. I shall now conclude this chapter and take up my story again in the next.

CHAPTER 3

In buying a girl, he obtains an older woman;
By keeping a mother, he acquires a charming wife.

After embarking, Yin put a question to Yao: "Since you make such a good living, why are you still single at your age? Our first order of business when we get home must be to arrange a marriage for you. You can't put it off a moment longer."

"A marriage *was* arranged, although we were never formally engaged. The girl is also from Hankou, so I'll need to stop there on our way home. Father, I'll have to trouble you to wait on the boat for a day or two while I go ashore and find out her situation. If she's married, that's that. But if she isn't, I'll arrange a wedding date with her parents and go back for her after we get home. What do you say?"

"What sort of family does she belong to? If you had an agreement, she is yours, formal engagement or no. Why do you need to find out her situation?"

"To be frank, she's the daughter of my former employer, Cao Yuyu. She's five or six years younger than I am and extraordinarily pretty. I had long been meaning to ask for her hand, and she indicated that she'd like to marry me, but her parents hedged, no doubt fearing that I hadn't the money to support a family. But they're so snobbish that when they hear about this change in my fortunes, they're sure to agree."

"In that case, by all means go ashore and find out."

When they reached Hankou, Yao Ji told the boatmen to wait while he went ashore. But the other passengers loudly protested: "At a time like this, when we don't even know if our wives and children are still alive, our only thought is to rush home and find them as quickly as possible. We can't afford to wait!"

There was nothing Yin could do. He brought out two packets of silver, about a hundred taels in all, from his shabby cloth bag and handed them to Yao Ji. "Obviously I'll have to go on ahead. You follow as soon as you can. Keep this money on you and use it either for a betrothal gift or as travel expenses. But see that you leave here the moment you find out about her. Don't delay and make me more anxious than ever."

Yao Ji bowed and took his leave. He would have liked to urge his father to take good care of himself on the journey and watch his health, but the other passengers, unwilling to wait a moment longer, kept urging him ashore. As it was, he had to make a frantic leap to get off the boat in time.

As soon as he had gone, the boatmen hoisted sail and in less than an hour were nine or ten miles away, at which point a great cry of anguish arose from one of the passengers: "I never told him the most important thing of all! Oh, what am I going to do?" The man began beating his chest and stamping his feet in disgust.

Who do you suppose it was? None other than Chalet Yin. He had revealed his secrets to Yao Ji—all except his true name and address. He had expected them to arrive home together, at which point Yao would learn everything anyway; there was no need to tell him now. How could he have imagined that Yao would be driven ashore with the most important thing of all unsaid, and that his own lapse would come to mind only after the boat had sailed? The other passengers would never allow him to turn back now, but if he continued his journey, how would Yao Ji ever find him? Hence his predicament, in which he could only cry out to Heaven and Earth and beat his chest and stamp his feet.

After a moment's panic, an idea came to him. He would draw up a notice and post a copy at each port of call. When Yao Ji saw the notices, he would know how to find him.

Our story now turns to a different subject. Let me tell how Yao Ji, after going ashore, rushed to Cao's house, nominally to visit the Caos but actually to find out the daughter's situation. He found one vast change; no women remained in the house. What had happened was that as news of the military collapse reached Huguang, numbers of local bandits posing as Mongol soldiers had split up into separate bands and begun plundering. All the women they came upon, old and young alike, were seized and brought aboard their boats, this girl among them. No one knew whether she was still alive and, if so, where she had been taken.

Yao Ji was heartbroken at the news and wept privately, then took leave of his former master and caught the next available boat for Yunyang.

After several days on the river, he came to a port named Peachtown or Fishmouth, where large numbers of rebels had moored their boats and set up a vast human market in which to sell off the women they had captured. Yao Ji had a good heart, and now he knew that the girl he loved had been abducted, he was determined to find her. He could not neglect this chance simply because his own life would be endangered.

Then he heard that the rebels were soliciting buyers and that this area would be off limits for plunder, so he stopped worrying and, taking a few taels with him, went straight to the market to do business. That would be his excuse for watching while the women were sold off. He would check all the women who had been abducted by the various bands and step forward when he found the girl he loved.

But the rebels were devilishly cunning. They feared that if they let their captives' faces be seen, the buyers would pick and choose among them, snapping up all the presentable women. To whom would they sell the rejects? With that thought in mind, they set new rules and established a different sales procedure. Bundling the women into sacks, like pickled or rotten fish, they offered people a choice.[4] With no way to tell which sacks held the pickled fish, the customer had to chance his luck. Crammed inside the sacks, the women were sold by weight, not quality, at a uniform tariff. The lucky buyers got a paragon, the unlucky a gorgon—it was undoubtedly the most equitable system of exchange ever devised.

Yao Ji realized his plan was unworkable and was about to leave when he saw a notice posted beside the road:

IDLE SPECTATORS ARE FORBIDDEN TO VISIT THE
HUMAN MARKET. ANYONE LEAVING
EMPTY-HANDED WILL BE CONVICTED OF SPYING
AND SUMMARILY EXECUTED WITHOUT REPRIEVE.
BY ORDER

Yao Ji was afraid. He had made a mistake in coming but knew he could not afford a similar mistake in leaving. He would just have to take his chances with the few taels in his pocket. Perhaps by some happy coincidence of their mar-

---

4. Pickled fish also smelled foul; you had to see the fish to tell the difference.

riage destinies he might pick out the girl he loved. But even if he was never able to meet her and chose some other girl, so long as she was nice-looking and would make a suitable wife for a rich man, he would take her in Miss Cao's place. Back home no one would know the facts.

He marched up to the pile of sacks and pointed to one at random. "I'll take this one," he said. The rebels weighed the sack, yelled out the price, and set up the scales to weigh the money. Fortunately the sack did not weigh much, and Yao Ji was easily able to cover the cost.

He couldn't wait to get back to the boat before seeing who was in the sack, so he opened it then and there. As he undid the knot, before the sack was even open, a flash of snow-white radiance came shining through. "If her face is as white as this," he thought, "she must be young and beautiful. Those taels of mine will have been well spent." But when he opened the sack and took a closer look, his excitement evaporated and he began to protest. For the snow-white radiance came not from the woman's face but from her hair. She was in her fifties with snowy hair and a face full of wrinkles.

When the rebels heard his protests, they bawled at him: "It's no good crying foul just because you're out of luck and have gotten yourself an old'un. Come on, take her off and be quick about it!" And drawing their swords, they chased him as far as the road.

Yao Ji had no choice but to pick the woman up in his arms and pull her out of the sack, then take her back with him to the boat, where he looked her up and down and noted that, elderly as she was, her looks were quite distinguished; she was not from humble or menial stock. The passion he had felt before opening the sack now transformed itself into a gentle affection and, far from regretting his choice, he felt rather proud of it. I put up ten taels for a father the other day and obtained all kinds of blessings, he told himself. Now I've paid a few taels for this treasure, and perhaps some blessings will flow from her, too. Moreover, having taken pity on an elderly widower, I ought to do as much for an elderly widow. All three of us are poor folk, with no one to turn to. Wouldn't it be wonderful to bring us all together—orphan, widow, and widower? Besides, I don't have any gift to take to my father. Why not consider this woman a gift and offer her to him as an senior concubine? Even if he has a wife, I don't imagine that people of that age feel jealous anymore. She shouldn't mind a few additions to the family.

"I meant to buy myself a wife," he told the woman, "instead of which I got you, who look old enough to be my mother. As an orphan myself I would like to consider you my mother, if you would agree."

She was astonished. "When I saw how young you were, sir, I was afraid you'd be so upset at getting an ugly old creature like me that you'd want to throw me in the river. At the very height of my fears, for no conceivable reason, you come out with this offer. Of course I'm only too happy to accept!"

Once she had consented, Yao Ji kowtowed and offered her food in case she was hungry and took off his coat in case she felt cold. She was so overcome with gratitude that she broke down.

"This great kindness you've done me will bring its own reward one day, but I can't wait that long," she said, after crying for some time. "At this very moment there is a good deed I want to urge on you. Among my fellow captives were a number of young women, one of whom is an extraordinary beauty by any standard. And she's not only virtuous, she also comes from an established family—the perfect match for you. The rebels wanted to sell off all the old and ugly women first. The unsaleable ones were disposed of today, and tomorrow it will be the others' turn. Hurry up and scrape together some silver and go and buy her."

"That's all very well, but there's one problem. The girl will be inside a sack that is mixed up with all the others. How am I going to find her?"

"Don't worry, I know a way. She has something or other in her sleeve. I don't know what it is, but it's a foot long and half an inch wide. She keeps it with her at all times and won't part with it. When you get to the market, feel the women's sleeves through the sacking. She'll be the only one with this object inside, so you can go ahead and buy her."

Yao Ji was so excited at the prospect that he could not sleep a wink all night. Next morning he arose and went off to the market with his money. Following the older woman's advice, he felt the women's sleeves and found one with a hard object tucked inside. Pointing at her, he agreed on a price and received in exchange this rare commodity. Fearing that if he took her out of the sack in the marketplace someone would snatch her away, he carried her all the way to the boat and told the captain to set sail. He then took the sack to a quiet corner and opened it.

Who do you suppose the girl was? Neither Zhang nor Li, but Cao—none other than the daughter of his former master and the very girl he was in love with! The young couple had fallen in love and agreed to marry, and the object in her sleeve was a jade rule used for measuring cloth that Yao had given her as a token. Throughout the worst dangers she had refused to be parted from it, a testament to her love for him.

Wouldn't you expect these two lovers to be happy, suddenly reunited as they were? The young girl and the old woman, companions in misfortune before and now mother-in-law and daughter-in-law, also felt a special affection for each other, as much as if Miss Cao had been married to the older woman's natural son. Yao Ji's reward for helping the old man had not yet come to hand, although there was every prospect of it, but his reward for rescuing the widow had been instantaneous. It should be clear from his experience that people who do good deeds do not lose out. I implore all my contemporaries, even if they cannot emulate Yao Ji in buying themselves a father and mother, at least not to do the opposite and ignore the plight of widows and widowers, the orphaned and the childless.

CHAPTER 4

In proving his parenthood a father uses an odd criterion, a single testicle;
In identifying his family a son has no name to go by, only a room.

Let us return to Yin, who was worried sick after parting from Yao Ji. At every port of call he put up a notice that ran:

WHAT I TOLD YOU BEFORE WAS WRONG.
IF YOU ARE LOOKING FOR ME, COME TO ZHUSHAN
AND ASK FOR YIN HOU.

However Yao Ji had no reason to question the address he had been given and never bothered to look at the notices. He went directly to his destination and tried to find his father, but everywhere he asked he received the same reply: "There's nobody here by that name. Someone must have been having you on."

Yao Ji did not know what to believe. He was at his wits' end when his mother realized that he had nowhere to go. "*My* home isn't very far from here," she said. "I have a husband, but no son. I don't want to presume, but why not take us there and let us all live together?" Despairing of finding his father, Yao had no choice but to accept.

At a point along the way a close relative was waiting for them. Spotting the boat a long way off, he shouted: "Is that my son Yao Ji's boat?"

Yao Ji was astonished. "That sounds *exactly* like my father's voice," he exclaimed, "but why is he *here*?"

His mother was equally astonished. "That sounds *exactly* like my husband's voice, but why is he calling to *him*?"

When the boat drew alongside, the old man jumped on board and then caught sight of the old woman. They fell into each other's arms and began weeping.

The old woman was none other than Yin's wife, who had been seized by the rebels after her husband left home. The two bands of rebels were commanded by a single chief; one band sailed downstream, plundering as it went, while the other headed upstream on the same mission. Their plan was to meet at that port, raise money by selling off the women they had abducted, and then surrender to the Mongol army when it arrived, using the money they had raised as bribes. By sheer chance both women were given the same berth and got to know each other. If the younger women had been sold off before the older ones, Yin and his wife could never have been reunited. Even if the older women had been sold off first but Yao Ji had bought someone else—and Yin's wife had gone to another man—he could never have been reunited with his fiancée. Who would ever have expected the Creator's ingenuity to be a hundred times greater than man's? It's as if he had deliberately combined these events so that they could be turned into a play or a story—uniting the two couples and then separating them, separating them and then uniting them, at a prodigious cost in mental effort! This plot rates as novel and ingenious to an extraordinary degree!

And yet, strange to say, there is another equally novel and ingenious episode that has taken place but which has not been fully revealed.

Yin and his wife led their son and daughter-in-law into the reception room, where they made their ceremonial bows. The young couple were then told about the chalet. "It's the *luckiest* place! When it was built, we moved in there to sleep and promptly had a boy. Tragically, we lost him to a tiger, but if he were alive today, he'd be about the same age as you two. We're going to let you have the upstairs as a bedroom. You're sure to be as lucky as we were and have a child right away." They showed the young couple to the second floor of the chalet and asked them to make it ready for their own use.

On arriving upstairs, Yao Ji examined the doors, windows, and furnishings—and was amazed. "This bedroom is the same one I had as a child, the one I see all the time in my dreams," he told Yin and his wife. "But why is it here instead of in my home?"

"What makes you think it's the same?" asked the Yins.

"From childhood on, whenever I drop off to sleep, I dream of a room whose doors, windows, and furnishings are *exactly* like these! One night I even asked a question in my dream. 'Whenever I dream,' I said, 'it's always of this room, never of anywhere else. Why is that?' And someone in my dream answered me: 'This is where you were born. That trunk over there contains the toys you used to play with. If you don't believe me, take them out and see.' I opened the trunk and found a great many toys—earthenware men and horses, cudgels, banners. When I looked at them, I felt as if I were meeting long-lost friends. On awakening, I compared the room of my dreams with the one I was in; they were entirely different, which puzzled me no end. But as I came in here just now and looked about, the whole scene struck me as exactly the same as in my dreams. I can't be dreaming *now*, can I, in broad daylight?"

It was the Yins' turn to be astonished. "There *is* a trunk behind that bed–curtain that is full of our son's toys. We couldn't bear to look at them after his death, so we piled them in a trunk and stowed it behind the bed. It's *exactly* as you described it. What possible explanation could there be for such an extraordinary thing? Is it conceivable that our son wasn't carried off by a tiger after all, but that he was kidnapped and sold, and now Heaven and Earth have taken pity on us because of our good deeds and brought him back, reuniting us with our flesh and blood?"

"In all my twenty years," said Yao, "I've never heard any suggestion that I wasn't born a Yao."

His wife burst out laughing. "In that case you still *are* dreaming!" she said. "Everybody in our family knew about your origins; they were just too polite to mention them. When you asked if you could marry me, my parents knew what a good person you were and were going to accept you, when they heard from someone outside the family that you weren't a natural son of the Yaos, but an illegitimate child they had bought from a dealer. That's why my parents were so reluctant. For all your cleverness you don't even know where you came from!"

Yao Ji was speechless.

Yin thought for a moment, then had an inspiration: "No more guesswork! I know how to prove it one way or the other."

He pulled Yao Ji aside and told him to open up his trousers, then felt the young man's scrotum and began shouting: "My son, my own son! *Now* we have our proof! The other things might have been sheer coincidence, but the fact that you have only one testicle—how could *that* be coincidence? No question about it, this is a wonderful stroke of good fortune granted us by Heaven to reunite our family! It's obvious, when you come to think of it, that if someone meets a couple of strangers, willingly takes them as his own parents and shows them so much genuine love, it can only be Heaven's doing. It cannot be mere chance."

All four knelt down and kowtowed innumerable times to Heaven and Earth. They also sacrificed a pig and a sheep to the gods in fulfillment of their vow. Finally they invited in the local people and told them the whole story. Lest they find it hard to believe, Yin told his son to take down his trousers in front of everyone and asked them to check the single testicle. From the incident his son acquired a new name: Singular Yin.

Afterwards he continued his father's tradition of good deeds. And this unitesticular man showed himself as capable of fathering sons as other men; in fact he left numerous descendants behind, each of them born with a single testicle. This branch of the family retained their lands and their prosperity right up until the Hongzhi era of the Ming dynasty.[5] They even acquired their own name: the Singular Yins. There is a poem on the subject that runs:

> "When lines converge at the mouth, it means high rank."
> Singular fathers—*that* we can comprehend.
> Better to have a good heart than a lucky face,
> For on Mayi's prophecies you cannot depend.[6]

CRITIQUE

Everything that the Romancer Who Awakens the World has written falls within the bounds of plausibility except the episode in which the young man buys a father, which does seem a trifle fantastic. When readers get to that point, they will think they have discovered a flaw in his writing and will apply their harshest critical standards. However, when they read on and see that the pair were originally father and son and that the adoption was "all Heaven's doing," they will find it quite normal and not in the least implausible. From this example we can see that writing well is like being

5. 1488–1505.
6. Mayi was a famous Song dynasty physiognomer who gave his name to a system for reading faces.

a good man and doing good deeds; first you must surprise people, then tempt them to criticize you; and finally, when their suspicions have gathered and their resentment is on the rise, you suddenly reveal all the good things that accrue to your hero and convince them that it takes patient effort to be a good man and do good deeds, after which they will be loud in their praise. Grasp this point and you will know how to write—and also how to read.

OTHER WORKS IN THE COLUMBIA ASIAN STUDIES SERIES

Burton Watson. Also in separate paperback eds. 1967

The Awakening of Faith, Attributed to Aśvaghosha, tr.
Yoshito S. Hakeda. Also in paperback ed. 1967

Reflections on Things at Hand: The Neo-Confucian Anthology,
comp. Chu Hsi and Lü Tsu-ch'ien, tr. Wing-tsit Chan 1967

The Platform Sutra of the Sixth Patriarch, tr. Philip B.
Yampolsky. Also in paperback ed. 1967

Essays in Idleness: The Tsurezuregusa of Kenkō, tr. Donald
Keene. Also in paperback ed. 1967

The Pillow Book of Sei Shōnagon, tr. Ivan Morris, 2 vols. 1967

*Two Plays of Ancient India: The Little Clay Cart and the
Minister's Seal*, tr. J. A. B. van Buitenen 1968

The Complete Works of Chuang Tzu, tr. Burton Watson 1968

The Romance of the Western Chamber (Hsi Hsiang chi), tr.
S. I. Hsiung. Also in paperback ed. 1968

The Manyōshu, Nippon Gakujutsu Shinkōkai edition.
Paperback ed. only. 1969

*Records of the Historian: Chapters from the Shih chi of
Ssu-ma Ch'ien*, tr. Burton Watson. Paperback ed. only. 1969

Cold Mountain: 100 Poems by the T'ang Poet Han-shan, tr.
Burton Watson. Also in paperback ed. 1970

Twenty Plays of the Nō Theatre, ed. Donald Keene. Also in
paperback ed. 1970

Chūshingura: The Treasury of Loyal Retainers, tr. Donald
Keene. Also in paperback ed. 1971;
rev. ed. 1997

The Zen Master Hakuin: Selected Writings, tr. Philip B.
Yampolsky 1971

*Chinese Rhyme-Prose: Poems in the Fu Form from the Han
and Six Dynasties Periods*, tr. Burton Watson. Also in
paperback ed. 1971

Kūkai: Major Works, tr. Yoshito S. Hakeda. Also in
paperback ed. 1972

*The Old Man Who Does as He Pleases: Selections from the
Poetry and Prose of Lu Yu*, tr. Burton Watson 1973

The Lion's Roar of Queen Śrīmālā, tr. Alex and Hideko
    Wayman   1974
Courtier and Commoner in Ancient China: Selections from
    the History of the Former Han by Pan Ku, tr. Burton
    Watson. Also in paperback ed.   1974
Japanese Literature in Chinese, vol. 1: *Poetry and Prose in*
    Chinese by Japanese Writers of the Early Period, tr.
    Burton Watson   1975
Japanese Literature in Chinese, vol. 2: *Poetry and Prose in*
    Chinese by Japanese Writers of the Later Period, tr.
    Burton Watson   1976
Scripture of the Lotus Blossom of the Fine Dharma, tr. Leon
    Hurvitz. Also in paperback ed.   1976
Love Song of the Dark Lord: Jayadeva's Gītagovinda, tr.
    Barbara Stoler Miller. Also in paperback ed. Cloth ed.
    includes critical text of the Sanskrit.   1977;
                                rev. ed. 1997
Ryōkan: Zen Monk-Poet of Japan, tr. Burton Watson   1977
Calming the Mind and Discerning the Real: From the Lam
    rim chen mo of Tsoṇ-kha-pa, tr. Alex Wayman   1978
The Hermit and the Love-Thief: Sanskrit Poems of Bhartri-
    hari and Bilhaṇa, tr. Barbara Stoler Miller   1978
The Lute: Kao Ming's P'i-p'a chi, tr. Jean Mulligan. Also in
    paperback ed.   1980
A Chronicle of Gods and Sovereigns: Jinnō Shōtōki of
    Kitabatake Chikafusa, tr. H. Paul Varley.   1980
Among the Flowers: The Hua-chien chi, tr. Lois Fusek   1982
Grass Hill: Poems and Prose by the Japanese Monk Gensei,
    tr. Burton Watson   1983
Doctors, Diviners, and Magicians of Ancient China:
    Biographies of Fang-shih, tr. Kenneth J. DeWoskin.
    Also in paperback ed.   1983
Theater of Memory: The Plays of Kālidāsa, ed. Barbara
    Stoler Miller. Also in paperback ed.   1984
The Columbia Book of Chinese Poetry: From Early Times to

Steven D. Carter 1997
The Vimalakirti Sutra, tr. by Burton Watson 1997
Japanese and Chinese Poems to Sing: The Wakan rōei shū,
    tr. J. Thomas Rimer and Jonathan Chaves 1997

MODERN ASIAN LITERATURE SERIES

Modern Japanese Drama: An Anthology, ed. and tr. Ted.
    Takaya. Also in paperback ed. 1979
*Mask and Sword: Two Plays for the Contemporary Japanese
    Theater*, by Yamazaki Masakazu, tr. J. Thomas Rimer 1980
Yokomitsu Riichi, Modernist, Dennis Keene 1980
*Nepali Visions, Nepali Dreams: The Poetry of Laxmiprasad
    Devkota*, tr. David Rubin 1980
Literature of the Hundred Flowers, vol. 1: *Criticism and
    Polemics*, ed. Hualing Nieh 1981
Literature of the Hundred Flowers, vol. 2: *Poetry and Fiction*,
    ed. Hualing Nieh 1981
Modern Chinese Stories and Novellas, 1919–1949, ed. Joseph
    S. M. Lau, C. T. Hsia, and Leo Ou-fan Lee. Also in
    paperback ed. 1984
A View by the Sea, by Yasuoka Shōtarō, tr. Kären
    Wigen Lewis 1984
*Other Worlds; Arishima Takeo and the Bounds of Modern
    Japanese Fiction*, by Paul Anderer 1984
Selected Poems of Sŏ Chŏngju, tr. with introduction by
    David R. McCann 1989
The Sting of Life: Four Contemporary Japanese Novelists, by
    Van C. Gessel 1989
Stories of Osaka Life, by Oda Sakunosuke, tr. Burton Watson 1990
The Bodhisattva, or Samantabhadra, by Ishikawa Jun, tr.
    with introduction by William Jefferson Tyler 1990
The Travels of Lao Ts'an, by Liu T'ieh-yün, tr. Harold Shadick.
    Morningside ed. 1990
Three Plays by Kōbō Abe, tr. with introduction by Donald Keene 1993

STUDIES IN ASIAN CULTURE

COMPANIONS TO ASIAN STUDIES

Practical Learning, eds. Wm. Theodore de Bary and
  Irene Bloom. Also in paperback ed.   1979
The Syncretic Religion of Lin Chao-en, by Judith A. Berling   1980
*The Renewal of Buddhism in China: Chu-hung and the Late
  Ming Synthesis*, by Chün-fang Yü   1981
*Neo-Confucian Orthodoxy and the Learning of the Mind-
  and-Heart*, by Wm. Theodore de Bary   1981
*Yüan Thought: Chinese Thought and Religion Under the
  Mongols*, eds. Hok-lam Chan and Wm. Theodore de Bary   1982
The Liberal Tradition in China, by Wm. Theodore de Bary   1983
The Development and Decline of Chinese Cosmology, by
  John B. Henderson   1984
The Rise of Neo-Confucianism in Korea, by Wm. Theodore
  de Bary and JaHyun Kim Haboush   1985
*Chiao Hung and the Restructuring of Neo-Confucianism in
  Late Ming*, by Edward T. Ch'ien   1985
Neo-Confucian Terms Explained: Pei-hsi tzu-i, by Ch'en
  Ch'un, ed. and trans. Wing-tsit Chan   1986
Knowledge Painfully Acquired: K'un-chih chi, by Lo Ch'in-
  shun, ed. and trans. Irene Bloom   1987
To Become a Sage: The Ten Diagrams on Sage Learning, by
  Yi T'oegye, ed. and trans. Michael C. Kalton   1988
The Message of the Mind in Neo-Confucian Thought, by
  Wm. Theodore de Bary   1989